I
A
a
tailor...

a surgeon at the Middlesex Hospital Medical College taught for a while and joined the colonial service, offering his as an assistant surgeon along the Gold Coast of Africa. He became embroiled in a diplomatic mission when a British expeditionary party was sent to investigate the activities of the French. Through his tact and formidable intelligence, a massacre was narrowly avoided. His future was assured in the colonial service. However, after becoming ill with blackwater fever, Freeman was sent back to England to recover and, finding his finances precarious, embarked on a career as acting physician in Holloway Prison. In desperation, he turned to writing and went on to dominate the world of British detective fiction, taking pride in testing different criminal techniques. So keen were his powers as a writer that part of one of his best novels was written in a bomb shelter.

BY THE SAME AUTHOR
ALL PUBLISHED BY HOUSE OF STRATUS

The Shadow of the Wolf

R Austin Freeman

HOUSE OF
STRATUS

This edition published in 2001 by House of Stratus, an imprint of Stratus Books Ltd., 21 Beeching Park, Kelly Bray, Cornwall, PL17 8QS, UK.

www.houseofstratus.com

Typeset, printed and bound by House of Stratus.

A catalogue record for this book is available from the British Library and the Library of Congress.

ISBN 0-7551-0376-9

CONTENTS

CHAPTER ONE

In Which Two Men Go Forth and One Arrives

About half-past eight on a fine, sunny June morning a small yacht crept out of Sennen Cove, near the Land's End, and headed for the open sea. On the shelving beach of the Cove two women and a man, evidently visitors (or "foreigners," to use the local term), stood watching her departure with valedictory waving of cap or handkerchief; and the boatman who had put the crew on board, aided by two of his comrades, was hauling his boat up above the tide-mark.

A light northerly breeze filled the yacht's sails and drew her gradually seaward. The figures of her crew dwindled to the size of a doll's, shrank with the increasing distance to the magnitude of insects, and at last, losing all individuality, became mere specks merged in the form of the fabric that bore them. At this point the visitors turned their faces inland and walked away up the beach, and the boatman, having opined that "she be fetchin' a tidy offing," dismissed the yacht from his mind and reverted to the consideration of a heap of netting and some invalid lobster-pots.

On board the receding craft two men sat in the little cockpit. They formed the entire crew, for the *Sandhopper* was only a ship's lifeboat, timbered and decked, of light draught, and, in the matter of spars and canvas, what the art critics would call "reticent."

Both men, despite the fineness of the weather, wore yellow oilskins and sou'westers, and that was about all they had in common. In other respects they made a curious contrast: the one small, slender, sharp-featured, dark almost to swarthiness, and restless and quick in his movements; the other large, massive, red-faced, blue-eyed, with the rounded outlines suggestive of ponderous strength – a great ox of a man, heavy, stolid, but much less unwieldy than he looked.

The conversation incidental to getting the yacht under way had ceased, and silence had fallen on the occupants of the cockpit. The big man grasped the tiller and looked sulky, which was probably his usual aspect, and the small man watched him furtively. The land was nearly two miles distant when the latter broke the silence with a remark very similar to that of the boatman on the beach.

"You're not going to take the shore on board, Purcell. Where are we supposed to be going to?"

"I am going outside the Longships," was the stolid answer.

"So I see," rejoined the other. "It's hardly the shortest course for Penzance, though."

"I like to keep an offing on this coast," said Purcell; and once more the conversation languished.

Presently the smaller man spoke again, this time a more cheerful and friendly tone.

"Joan Haygarth has come on wonderfully the last few months; getting quite a fine-looking girl. Don't you think so?"

"Yes," answered Purcell, "and so does Phil Rodney."

"You're right," agreed the other. "But she isn't a patch on her sister, though, and never will be. I was looking at Maggie as we came down the beach this morning and thinking what a handsome girl she is. Don't you agree with me?"

Purcell stooped to look under the boom, and answered without turning his head:

"Yes, she's all right."

"All right!" exclaimed the other. "Is that the way – "

2

"Look here, Varney," interrupted Purcell, "I don't want to discuss my wife's looks with you or any other man. She'll do for me, or I shouldn't have married her."

A deep coppery flush stole into Varney's cheeks. But he had brought the rather brutal snub on himself, and apparently had the fairness to recognize the fact, for he mumbled an apology and relapsed into silence.

When he next spoke he did so with a manner diffident and uneasy, as though approaching a disagreeable or difficult subject.

"There's a little matter, Dan, that I've been wanting to speak to you about when we got a chance of a private talk." He glanced a little anxiously at his stolid companion, who grunted, and then, without removing his gaze from the horizon ahead, replied: "You've a pretty fair chance now, seeing that we shall be bottled up together for another five or six hours. And it's private enough, unless you bawl loud enough to be heard at the Longships."

It was not a gracious invitation. But that Varney had hardly expected; and if he resented the rebuff he showed no signs of annoyance, for reasons which appeared when he opened his subject.

"What I wanted to say," he resumed, "was this. We're both doing pretty well now on the square. You must be positively piling up the shekels, and I can earn a decent living, which is all I want. Why shouldn't we drop this flash note business?"

Purcell kept his blue eye fixed on the horizon, and appeared to ignore the question; but after an interval, and without moving a muscle, he said gruffly, "Go on," and Varney continued:

"The lay isn't what it was, you know. At first it was all plain sailing. The notes were first-class copies, and not a soul suspected anything until they were presented at the bank. Then the murder was out, and the next little trip that I made was a very different affair. Two or three of the notes were suspected quite soon after I had changed them, and I had to be precious fly, I can tell you, to avoid complications. And now that the second batch has come into the bank, the planting of fresh specimens is going to be no sinecure. There isn't a moneychanger on the Continent of Europe that isn't keeping his weather eyeball peeled, to say nothing of the detectives that the bank people have sent abroad."

He paused and looked appealingly at his companion. But Purcell, still minding his helm, only growled: "Well?"

"Well, I want to chuck it, Dan. When you've had a run of luck and pocketed your winnings is the time to stop play."

"You've come into some money then, I take it," said Purcell.

"No, I haven't. But I can make a living now by safe and respectable means, and I'm sick of all this scheming and dodging with the gaol everlastingly under my lee."

"The reason I asked," said Purcell, "is that there is a trifle outstanding. You hadn't forgotten that, I suppose?"

"No, I hadn't forgotten it, but I thought that perhaps you might be willing to let me down a bit easily."

The other man pursed up his thick lips, but continued to gaze stonily over the bow.

"Oh, that's what you thought, hey?" he said; and then, after a pause, he continued: "I fancy you must have lost sight of some of the facts when you thought that. Let me just remind you how the case stands. To begin with, you start your career with a little playful forgery and embezzlement; you blue the proceeds, and you are mug enough to be found out. Then I come in. I compound the affair with old Marston for a couple of thousand, and practically clean myself out of every penny I possess, and he consents to regard your temporary absence in the light of a holiday.

"Now why do I do this? Am I a philanthropist? Devil a bit. I'm a man of business. Before I ladle out that two thousand, I make a business contract with you. I happen to possess the means of making and the skill to make a passable imitation of the Bank of England paper; you are a skilled engraver and a plausible scamp. I am to supply you with paper blanks; you are to engrave plates, print the notes, and get them changed. I am to take two-thirds of the proceeds, and, although I have done the most difficult part of the work, I agree to regard my share of the profits as constituting repayment of the loan. Our contract amounts to this: I lend you two thousand without security – with an infernal amount of insecurity, in fact – you promise, covenant, and agree,' as the lawyers say, to hand me back ten thousand in instalments, being the products of our joint industry. It is a verbal contract which I have no means of enforcing; but I trust you to keep your word, and up to the present you have kept it. You have paid me a little over four thousand. Now you want to cry off and leave the balance unpaid. Isn't that the position?"

"Not exactly," said Varney. "I'm not crying off the debt; I only want time. Look here, Dan: I'm making about five-fifty a year now. That isn't much, but I'll manage to let you have a hundred a year out of it. What do you say to that?"

Purcell laughed scornfully. "A hundred a year to pay off six thousand! That'll take just sixty years, and as I'm now forty-three, I shall be exactly a hundred and three years of age when the last instalment is paid. I think, Varney, you'll admit that a man of a hundred and three is getting a bit past his prime."

"Well, I'll pay you something down to start. I've saved about eighteen hundred pounds out of the note business. You can have that now, and I'll pay off as much as I can at a time until I'm clear. Remember that if I should happen to get clapped in chokee for twenty years or so you won't get anything. And, I tell you, it's getting a risky business."

"I'm willing to take the risk," said Purcell.

"I dare say you are!" Varney retorted passionately, "because it's my risk. If I am grabbed, it's my racket. You sit out. It's I who passed the notes, and I'm known to be a skilled engraver. That'll be good enough for them. They won't trouble about who made the paper."

"I hope not," said Purcell.

"Of course they wouldn't, and you know I shouldn't give you away."

"Naturally. Why should you? Wouldn't do you any good."

"Well, give me a chance, Dan," Varney pleaded. "This business is getting on my nerves. I want to be quit of it. You've had four thousand; that's a hundred per cent. You haven't done so badly."

"I didn't expect to do badly. I took a big risk. I gambled two thousand for ten."

"Yes, and you got me out of the way while you put the screw on to poor old Haygarth to make his daughter marry you."

It was an indiscreet thing to say, but Purcell's stolid indifference to his danger and distress had ruffled Varney's temper somewhat.

Purcell, however, was unmoved. "I don't know," he said, "what you mean by getting you out of the way. You were never in the way. You were always hankering after Maggie, but I could never see that she wanted you."

"Well, she certainly didn't want you," Varney retorted, "and, for that matter, I don't much think she wants you now."

For the first time Purcell withdrew his eye from the horizon to turn it on his companion. And an evil eye it was, set in the great sensual face, now purple with anger.

"What the devil do you mean?" he exclaimed furiously, "you infernal sallow-faced little whippersnapper! If you mention my wife's name again I'll knock you on the head and pitch you overboard."

Varney's face flushed darkly, and for a moment he was inclined to try the wager of battle. But the odds were impossible, and if Varney was not a coward, neither was he a fool. But the discussion was at an end. Nothing was to be hoped for now. Those indiscreet words of provocation had rendered further pleading impossible; and as Varney relapsed into sullen silence, it was with the knowledge that, for weary years to come, he was doomed, at best, to tread the perilous path of crime, or, more probably, to waste the brightest years of his life in a convict prison. For it is a strange fact, and a curious commentary on our current ethical notions, that neither of these rascals even contemplated as a possibility the breach of a merely verbal covenant. A promise had been given. That was enough. Without a specific release, the terms of that promise must be fulfilled to the letter. How many righteous men – prim lawyers or strait-laced, church-going men of business – would have looked at the matter in the same way?

The silence that settled down on the yacht and the aloofness that encompassed the two men were conducive to reflection. Each of the men ignored the presence of the other. When the course was altered southerly, Purcell slacked out the sheets with his own hand as he put up the helm. He might have been sailing single-handed. And Varney watched him askance, but made no move, sitting hunched up on the locker, nursing a slowly matured hatred and thinking his thoughts.

Very queer thoughts they were, rambling, but yet connected and very vivid. He was following out the train of events that might have happened, pursuing them to their possible consequences. Supposing Purcell had carried out his threat? Well, there would have been a pretty tough struggle, for Varney was no weakling. But a struggle with that solid fifteen stone of flesh could end only in one way. He glanced at the great purple, shiny hand that grasped the knob of the tiller. Not the sort of hand that you would want at your throat! No, there was no doubt; he would have gone overboard.

And what then? Would Purcell have gone back to Sennen Cove, or sailed alone into Penzance? In either case, he would have had to make up some sort of story, and no one could have contradicted him, whether the story was believed or not. But it would have been awkward for Purcell.

Then there was the body. That would have washed up sooner or later, as much of it as the lobsters had left. Well, lobsters don't eat clothes or bones, and a dent in the skull might take some accounting for. Very awkward, this, for Purcell. He would probably have had to clear out – to make a bolt for it, in short.

The mental picture of this great bully fleeing in terror from the vengeance of the law gave Varney appreciable pleasure. Most of his life he had been borne down by the moral and physical weight of this domineering brute. At school Purcell had fagged him; he had even bullied him up at Cambridge; and now he had fastened on for ever like the Old Man of the Sea. And Purcell always got the best of it. When he, Varney, had come back from Italy after that unfortunate little affair, behold! the girl whom they had both wanted (and who had wanted neither of them) had changed from Maggie Haygarth into Maggie Purcell. And so it was even unto this day. Purcell, once a book-keeper in a paper-mill, now a prosperous "financier" − a money-lender, as Varney more than suspected − spent a part of his secret leisure making, in absolute safety, those paper blanks, which he, Varney, must risk his liberty to change into money. Yes, it was quite pleasant to think of Purcell sneaking from town to town, from country to country, with the police at his heels.

But in these days of telegraphs and extradition there isn't much chance for a fugitive. Purcell would have been caught to a certainty, and he would have been hanged; no doubt of it. And, passing lightly over less attractive details, Varney considered luxuriously the circumstances of the execution. What a figure he would have made, that great human ox, turning round and round at the end of a taut rope, like a baron of beef on a colossal roasting-jack! Varney looked gloatingly at his companion, considered his large sullen face, and thought how it would swell and grow purple as the rope tightened round the thick crimson neck.

A disagreeable picture, perhaps, but not to Varney, who saw it through the distorting medium of years of accumulated dislike. Then, too, there was the consideration that in the very moment that those brawny limbs had ceased to twitch Maggie would have been free − would have been a widow. Not that that would have concerned him, Varney: he would have been in some Cornish churchyard, with a dent in his skull. Still, it was a pleasant reflection.

The imagined picture of the execution gave him quite a lengthy entertainment. Then his errant thoughts began to spread out in search of other possibilities. For, after all, it was not an absolute certainty that Purcell could have got him overboard. There was just the chance that he might have gone overboard himself. That would have been a very different affair.

Varney settled himself composedly to consider the new and interesting train of consequences that would thus have been set going. They were more agreeable to contemplate than the others, because they did not include his own demise. The execution scene made no appearance in this version. The salient fact was that his oppressor would have vanished; that the intolerable burden of his servitude would have been lifted for ever; that he would have been free.

The thought of his regained freedom set him dreaming of the future – the future that might have been if he could have been rid of this monstrous parasite; the future that might even have held a place for Maggie – for she would have been free, too. It was all very pleasant to think about, though rather tantalizing. He almost wished he had let Purcell try to put him over.

Of course, some explanation would have to be given, some sort of story told, and people might not have believed him. Well, they could have pleased themselves about that. To be sure, there would have been the body; but if there were no marks of violence, what of it? Besides, it really need never have washed ashore: that could easily have been prevented, and if the body had never been found, who was to say that the man had gone overboard at all?

This, again, was a new view of the case, and it set his thoughts revolving afresh. He found himself roughly sketching out the conditions under which the body might have vanished for ever. It was mere idle speculation to while away a dull hour with an uncongenial companion, and he let his thoughts ramble at large. Now he was away in the imagined future, a future of peace and prosperity and honourable effort; and now his thoughts came back unbidden to fill in some forgotten detail. One moment he was dreamily wondering whether Maggie would ever have listened to him, ever have come to care for him; the next, he was back in the yacht's cabin, where hung from a hook on the bulkhead the revolver that the Rodneys used to practise at floating bottles. It was usually loaded, he knew, but if not, there was a canvas bag full of cartridges in the starboard locker. Again he found himself dreaming of the home that he would have had, a home very different from the cheerless lodgings in which he moped at present; and then his thoughts had flitted back to the yacht's hold, and were busying themselves with the row of half-hundredweights that rested on the timbers on either side of the kelson.

It was a curious mental state, rambling, seemingly incoherent, yet quite purposeful, the attention oscillating between the great general idea and its various component details. He was like a painter roughing out the preliminary sketch of a picture, at first carelessly smearing in the general effect, then pausing from time to time to sharpen an edge, to touch in a crisp light, to define the shape of a shadow, but never losing sight of the central motive. And as in the sketch definable shapes begin to grow out of the formless expanse, and a vague suggestion crystallizes into an intelligible composition, so in Varney's mind a process of gradual integration turned a vague and general idea into a clear picture, sharp, vivid, complete.

When Varney had thus brought his mental picture, so to speak, to a finish, its completeness surprised him. It was so simple, so secure. He had actually planned out the scheme of a murder; and behold! there was nothing in it. Anyone could have done it, and no one could have been any the wiser. Here he found himself wondering whether many murders passed undetected. They well might if murders were as easy and as safe as this. A dangerous reflection for an injured and angry man. And at this critical point his meditations were broken in on by Purcell, continuing the conversation as if there had been no pause.

"So you can take it from me, Varney, that I expect you to stick to your bargain. I paid down my money, and I'm going to have my pound of flesh."

"You won't agree to any sort of compromise?"

"No. There are six thousand pounds owing. If you've got the money you can hand it over. If you haven't, you'll have to go on the lay and get it. That's all I've got to say. So now you know."

It was a brutal thing to say, and it was brutally said. But more than that: it was inopportune − or opportune, as you will. For it came as a sort of infernal doxology to the devil's anthem that had been, all unknown, ringing in Varney's soul.

Purcell had spoken without looking round. That was his unpleasant habit. Had he looked at his companion, he might have been startled. A change in Varney's face might have given him pause: a warm flush, a sparkle of the eye, a look of elation, of settled purpose, deadly, inexorable. The look of a man who has made a fateful resolution. But he never looked, and the warning of the uplifted axe passed him by.

It was so simple, so secure! That was the burden of the song that echoed in Varney's brain. So safe! And there abroad were the watchful money-changers waiting for the clever forger to come once too often. There were the detectives lurking in ambush for him. No safety there! Rather the certainty of swift disaster, with the sequel of judge and jury, the clang of an iron door, and thereafter the dreary prison eating up the years of his life.

He glanced over the sea. They had opened the South Coast now, and he could see, afar off, a fleet of black-sailed luggers heading east. *They* wouldn't be in his way. Nor would the big four-master that was creeping away to the west, for she was hull down already; and other ships there were none. There was one hindrance, though. Dead ahead the Wolf Rock lighthouse rose from the blue water, its red-and-white-ringed tower looking like some gaudily painted toy. The keepers of lonely lighthouses have a natural habit of watching the passing shipping through their glasses, and it was possible that one of their telescopes might be pointed at the yacht at this very moment. That was a complication.

Suddenly there came down the wind a sharp report like the firing of a gun, quickly followed by a second. Both men recognized the duplicate report and both looked round. It was the explosive signal from the Longships lighthouse; but when they looked there was no lighthouse to be seen, and the dark blue heaving water faded away at the foot of an advancing wall of vapour.

Purcell cursed volubly. A pretty place, this, to be caught in a fog! And then, as his eye lighted on his companion, he demanded angrily: "What the devil are you grinning at?" For Varney, drunk with suppressed excitement, snapped his fingers at rocks and shoals; he was thinking only of the light-keeper's telescope and of the revolver that hung on the bulkhead. He must make some excuse presently to go below and secure that revolver.

But no excuse was necessary. The opportunity came of itself. After a hasty glance at the vanishing land and another at the compass, Purcell put up the helm to jibe the yacht round on to an easterly course. As she came round, the single headsail that she carried in place of jib and foresail shivered for a few seconds and then filled suddenly on the opposite tack. And at this moment the halyard parted with a loud snap, the end of the rope flew through the blocks, and, in an instant, the sail was down and its upper half trailing in the water alongside.

Purcell swore furiously, but kept an eye to business. "Run below, Varney," said he, "and fetch up that coil of new rope out of the starboard locker while I haul the sail on board. And look alive. We don't want to drift down on to the Wolf."

Varney obeyed with silent alacrity and a curious feeling of elation. It was going to be even easier and safer than he had thought. He slipped through the hatch into the cabin, and, as he heard Purcell scrambling along the side-deck overhead, he quietly took the revolver from its hook and examined the chambers. Finding them all loaded, he cocked the hammer and slipped the weapon carefully into the inside breast-pocket of his oilskin coat. Then he took the coil of rope from the locker and went on deck.

As he emerged from the hatch he perceived that the yacht was already enveloped in fog, which drifted past in steamy clouds and swirling streamers, and that she had come up head to wind. Purcell was kneeling on the forecastle, tugging at the sail, which had caught under the forefoot, and punctuating his efforts with deep-voiced curses.

Varney stole silently along the deck, steadying himself by mast and shroud, softly laid down the coil of rope, and approached. Purcell was quite engrossed with his task; his back was towards Varney, his face over the side, intent on the entangled sail. It was a chance in a thousand.

With scarcely a moment's hesitation Varney stooped forward, steadying himself with a hand on the little windlass, and, softly drawing forth the revolver, pointed it at the back of Purcell's head, at the spot where the back seam of his sou'wester met the brim. The report rang out, but weak and flat in that open space, and a cloud of smoke mingled with the fog; but it blew away immediately, and showed Purcell almost unchanged in posture, crouching on the sail with his chin resting on the little rim of bulwark, while behind him his murderer, as if turned into bronze, still stood stooping forward, one hand grasping the windlass, the other still pointing the revolver.

Thus the two figures remained for some seconds motionless like some horrible waxworks, until the little yacht, lifting to the swell, gave a more than usually lively curvet, when Purcell rolled over on to his back, and Varney relaxed the rigidity of his posture like a golf player who has watched his ball drop. He bent over the prostrate figure with no emotion but curiosity. Looked into the wide-open, clear blue eyes, noted how the great red face had faded to a pallid mauve, against which the blood on lips and chin stood out like the painted patches on a clown's face; but he felt not a single twinge of compunction.

Purcell was dead. That was the salient fact. The head wagged to and fro as the yacht pitched and rolled, the limp arms and legs seemed to twitch, the limp body to writhe uneasily. But Varney was not disturbed. Lifeless things will move on an unsteady deck. He was only interested to notice how the passive movements produced the illusion of life. But it was only illusion. Purcell was dead. There was no doubt of that.

The double report from the Longships came down the wind, and then, as if in answer, a prolonged deep bellow. That was the fog-horn of the lighthouse on the Wolf Rock, and it sounded surprisingly near. But, of course, these signals were meant to be heard at a distance. Then a stream of hot sunshine, pouring down on deck, startled him and made him hurry. The body must be got overboard before the fog lifted. With an uneasy glance at the clear sky overhead, he hastily cast off the broken halyard from its cleat and cut off a couple of fathoms. Then he hurried below and, lifting the trap in the cabin floor, hoisted out one of the iron half-hundredweights with which the yacht was ballasted. As he stepped on deck with the weight in his hand the sun was shining overhead; but the fog was still thick below, and the horn sounded once more from the Wolf. And again it struck him as surprisingly near.

He passed the length of rope that he had cut off twice round Purcell's body, hauled it tight, and secured it with a knot. Then he made the ends fast to the handle of the iron weight.

Not much fear of Purcell drifting ashore now! That weight would hold him as long as there was anything to hold. But it had taken some time to do, and the warning bellow from the Wolf seemed to draw nearer and nearer. He was about to heave the body over when his eye fell on the dead man's sou'wester, which had fallen off when the body rolled over. That hat must be got rid of, for Purcell's name was worked in silk on the lining, and there was an unmistakable bullet-hole through the back. It must be destroyed, or, which would be simpler and quicker, lashed securely on the dead man's head.

Hurriedly, Varney ran aft and descended to the cabin. He had noticed a new ball of spun-yarn in the locker when he had fetched the rope. This would be the very thing.

He was back again in a few moments with the ball in his hand, unwinding it as he came, and without wasting time he knelt down by the body and fell to work. There was a curious absence of repugnance in his manner, horrible as his task would have seemed. He had to raise the dead man's head to fit on the hat, and in so doing covered his left hand with blood. But he appeared to mind no more than if he had been handling a seal that he had shot or a large and dirty fish. Quite composedly, and with that featness in the handling of cordage that marks the sailor-man, whether amateur or professional, he proceeded with his task, intent only on making the lashing secure and getting it done quickly.

And every half minute the deep-voiced growl of the Wolf came to him out of the fog, and each time it sounded nearer and yet nearer.

By the time he had made the sou'wester secure, the dead man's face and chin were encaged in a web of spun-yarn that made him look like some old-time, grotesque-vizored Samurai warrior. But the hat was now immovable. Long after that burly corpse had dwindled to a mere skeleton it would hold, would still cling to the dead head when the face that looked through the lacing of cords was the face of a bare and grinning skull.

Varney rose to his feet. But his task was not finished yet. There was Purcell's suitcase. That must be sunk, too; and there was something in it that had figured in the detailed picture that his imagination had drawn. He ran to the cockpit, where the suitcase lay, and having tried its fastenings and found it unlocked, he opened it and took out with his right hand – the clean one – a letter that lay on top of the other contents. This he tossed through the hatch into the cabin. Then his eye caught Purcell's fountain-pen, slipped neatly through a loop in the lid. It was filled, he knew, with the peculiar black ink that Purcell always used. The thought passed swiftly through his mind that perchance it might be of use to him. In a moment he had drawn it from its loop and slipped it into his pocket. Then, having closed and fastened the suitcase, he carried it forward and made it fast to the iron weight with a half-dozen turns of spun-yarn.

That was really all, and, indeed, it was time. As he rose, once more, to his feet, the growl of the foghorn burst out, as it seemed, right over the stern of the yacht, and she was drifting stern foremost, who could say how fast? Now, too, he caught a more ominous sound, which he might have heard sooner had he listened – the wash of water, the boom of breakers bursting on a rock.

A sudden revulsion came over him. He burst into a wild sardonic laugh. And had it come to this, after all? Had he schemed and laboured only to leave himself alone on an unmanageable craft drifting down to shipwreck and certain death? Had he taken all this thought and care to secure Purcell's body, when his own might be resting beside it on the sea bottom within an hour?

But his reverie was brief. Suddenly from the white void over his very head, as it seemed, there issued a stunning, thunderous roar that shook the very deck under his feet. The water around him boiled into a foamy chaos, the din of bursting waves was in his ears, the yacht plunged and wallowed amidst clouds of spray, and, for an instant, a dim, gigantic shadow loomed through the fog and was gone.

In that moment his nerve had come back. Holding on, with one hand, to the windlass, he dragged the body to the edge of the forecastle, hoisted the weight out-board, and then, taking advantage of a heavy lurch, gave the corpse a vigorous shove. There was a rattle and a hollow splash, and corpse and weight and suitcase had vanished into the seething water.

He clung to the swinging mast and waited. Breathlessly he told out the allotted seconds until, once again, the invisible Titan belched forth his thunderous warning. But this time the roar came over the yacht's bow. She had drifted past the Rock, then. The danger was over, and Purcell would have to go down to Davy Jones' Locker companionless after all.

Very soon the water around ceased to boil and tumble, and as the yacht's wild plunging settled down once more into the normal rise and fall on the long swell, Varney turned his attention to the refitting of the halyard. But what was this on the creamy duck sail? A pool of blood and a gory imprint of his own hand! That wouldn't do at all. He would have to clear that away before he could hoist the sail, which was annoying, as the yacht was helpless without her head-sail and was evidently drifting out to sea.

He fetched a bucket, a swab, and a scrubbing-brush, and set to work. The bulk of the large bloodstain cleared off pretty completely after he had drenched the sail with a bucketful or two and given it a good scrubbing. But the edge of the stain, where the heat of the deck had dried it, remained like the painted boundary on a map; and the hand-print, which had also dried, though it faded to a pale buff, continued clearly visible.

Varney began to grow uneasy. If those stains would not come out, especially the hand-print, it would be very awkward; they would take such a deal of explaining. He decided to try the effect of marine soap, and fetched a cake from the cabin; but even this did not obliterate the stains completely, though it turned them a faint greenish brown, very unlike the colour of blood. Still he scrubbed on, until at last the hand-print faded away entirely and the large stain was reduced to a faint green wavy line, and that was the best he could do; and quite good enough, for if that faint line should ever be noticed, no one would ever suspect its origin.

He put away the bucket and proceeded with the refitting. The sea had disengaged the sail from the forefoot, and he hauled it on board without difficulty. Then there was the reeving of the new halyard – a troublesome business, involving the necessity of his going aloft, where his weight, small man as he was, made the yacht roll most infernally, and set him swinging to and fro like the bob of a metronome. But he was a smart yachtsman and active, though not powerful, and a few minutes' strenuous exertion ended in his sliding down the shrouds with the new halyard running fairly through the upper block. A vigorous haul or two at the new hairy rope sent the head of the dripping sail aloft, and the yacht was once more under control.

The rig of the *Sandhopper* was not smart, but it was handy. She carried a short bowsprit to accommodate the single head-sail and a relatively large mizzen, of which the advantage was that by judicious management of the mizzen-sheet the yacht would sail with very little attention to the helm. Of this advantage Varney was keenly appreciative just now, for he had several things to do before entering port. The excitement of the last hour and the bodily exertions had left him shaky and faint. He wanted refreshment, he wanted a wash, and the various traces of recent events had to be removed. Also, there was that letter to be attended to. So that it was convenient to be able to leave the helm in charge of a lashing for a minute now and again.

When he had washed he put the kettle on the spirit-stove, and, while it was heating, busied himself in cleaning the revolver, flinging the empty cartridge-case overboard, and replacing it with a cartridge from the bag in the locker. Then he picked up the letter that he had taken from Purcell's suitcase and examined it. It was addressed to "Joseph Penfield, Esq., George Yard, Lombard Street," and was unstamped, though the envelope was fastened up. He affixed a stamp from his pocket-book, and, when the kettle began to boil, he held the envelope in the steam that issued from spout. Very soon the flap of the envelope loosened and curled back, when he laid it aside to mix himself a mug of hot grog, which, together with the letter and a biscuit-tin, he took out into the cockpit. The fog was still dense, and the hoot of a steamer's whistle from somewhere to the westward caused him to reach the fog-horn out of the locker and blow a long blast on it. As if in answer to his treble squeak came the deep bass note from the Wolf, and, unconsciously, he looked round. He turned automatically, as one does towards a sudden noise, not expecting to see anything but fog, and what he did see startled him not a little.

For there was the lighthouse – or half of it, rather – standing up above the fogbank, clear, distinct, and hardly a mile away. The gilded vane, the sparkling lantern, the gallery, and the upper half of the red-and-white-ringed tower, stood sharp against the pallid sky, but the lower half was invisible. It was a strange apparition – like half a lighthouse suspended in mid-air – and uncommonly disturbing, too. It raised a very awkward question. If he could see the lantern the light-keepers could see him. But how long had the lantern been clear of the fog? That was the question, and the answer to it might come in a highly disagreeable form.

Thus he meditated as, with one hand on the tiller, he munched his biscuit and sipped his grog. Presently he picked up the stamped envelope and drew from it a letter, which he tore into fragments and dropped overboard. Then, from his pocket-book, he took a similar but unaddressed envelope, from which he drew out its contents, and very curious those contents were. There was a letter, brief and laconic, which he read thoughtfully. "These," it ran, "are all I have by me, but they will do for the present, and when you have planted them I will let you have a fresh supply." There was no date and no signature, but the rather peculiar handwriting, in jet-black ink, was similar to that on the envelope addressed to Joseph Penfield, Esq.

The other contents consisted of a dozen sheets of blank paper, each of the size of a Bank of England note. But they were not quite blank, for each bore an elaborate water-mark, identical with that of a twenty-pound banknote. They were, in fact, the "paper blanks" of which Purcell had spoken. The envelope with its contents had been slipped into his hand by Purcell, without remark, only three days ago.

Varney refolded the "blanks," enclosed them within the letter, and slipped letter and "blanks" together into the stamped envelope, the flap of which he licked and reclosed.

"I should like to see old Penfield's face when he opens that envelope," was his reflection as, with a grim smile, he put it away in his pocket-book. "And I wonder what he will do," he added mentally; "however, I shall see before many days are over."

Varney looked at his watch. He was to meet Jack Rodney on Penzance Pier at a quarter to three. He would never do it at this rate, for when he opened Mount's Bay, Penzance would be right in the wind's eye. That would mean a long beat to windward. Then Rodney would be there first, waiting for him. Deuced awkward, this. He would have to account for his being alone on board, would have to invent some lie about having put Purcell ashore at

Mousehole or Newlyn. But a lie is a very pernicious thing. Its effects are cumulative. You never know when you have done with it. Apart from moral considerations, lies should be avoided at all cost of present inconvenience; that is, unless they are absolutely unavoidable, and then they should be as probable as can be managed, and not calculated to provoke inquiry. Now, if he had reached Penzance before Rodney, he need have said nothing about Purcell – for the present, at any rate, and that would have been so much safer.

When the yacht was about abreast of Lamorna Cove, though some seven miles to the south, the breeze began to draw ahead, and the fog cleared off quite suddenly. The change of wind was unfavourable for the moment, but when it veered round yet a little more until it blew from east-north-east, Varney brightened up considerably. There was still a chance of reaching Penzance before Rodney arrived; for now, as soon as he had fairly opened Mount's Bay, he could head straight for his destination and make it on a single board.

Between two and three hours later the *Sandhopper* entered Penzance Harbour, and, threading her way among an assemblage of luggers and small coasters, brought up alongside the Albert Pier, at the foot of a vacant ladder.

Having made the yacht fast to a couple of rings, Varney divested himself of his oilskins, locked the cabin scuttle, and climbed the ladder. The change of wind had saved him after all, and as he strode away along the pier he glanced complacently at his watch. He still had nearly half an hour to the good.

He seemed to know the place well and to have a definite objective, for he struck out briskly from the foot of the pier into Market Jew Street, and from thence, by a somewhat zigzag route, to a road which eventually brought him out about the middle of the esplanade. Continuing westward, he entered the Newlyn Road, along which he walked rapidly for about a third of a mile, when he drew up opposite a small letter-box, which was let into a wall. Here he stopped to read the tablet, on which was printed the hours of collection, and then, having glanced at his watch, he walked on again, but at a less rapid pace.

When he reached the outskirts of Newlyn, he turned and began slowly to retrace his steps, looking at his watch from time to time with a certain air of impatience. Presently a quick step behind him caused him to look round. The newcomer was a postman, striding along, bag on shoulder, with the noisy tread of a heavily shod man and evidently collecting letters. Varney let him pass, watched him halt at the little letter-box, unlock the door, gather up the letters, and stow them in his bag, heard the clang of the iron door, and finally saw the man set forth again on his pilgrimage. Then he brought forth his pocket-book, and drawing from it the letter addressed to Joseph Penfield, Esq., stepped up to the letter-box. The tablet now announced that the next collection would be at 8.30 p.m. Varney read the announcement with a faint smile, glanced again at his watch, which stood at two minutes past four, and dropped the letter into the box.

As he walked up the pier with a large paper bag under his arm, he became aware of a tall man who was doing sentry-go before a Gladstone bag that stood on the coping opposite the ladder, and who, observing his approach, came forward to meet him.

"Here you are, then, Rodney," was Varney's rather unoriginal greeting.

"Yes," replied Rodney, "and here I've been for nearly half an hour. Purcell gone?"

"Bless you! yes, long ago," answered Varney.

"I didn't see him at the station. What train was he going by?"

"I don't know. He said something about taking Falmouth on the way; had some business or other there. But I expect he's gone to have a feed at one of the hotels. We got hung up in a fog; that's why I'm so late. I've been up to buy some prog."

"Well," said Rodney, "bring it on board. It's time we were under way. As soon as we are outside I'll take charge, and you can go below and stoke up at your ease."

The two men descended the ladder and proceeded at once to hoist the sails and cast off the shore ropes. A few strokes of an oar sent them clear of the lee of the pier, and in a few minutes the yacht *Sandhopper* was once more outside, heading south with a steady breeze from east–north-east.

CHAPTER TWO

In Which Margaret Purcell Receives a Letter

Daylight dies hard in the month of June, and Night comes but tardily into her scanty reversion. The clock on the mantelpiece stood at half-past nine, and candles twinkled on the supper table, but even now the slaty-grey band of twilight was only just stealing up behind the horizon to veil the fading glories of the western sky.

Varney sat at the old-fashioned, oval, gate-legged table with an air of placid contentment, listening to and joining in the rather disconnected talk (for hungry people are poor conversationalists) with quiet geniality but with a certain remoteness and abstraction. From where he sat he could see out through the open window the great ocean stretching away to the south and west, the glittering horizon, and the gorgeous evening sky. With quiet pleasure he had watched the changing scene – the crimson disc of the setting sun, the flaming gold softening down into the sober tints of the afterglow – and now, as the grey herald of the night spread upwards, his eye dwelt steadily on one spot away in the south-west. At first faintly visible, then waxing as the daylight waned, a momentary spark flashed in the heart of the twilight grey, now white like the sparkle of a diamond, now crimson like the flash of a ruby. It was the light on the Wolf Rock.

He watched it thoughtfully as he talked: white – red, white – red, diamond – ruby, so it would go on every fifteen seconds through the short summer night – to mariners a warning and a guide; to him, a message of release; for another, a memorial.

As he looked at the changing light, he thought of his enemy lying out there in the chilly depths on the bed of the sea. It was strange how often he thought of Purcell. For the man was dead; had gone out of his life utterly. And yet, in the two days that had passed, every trivial incident had seemed to connect itself and him with the man who was gone. And so it was now. All roads seemed to lead to Purcell. If he looked out seaward, there was the lighthouse flashing its secret message, as if it should say, "We know, you and I; he is down here." If he looked around the table, still everything spoke of the dead man. There was Philip Rodney – Purcell and he had talked of him on the yacht. There was Jack Rodney who had waited on the pier for the man who had not come. There, at the hostess' right hand, was the quiet, keen-faced stranger whom Purcell, for some reason, had not wished to meet; and there, at the head of the table, was Margaret herself, the determining cause of it all. Even the very lobsters on the table (lobsters are plentiful at the Land's End) set him thinking of dark crawling shapes down in that dim underworld, groping around a larger shape tethered to an iron weight.

He turned his face resolutely away from the sea. He would think no more of Purcell. The fellow had dogged him through life, but now he was gone. Enough of Purcell. Let him think of something more pleasant.

The most agreeable object of contemplation within his field of vision was the woman who sat at the head of the table, his hostess. And, in fact, Margaret Purcell was very pleasant to look upon, not only for her comeliness – though she was undoubtedly a pretty, almost a beautiful, woman – but because she was sweet-faced and gracious, and what men compliment the sex by calling "womanly." She was evidently under thirty, though she carried a certain matronly sedateness and an air of being older than she either looked or was, which was accentuated by the fashion in which she wore her hair, primly parted in the middle; a rather big woman, quiet and reposeful, as big women often are.

Varney looked at her with a kind of wonder. He had always thought her lovely, and now she seemed lovelier than ever. And she was a widow, little as she suspected it, little as anyone but he suspected it. But it was a fact. She was free to marry, if she only knew it.

He hugged himself at the thought and listened dreamily to the mellow tones of her voice. She was talking to her guest and the elder Rodney, but he had only a dim idea of what she was saying; he was enjoying the music of her speech rather than attending to the matter. Suddenly she turned to him and asked:

"Don't you agree with me, Mr Varney?"

He pulled himself together, and, after a momentarily vacant look, answered:

"I always agree with you, Mrs Purcell."

"And so," said Jack Rodney, "as the greater includes the less, he agrees with you now. I am admiring your self-possession, Varney; you haven't the least idea what we were talking about."

Varney laughed and reddened, and Margaret looked at him with playful reproach.

"Haven't you?" she asked. "But how deceitful of you to answer so readily! I was remarking that lawyers have a way of making a solemn parade of exactness and secrecy when there is no occasion. That was my statement."

"And it is perfectly correct," said Varney. "You know it is, Rodney. You're always doing it. I've noticed it constantly."

"Oh, this is mere vindictiveness, because he unmasked your deceit. I wasn't alluding to Mr Rodney or anyone in particular. I was just speaking generally."

"But," said Varney, "something must have suggested the reflection."

"Certainly. Something did: a letter that I have just received from Mr Penfield; a most portentous document, and all about nothing."

At the mention of the lawyer's name Varney's attention came to a sharp focus.

"It seems," Margaret continued, "that Dan, when he wrote to Mr Penfield the other day, put the wrong letter in the envelope – a silly thing to do, but we all do silly things sometimes."

"I don't," said Rodney.

"Well, ordinary persons, I mean. Then Mr Penfield, instead of simply stating the fact and returning the letter, becomes mysterious and alarming. He informs me that the envelope was addressed in Dan's handwriting, that the letter was posted at Penzance at eight-thirty p.m., that it was opened by him in person, and that the contents, which have been seen by no one but himself, are at present reposing in his private safe, of which he alone has the key. What he does not tell us is what the contents of the envelope were, which is the only thing that matters. It is most extraordinary. From the tone of his letter one would think that the envelope had contained something dreadful and incriminating."

"Perhaps it did," said Varney. "Dan's political views are distinctly revolutionary, and he is as secret as a whole barrel of oysters. That letter may have contained particulars of some sort of Guy Fawkes conspiracy, enclosing samples of suitable explosives. Who knows?"

Margaret was about to reply, when her glance happened to light on Jack Rodney, and something in that gentleman's expressive and handsome face gave her pause. Had she been chattering indiscreetly? And might Mr Penfield have meant something after all? There were some curious points about his letter. She smilingly accepted the Guy Fawkes theory and then adroitly changed the subject.

"Speaking of Penzance, Mr Varney, reminds me that you haven't told us what sort of voyage you had. There was quite a thick fog wasn't there?"

"Yes. It delayed us a lot. Purcell would steer right out to sea for fear of going ashore. Then the breeze failed for a time, and then it veered round easterly and headed us, and, as a wind up to the chapter of accidents, the jib-halyards carried away and we had to reeve a new one. Nice crazy gear you keep on your craft, Rodney."

"I suspected that rope," said Rodney – "in fact, I had meant to fit a new halyard before I went up to town. But I should have liked to see Purcell shinning up aloft."

"So should I – from the shore," said Varney. "He'd have carried away the mast or capsized the yacht: No, my friend; I left him below as a counterpoise and went aloft myself."

"Did Dan go straight off to the station?" Margaret asked.

"I should say not," replied Varney. "He was in a mighty hurry to be off – said he had some things to see to; I fancy one of them was a grilled steak and a bottle of Bass. We were both pretty ravenous."

"But why didn't you go with him if you were ravenous too?"

"I had to snug up the yacht and he wouldn't wait. He was up the ladder like a lamplighter almost before we had made fast. I can see him now, with that great suitcase in his hand, going up as light as a feather. He is wonderfully active for his size."

"Isn't he?" said Rodney. "But these big men often are. Look at the way those great lumping pilots will drop down into a boat: as light as cats."

"He is a big fellow, too," said Varney. "I was looking at him as he stopped at the top of the ladder to sing out 'So long.' He looked quite gigantic in his oilskins."

"He actually went up into town in his oilskins, did he?" exclaimed Margaret. "He must have been impatient for his meal! Oh, how silly of me! I never sewed on that button that had come off the collar of his oilskin coat. I hope you didn't have a wet passage."

"You need not reproach yourself, Mrs Purcell," interposed Philip Rodney. "Your neglect was made good by my providence. I sewed on that button when I borrowed the coat on Friday evening to go to my diggings in."

"You told me you hadn't a spare oilskin button," said Margaret.

"I hadn't, but I made one – out of a cork."

"A cork!" Margaret exclaimed, with an incredulous laugh.

"Not a common cork, you know," Philip explained. "It was a flat circular cork from one of my collecting jars, waterproofed with paraffin wax; a most superior affair, with a beautiful round label – also waterproofed by the wax – on which was typed 'Marine Worms.' The label was very decorative. It's my own invention, and I'm rather proud of it."

"You may well be. And I suppose you sewed it on with rope-yarn and a sail-needle?" Margaret suggested.

"Not at all. It was secured with catgut, the fag end of an E string that I happened to have in my pocket. You see, I had no needle or thread, so I made two holes in the cork with the marlinspike in my pocket-knife, two similar holes in the coat, poked the ends of the fiddlestring through, tied a reef-knot inside, and there it was, tight as wax – paraffin wax."

"It was very ingenious and resourceful of you", Varney commented, "but the product wasn't very happily disposed of on Dan's coat – I mean as to your decorative label. I take it that Dan's interest in marine worms is limited to their use as bait. Now if you could have fitted out Dr Thorndyke with a set there would have been some appropriateness in it, since marine worms are the objects of his devotion – at least, so I understand," and he looked interrogatively at Margaret's guest.

Dr Thorndyke smiled. "You are draping me in the mantle of my friend, Professor D'Arcy," he said. "He is the real devotee. I have merely come down for a few days to stay with him and be an interested spectator of the chase. It is he who should have the buttons."

"Still," said Varney, "you aid and abet him. I suppose you help him to dig them up."

Philip laughed scornfully. "Why, you are as bad as Dan, Varney. You are thinking in terms of bait. Do you imagine Dr Thorndyke and the professor go a-worming with a bully-beef tin and a garden fork as you do when you are getting ready for a fishing jaunt?"

"Well, how was I to know?" retorted Varney. "I am not a naturalist. What do they do? Set traps for 'em with bits of cheese inside?"

"Of course they don't," laughed Margaret. "How absurd you are, Mr Varney! They go out with a boat and a dredge, and very interesting it must be to bring up all those curious creatures from the bottom of the sea."

She spoke rather absently, for her thoughts had gone back to Mr Penfield's letter. There was certainly something a little cryptic in its tone, which she had taken for mere professional pedantry, but which she now recalled with vague uneasiness. Could the old lawyer have stumbled on something discreditable and written this ambiguously worded letter as a warning? Her husband was not a communicative man, and she could not pretend to herself that she had an exalted opinion of his moral character. It was all very disquieting.

The housekeeper, who had been retained with the furnished house, brought in the coffee, and as Margaret poured it out she continued her reflections, watching Varney with unconscious curiosity as he rolled a cigarette. The ring-finger of his left hand had a stiff joint, the result of an old injury, and was permanently bent at a sharp angle. It gave his hand an appearance of awkwardness, but she noted that he rolled his cigarette as quickly and neatly as if all his fingers were sound. The stiff finger had become normal to him. And she also noted that Dr Thorndyke appeared quite interested in the contrast between the appearance of awkwardness and the actual efficiency of the maimed finger.

From Varney her attention – or inattention – wandered to her guest. Absently she dwelt on his powerful, intellectual face, his bold, clean-cut features, his shapely mouth, firm almost to severity; and all the time she was thinking of Mr Penfield's letter.

"Have we all finished?" she asked at length;" and if so, where are we going to smoke our pipes and cigars?"

"I propose that we go into the garden," said Philip. "It is a lovely evening, and we can look at the moonlight on the sea while we smoke."

"Yes," Margaret agreed, "it will be more pleasant out there. Don't wait for me. I will join you in a few minutes, but I want first to have a few words with Mr Rodney."

Philip, who, like the others, understood that this was a consultation on the subject of Mr Penfield's letter, rose and playfully shepherded Varney out of the door which his brother held invitingly open.

"Now then, Varney, out you go. No lagging behind and eavesdropping. The pronouncements of the oracle are not for the likes of you and me."

Varney took his dismissal with a smile and followed Dr Thorndyke out, though, as he looked at the barrister's commanding figure and handsome face, he could not repress a twinge of jealousy. Why could not Maggie have consulted him? He was an old friend, and he knew more about old Penfield's letter than Rodney did. But, of course, she had no idea of that.

As soon as they were alone, Margaret and Rodney resumed their seats, and the former opened the subject without preamble.

"What do you really think of Mr Penfield's letter?" she asked.

"Could you give me, in general terms, the substance of what he says?" Rodney answered cautiously.

"I had better show you the letter itself," said Margaret.

She rose and left the room, returning almost immediately with an official-looking envelope, which she handed to Rodney. The letter, which he extracted from it and spread out on the table, was not remarkably legible; an elderly solicitor's autograph letters seldom are. But barristers, like old-fashioned druggists, are usually expert decipherers, and Rodney read the letter without difficulty. It ran thus:

"George Yard,
Lombard Street, EC
25th June, 1911

Dear Mrs Purcell,

"I have just received from your husband a letter with certain enclosures, which have caused me some surprise. The envelope is addressed to me in his handwriting, and the letter, which is unsigned, is also in his hand; but neither the letter nor the other contents could possibly have been intended for me, and it is manifest that they have been placed in the wrong envelope.

"The postmark shows that the letter was posted at Penzance at 8.30 p.m. on the 23rd instant. It was opened by me, and the contents, which have been seen by no one but me, have been deposited in my private safe, of which I alone have the key.

"Will you very kindly acquaint your husband with these facts and request him to call on me at his early convenience?

I am,

Dear Mrs Purcell,

Yours sincerely,

Joseph Penfield.

Mrs Daniel Purcell,
Sennen
Cornwall."

Rodney read the solicitor's letter through twice, refolded it, replaced it in its envelope, and returned it to Margaret.

"Well, what do you think of it?" the latter asked.

Rodney reflected for some moments.

"It's a very careful letter," he replied at length.

"Yes, I know; and that is a very careful answer, but not very helpful. Now do drop the lawyer and tell me just what you think like a good friend."

Rodney looked at her quickly with a faint smile and yet very earnestly. He found it strangely pleasant to be called a good friend by Margaret Purcell.

"I gather," he said slowly, "from the tone of Mr Penfield's letter, that he found something in that envelope that your husband would not have wished him to see – something that he had reasons for wishing no one to see but the person for whom it was meant."

"Do you mean something discreditable or compromising?"

"We mustn't jump at conclusions. Mr Penfield is very reticent, so, presumably, he has some reasons for reticence, otherwise he would have said plainly what the envelope contained. But why does he write to you? Doesn't he know your husband's address?"

"No, but he could have got it from Dan's office. I have been wondering myself why he wrote to me."

"Has your husband arrived at Oulton yet?"

"Heavens! Yes. It doesn't take two days and a half to get to Norfolk."

"Oh, then he wasn't staying at Falmouth?"

Margaret stared at him. "Falmouth!" she exclaimed. "What do you mean?"

"I understood Varney to say that he was going to call at Falmouth."

"No, certainly not. He was going straight to London and so on to Oulton the same night. I wonder what Mr Varney can have meant."

"We must find out presently. Have you heard from your husband since he left?"

"No. Oddly enough, he hasn't written, which is unlike him. He generally sends me a line as soon as he arrives anywhere."

"You had better send him a telegram in the morning to make sure of his whereabouts, and then let him have a copy of Mr Penfield's letter at once. And I think I wouldn't refer to the subject before any of our friends if I were you."

"No. I oughtn't to have said what I did. But, of course, I didn't dream that Mr Penfield really meant anything. Shall we go out into the garden?"

Rodney opened the door for her, and they passed out to where their three companions sat in deckchairs facing the sea. Two chairs had been placed for them, and, as they seated themselves, Varney remarked:

"I take it that the oracle has spoken, and I hope he was more explicit than oracles are usually."

"He was explicit and discreet – especially discreet," Margaret replied.

"Oh, they are always that," said Varney; "discretion is the oracular speciality. The explicitness is exceptional."

"I believe it is," replied Margaret, "and I am glad you set so much value on it because I am coming to you now for information. Mr Rodney tells me that Dan said something to you about Falmouth. What was it?"

"He said he was going to call in there – at least, so I understood."

"But he wasn't, you know. He was going direct to London and straight on to Oulton the same night. You must have mis-understood him."

"I may have done, but I don't think I did. Still, he only mentioned the matter casually, and I wasn't paying particular attention."

Margaret made no rejoinder, and the party became somewhat silent. Philip, realizing Margaret's uneasy preoccupation, engaged Dr Thorndyke in an animated conversation respecting the natural history of the Cornish coast and the pleasures of dredging.

The other three became profoundly thoughtful. To each the solicitor's letter had its special message, though to one only was that message clearly intelligible. Rodney was puzzled and deeply suspicious. To him the letter had read like that of a man washing his hands of a disagreeable responsibility. The curious reticence as to the nature of the enclosures and the reference to the private safe sounded ominous. He knew little of Purcell – he had been a friend of the Haygarth's – and had no great opinion of him. Purcell was a financier, and financiers sometimes did queer things. At any rate, Penfield's excessive caution suggested something fishy – possibly something illicit. In fact, to speak colloquially, Rodney smelt a rat.

Margaret also was puzzled and suspicious, but, womanlike, she allowed her suspicions to take a more special form. She, too, smelt a rat, but it was a feminine rat. The lawyer's silence as to the contents of that mysterious envelope seemed to admit of no other interpretation. It was so pointed. Of course he could not tell her, though he was an old friend and her trustee, so he had said nothing.

She reflected on the matter with lukewarm displeasure. Her relations with her husband were not such as to admit of jealousy in the ordinary sense; but still, she was married to him, and any affair on his part with another woman would be very disagreeable and humiliating to her. It might lead to a scandal, too, and from that her ingrained delicacy revolted.

Varney, meanwhile, sat with his head thrown back wrapped in thought of a more dreamy quality. He knew all about the letter, and his mind was occupying itself with speculation as to its effects. Rodney's view of it he gauged pretty accurately, but what did *she* think of it? Was she anxious – worried at the prospect of some unpleasant disclosure? He hoped not. At any rate, it could not be helped. And she was free, if she only knew it.

He had smoked out his cigarette, and now, as he abstractedly filled his pipe, his eye insensibly sought the spot where the diamond and ruby flashed out alternately from the bosom of the night. A cloud had crept over the moon, and the transitory golden and crimson gleam shone out bright and clear amidst the encompassing darkness, white – red, white – red, diamond – ruby, a message in a secret code from the tall, unseen sentinel on that solitary, wave-washed rock, bidding him be of good cheer, reminding him again and again of the freedom that was his – and hers, made everlastingly secure by a friendly iron sinker.

The cloud turned silvery at the edge and the moon sailed out into the open. Margaret looked up at it thoughtfully.

"I wonder where Dan is tonight," she said; and in the pause that followed a crimson spark from the dim horizon seemed to Varney to signal, "Here," and instantly fade into discreet darkness.

"Perhaps," suggested Philip, "he is having a moonlight sail on the Broad, or, more probably, taking a whisky-and-soda with Bradford in the inn-parlour where the stuffed pike is. You remember that stuffed pike, Jack?"

His brother nodded. "Can I ever forget it, or the landlord's interminable story of its capture? I wonder why people become so intolerably boresome about their fishing exploits. The angler is nearly as bad as the golfer."

"Still," said Varney, "he has more excuse. It is more of an achievement to catch a pike or a salmon than merely to whack a ball with a stick."

"Isn't that rather a crude description of the game?" asked Margaret. "It is to be hoped that Dr Thorndyke is not an enthusiast."

"I am not," he assured her — "in fact, I was admiring Mr Varney's simplification. His definition of the game is worthy of Dr Johnson. But I must tear myself away. My host is an early bird, and I expect you are, too. Good night, Mrs Purcell. It has been very delightful to meet you again. I am only sorry that I should have missed your husband."

"So am I," said Margaret, shaking his hand warmly, "but I think it most kind of you to have remembered me after all these years."

As Dr Thorndyke rose, the other three men stood up. "It is time for us to go, too," said Rodney, "so we will see you to the end of the road, Thorndyke. Good night, Mrs Purcell."

"Good night, gentlemen all," she replied. "Eight o'clock breakfast, remember."

The four men went into the house to fetch their hats and took their departure, walking together as far as the cross-roads, where

Thorndyke wished the other three "good night" and left them to pursue their way to the village.

The lodging accommodation in this neighbourhood was not sumptuous, but our three friends were not soft or fastidious. Besides, they only slept at their "diggings," taking their meals and making their home at the house which Purcell had hired, furnished, for the holiday. It was a somewhat unconventional arrangement, now that Purcell had gone, and spoke eloquently of his confidence in the discretion of his attractive wife.

The three men were not in the same lodgings. Varney was "putting up" at the "First and Last" inn in the adjoining village – or "church-town," to give it its local title – of Sennen, while the Rodney's shared a room at the "Ship" down in Sennen Cove, more than a mile away. They proceeded together as far as Varney's hostel, when, having wished him "good night," the two brothers strode away along the moonlit road towards the Cove.

For a while neither spoke, though the thoughts of both were occupied by the same subject, the solicitor's letter. Philip had fully taken in the situation, although he had made no remark on it, and the fact that his brother had been consulted quasi-professionally on the subject made him hesitate to refer to it. For in spite of his gay, almost frivolous, manner, Philip Rodney was a responsible medical practitioner, and really a man of sound judgment and discretion.

Presently his scruples yielded to the consideration that his brother was not likely to divulge any confidence, and he remarked:

"I hope Purcell hasn't been doing anything shady. It sounded to me as if there was a touch of Pontius Pilate in the tone of Penfield's letter."

"Yes, a very guarded tone, with a certain note of preparation for unpleasant possibilities. So it struck me. I do sincerely hope there isn't anything in it."

"So do I, by Jove! but I shouldn't be so very astonished. Of course we don't know anything against Purcell – at least, I don't – but somehow he doesn't strike me as a very scrupulous man. His outlook on life jars a bit; don't you feel that sometimes?"

"The commercial standard isn't quite the same as the professional, you know," Jack Rodney answered evasively, "and financial circles are not exactly hotbeds of the higher morality. But I know of nothing to Purcell's discredit."

"No, of course not. But he isn't the same class as his wife; she's a lot too good for a coarse, bucolic fellow like that. I wonder why the deuce she married him. I used to think she rather liked you."

"A woman can't marry every man she rather likes, you know, Phil, unless she happens to live in Ladak; and even there I believe there are limits. But to come back to Purcell, we may be worrying ourselves about nothing. Tomorrow we shall get into touch with him by telegraph, and then we may hear something from him."

Here the consideration of Purcell and his affairs dropped so far as conversation went; but in the elder man's mind certain memories had been revived by his brother's remark and occupied it during the remainder of the walk. For he, too, had once thought that Maggie Haygarth rather liked him, and he now recalled the shock of disagreeable surprise with which he had heard of her marriage. But that was over and done with long ago, and the question now was, how was the *Sandhopper*, at present moored in Whitesand Bay, to be got from the Land's End to her moorings above Westminster Bridge? – a problem that engaged the attention of the two brothers until they turned into their respective beds and the laggard, according to immemorial custom, blew out the light.

In spite of Mrs Purcell's admonition they were some minutes late on the following morning. Their two friends were already seated at the breakfast table, and it needed no extraordinary powers of observation to see that something had happened. Their hostess was pale and looked worried and somewhat frightened, and Varney was preternaturally grave. A telegram lay open on the table by Margaret's place, and as Rodney advanced to shake hands, she held it out to him without a word. He took the paper and read the brief but ominous message that confirmed but too plainly his misgivings of the previous night.

"Where is Dan? Expected him here Tuesday night. Hope nothing wrong – BRADFORD Angler's Hotel, Oulton."

Rodney laid down the telegram and looked at Margaret. "This is a queer business," said he. "Have you done anything?"

"No," she replied. "What can we do?"

Rodney took a slip of paper and a pencil from his pocket. "If you will write down the name of the partner or clerk who is attending at the office and the address, and that of the caretaker of your flat, I will go and send off reply-paid telegrams to them asking for information as to your husband's whereabouts, and I will also reply to Mr Bradford. It is just possible that Purcell may have gone home after all."

"It's very unlikely," said Margaret. "The flat is shut up, and he would surely have written. Still, we may as well make sure, if you will be so kind. But won't you have your breakfast first?"

"We'd better waste no time," he answered, and, pocketing the paper, strode away on his errand.

Little was said until he returned, and even then the breakfast proceeded in a gloomy silence that contrasted strangely with the usual vivacity of the gatherings around that hospitable table. A feeling of tense expectation pervaded the party and a vivid sense of impending disaster. Dreary efforts were made to keep some kind of conversation going, but the talk was colourless and disjointed with long and awkward pauses.

Varney especially was wrapped in deep meditation. Outwardly he preserved an appearance of sympathetic anxiety, but inwardly he was conscious of a strange, rather agreeable excitement, almost of elation. When he looked at Margaret's troubled face he felt a pang of regret, of contrition; but principally he was sensible of a feeling of power, of knowledge. He sat apart, as it were, Godlike, omniscient. He knew all the facts that were hidden from the others. The past lay clear before him to the smallest detail; the involved present was as an open book which he read with ease, and he could even peer confidently into the future.

And these men and the woman before him, and those others afar off – the men at the office, the caretaker, Penfield the lawyer, and Bradford at his inn in Norfolk – what were they but so many puppets, moving feverishly hither and thither as he, the unseen master-spirit, directed them by a pull at the strings? It was he who had wound them up and set them going; and here he sat, motionless and quiet, watching them do his bidding. He was reminded of an occasion when he had been permitted for a short time to steer a five-thousand-ton steamer. What a sense of power it had given him to watch the stupendous consequences of his own trifling movements! A touch of the little wheel, the movement of a spoke or two to right or left, and what a commotion followed! How the steam gear had clanked with furious haste to obey, and the great ship had presently swerved round, responsive to the pressure of his fingers! What a wonderful thing it had been! There was that colossal structure with its enormous burden of merchandise, its teeming population sweating in the stokehold or sleeping in the dark forecastle, its unconscious passengers chatting on the decks, reading, writing, or playing cards in saloon or smoking-room; and he had had it all in the grasp of one hand, had moved it and turned it about with the mere touch of a finger.

And so it was now. The magical pressure of his finger on the trigger, a few turns of a rope, the hoisting of an iron weight, and behold! the whole course of a human life – probably of several human lives – was changed utterly.

It was a tremendous thought.

In a little over an hour the replies to Rodney's discreetly worded inquiries had come in. Mr Purcell had not been home nor had he been heard of at the office. Mr Penfield had been inquiring as to his whereabouts and so had Mr Bradford. That was all. And what it amounted to was that Daniel Purcell had disappeared.

"Can't you remember exactly what Dan said about going to Falmouth, Mr Varney?" Margaret asked.

"I am sorry to say I can't," replied Varney. "You see, he just threw the remark off casually, and I didn't ask any questions. He isn't very fond of being questioned, you know."

"I wonder what he could have been going to Falmouth for," she mused. In reality she did not wonder at all. She felt pretty certain that she knew. But pride would not allow her publicly to adopt that explanation until it was forced on her. "It seems to me that there is only one course," she continued. "I must go up to town and see Mr Penfield. Don't you think so, Mr Rodney?"

"Certainly. He is the only one who knows anything and is able to advise." He hesitated a moment, and then added: "Hadn't we better come up with you?"

"Yes," said Varney eagerly; "let us all go up."

Margaret considered for a few moments." It is excessively kind and sympathetic of you all, and I am glad you offered, because it makes me feel that I have good loyal friends, which is a great deal to know just now. But, really, there would be no use in breaking up your holidays. What could you do? We can't make a search in person. Why not take over the house and stay on here?"

"We don't want the house if you're not in it", said Philip.

"No," agreed Jack Rodney; "if we can't be of use to you we shall get afloat and begin to crawl round the coast homewards."

"I think I shall run over to Falmouth and see if I can pick up any news," said Varney.

"Thank you," said Margaret. "I think that would be really useful," and Rodney agreed heartily, adding: "Why not come round in the yacht, Varney? We shall probably get there tomorrow night."

Varney reflected. And suddenly it was borne in upon him that he felt an unspeakable repugnance to the idea of going on board the yacht, and especially to making the voyage from Sennen to Penzance. The feeling came to him as an utter surprise, but there was no doubt of its reality.

"I think I'll go over by train," he said. "It will save a day, you know."

"Then we will meet you there," said Rodney; "and, Mrs Purcell, will you send us a letter to the Green Banks Hotel, Falmouth, and let us know what Mr Penfield says, and if you would like us to come up to town to help you?"

"Thank you, yes, I will," Margaret replied heartily. "And I promise that, if I want your help, I will ask for it."

"That is a solemn promise, mind," said Rodney.

"Yes, I mean it – a solemn promise."

So the matter was arranged. By twelve o'clock, the weather being calm, the yacht was got under way for Penzance. And even as on that other occasion, she headed seaward with her crew of two, watched from the shore by a woman and a man.

CHAPTER THREE

In Which Margaret Purcell Consults Mr Penfield

Mr Joseph Penfield was undeniably in a rather awkward dilemma. For he had hooked the wrong fish. His letter to Maggie Purcell had been designed to put him immediately in touch with Purcell himself, whereas it had evoked an urgent telegram from Maggie announcing her intention of calling on him "on important business" and entreating him to arrange an interview.

It was really most unfortunate. There was no one in the world whom he had less desire to see, at the present moment, than Margaret Purcell. And yet there was no possible escape; for not only was he her solicitor and her trustee, but he was an old family friend, and not a little attached to her in his dry way. But he didn't want her just now. He wanted Purcell, and he wanted him very badly.

For a solicitor of irreproachable character and spotless reputation his position was highly unpleasant. As soon as he had opened the letter from Penzance he had recognised the nature of the enclosures, and had instantly connected them with the forgeries of Bank of England notes of which he had heard. The intricate water-marks on the "blanks" were unmistakable. But so was the handwriting of the accompanying letter. It was Daniel Purcell's beyond a doubt, and the peculiar, intensely black ink was equally characteristic. And, short as the note was, it made perfectly clear its connection with the incriminating enclosures. It wrote down Daniel Purcell a banknote forger.

Now Mr Penfield was, as we have said, a man of irreproachable character. But he was a very secretive and rather casuistical old gentleman; and his regard for Margaret had led him to apply his casuistry to the present case, pretending to himself that his discovery of the illicit blanks came within the category of "clients' secrets," which he need not divulge. But in his heart he knew that he was conniving at a felony, that he ought to give information to the police or to the Bank, and that he wasn't going to. His plan was to get hold of Purcell, make him destroy the blanks in his presence, and deliver such a warning as would put a stop to the forgeries.

But if he did not propose to give Purcell away, neither did he intend to give himself away. He would share his compromising secret with no one – especially with a lady. And this consideration raised the difficult question, What on earth was he to say to Margaret Purcell when she arrived? A question which he was still debating, with her telegram spread out before him and his silver snuff-box in his hand, when a clerk entered his private office to announce the unwelcome visitor.

Fortifying himself with a pinch of snuff, he rose and advanced towards the door to receive her, and as she entered he made a quick mental note of her anxious and troubled expression.

"How do you do, Mrs Purcell?" said he, with a ceremonious bow. "You have had a long journey and rather an early one. How very unfortunate that this business, to which you refer in your telegram, should have arisen while you were on holiday so far away!"

"You have guessed what the business is, I suppose?" said Margaret.

Mr Penfield smiled deprecatingly. "We lawyers," said he, "are not much addicted to guessing, especially when definite information is available. Pray be seated. And now," he continued, as Margaret subsided into the clients' chair and he resumed his own, resting his elbows on the arms and placing his finger-tips together, "let us hear what this new and important business is."

"It is about that mysterious letter that you had from my husband," said Margaret.

"Dear, dear!" said Mr Penfield. "What a pity that you should have taken this long journey for such a trifling affair! And I thought I gave you all the particulars."

"You didn't mention whom the letter was from."

"For several excellent reasons," replied Mr Penfield, checking them off on his fingers. "First, I don't know; second, it is not my business; third, your husband, whose business it is, does know. My object in writing to you was to get into touch with him so that I could hand back to him this letter which should never have come into my possession. Shall I take down his address now?"

"I haven't it myself," Margaret replied with a faint flush. "I have no idea where he is at present. He left Sennen on the 23rd to go to Oulton via Penzance. But he never arrived at Oulton. He has not been home, he has not been to the office, and he has not written. It is rather alarming, especially in connection with your mysterious letter."

"Was my letter mysterious?" said Mr Penfield rapidly considering this new but not very surprising development. "I hardly think so. It was not intended to be. What was there mysterious about it?"

"Everything," she replied, producing the letter from her bag and glancing at it as she spoke. "You emphasise that Dan's letter and the other contents have been seen by no eye but yours, and that they are in a receptacle to which no one has access but yourself. There is a strong hint of something secret and compromising in the nature of Dan's letter and enclosures."

"I would rather say 'confidential,'" murmured Mr Penfield.

"And," Margaret continued, "you must see that there is an evident connection between this misdirected letter and Dan's disappearance."

Mr Penfield saw the connection very plainly, but he was admitting nothing. He did, indeed, allow that "it was a coincidence," but would not agree to "a necessary connection." "Probably you will hear from your husband in a day or two, and then the letter can be returned."

"Is there any reason why you should not show me Dan's letter?" Margaret demanded. "Surely I am entitled, as his wife, to see it."

Mr Penfield pursed up his lips and took a deliberate pinch of snuff.

"We must not confuse," said he, "the theological relations of married people with their legal relations. Theologically they are one; legally they are separate persons subject to a mutual contract. As to this letter, it is not mine, and consequently I can show it to no one; and I must assume that if your husband had desired you to see it he would have shown it to you himself."

"But," Margaret protested impatiently, "are not my husband's secrets my secrets?"

"That," replied the lawyer, "is a delicate question which we need not consider. There is the question of the secrets of a third party. If I had the felicity to be a married man, which unfortunately I have not, you would hardly expect me to communicate your private, and perhaps secret, affairs to my wife. Now would you?"

Margaret had to admit that she would not. But she instantly countered the lawyer by inquiring: "Then I was apparently right in inferring that this letter and the enclosures contained matter of a secret and compromising character?"

"I have said nothing to that effect," replied Mr Penfield uncomfortably; and then, seeing that he had no choice between a downright lie and a flat refusal to answer any questions, he continued: "The fact is that it is not admissible for me to make any statement. This letter came to me by an error, and my position must be as if I had not seen it."

"But it can't be," Margaret persisted, "because you *have* seen it. I want to know if Dan's letter was addressed to anyone whom I know. You could tell me that, surely?"

"Unfortunately, I cannot," replied the lawyer, glad to be able to tell the literal truth for once. "The letter was without any formal opening. There was nothing to indicate the identity or even the sex of the person to whom it was addressed."

Margaret noted this curious fact and then asked: "With regard to the enclosures. Did they consist of money?"

"They did not," was the reply, "nor cheques."

A brief silence followed, during which Margaret reflected rapidly on what she had learned and what she had not learned. At length she looked up with a somewhat wry smile and said: "Well, Mr Penfield, I suppose that is all I shall get out of you?"

"I am afraid it is," he replied. "The necessity of so much reservation is most distasteful, I assure you; but it is the plain duty of a lawyer to keep not only his own counsel but other people's."

"Yes, of course, I quite understand that. And now, as we have finished with the letter, there is the writer to consider. What had I better do about Dan?"

"Why do anything? It is only four days since he left Sennen."

"Yes, but something has evidently happened. He may have met with an accident and be in some hospital. Do you think that I ought to notify the police that he is missing?"

"No; certainly not," Mr Penfield replied emphatically, for, in his mind, Purcell's disappearance was quite simply explained. He had discovered the mistake of the transposed letter, and knew that Penfield held the means of convicting him of a felony, and he had gone into hiding until he should discover what the lawyer meant to do. To put the police on his track would be to convince him of his danger and drive him hopelessly out of reach. But Mr Penfield could not explain this to Margaret, and to cover his emphatic rejection of police assistance he continued: "You see, he can hardly be said to be missing; he may merely have altered his plans and neglected to write. Have patience for a day or two, and if you still hear no tidings of him, send me a line, and I will take what measures seem advisable for trying to get into touch with him."

"Thank you," said Margaret, not very enthusiastically, rising to take her departure. She was in the act of shaking Mr Penfield's hand when, with a sudden afterthought, she asked: "By the way, was there anything in Dan's letter that might account for his disappearance in this fashion?"

This was rather a facer for Mr Penfield, who, like many casuists, hated telling a direct lie. For the answer was clearly "Yes," whereas the sense that he was compelled to convey was "No."

"You are forgetting that the letter was not addressed to me," he said. "And that reminds me that there must have been another letter – the one that was addressed to me and that must have been put into the other person's envelope. May I ask if that letter has been returned?"

"No, it has not," replied Margaret.

"Ha!" said Mr Penfield. "But it probably will be in the course of a day or two. Then we shall know what he was writing to me about and who is the other correspondent. Good day, good day, Mrs Purcell."

He shook her hand warmly, and hastened to open the door for her in the hope, justified by the result, that she would not realize until she had left that her very significant question had not been answered.

Indeed, she did not realize how adroitly the old solicitor had evaded that question until she was too far away to return and put it afresh, even if that had seemed worth while; for her attention was occupied by the other issue that he had so artfully raised. She had overlooked the presumable existence of the second transposed letter, the one that should have been in Mr Penfield's envelope. It ought to have been returned at once. Possibly it was even now waiting at Sennen to be forwarded. If it arrived, it would probably disclose the identity of the mysterious correspondent. On the other hand, it might not; and if it were not returned at all, that would confirm the suspicion that there was something gravely wrong. And it was at this point that Margaret became conscious of Mr Penfield's last evasion.

Its effect was to confirm the generally disagreeable impression that she had received from the interview. She was a little resentful of the lawyer's elaborate reticence, which, coupled with the strange precautionary terms of his letter to her, convinced her that her husband had embarked on some questionable transaction, and that Mr Penfield knew it and knew the nature of that transaction. His instant rejection of the suggestion that an accident might have occurred and that the police should be notified seemed to imply that he had some inkling of Purcell's proceedings, and his final evasion of her question strongly suggested that the letter, or the enclosures, or both, contained some clue to the disappearance.

Thus, as she took her way home, Margaret turned over again and again the puzzling elements of the mystery, and at each reshuffling of the scanty facts the same conclusion emerged: her husband had absconded, and he had not absconded alone. The secret that Mr Penfield was guarding was such a secret as might, if divulged, have pointed the way to the divorce court. And with this conclusion and a frown of disgust, she turned into the entry of her flat and ascended the stairs.

As she let herself in, the maid met her in the hall.

"Mr Varney is in the drawing-room, ma'am," she said. "He came about ten minutes ago. I am getting tea for him."

"Thank you, Nellie," said Margaret, "and you might get me some, too."

She passed on to her bedroom for a hasty wash and change, and then joined her visitor in time to pour out the tea.

"How good of you, Mr Varney," she said warmly, as they shook hands, "to come to me so quickly! You must have only just arrived."

"Yes," he replied, "I came straight on from the station. I thought you would be anxious to know if I had heard anything."

"And have you?"

"Well," Varney replied, hesitatingly, "I'm rather afraid not. I seem to have drawn a blank."

Margaret looked at him critically. There was something in his manner suggestive of doubt and reservation.

"Do you mean an absolute blank? Did you find out nothing at all?"

Again Varney seemed to hesitate, and Margaret's attention sharpened.

"There isn't much use in making guesses," said he. "I found no definite traces of Dan. He hadn't been at the 'Ship,' where I put up and where he used to stay when he went to Falmouth, and of course I couldn't go round the other hotels making inquiries. But I went down the quay-side and asked a few discreet questions about the craft that had left the port since Monday, especially the odd craft, bound for small ports. I felt that if Dan had any reason for slipping off quietly he wouldn't go by a passenger boat to a regular passenger port. He would go on a cargo boat bound to some out-of-the-way place. So I found out what I could about the cargo boats that had put out of Falmouth; but I didn't have much luck."

Again he paused irresolutely, and Margaret asked, with a shade of impatience:

"Did you find out anything at all?"

"Well, no; I can't say that I did," Varney replied, in the same slow, inconclusive manner. "It's disappointing in a way, especially as I really thought at one time that I had got on his track. But that turned out a mistake after all."

"You are sure it was a mistake," said Margaret eagerly. "Tell me about it."

"I picked up the clue when I was asking about a Swedish steamer that had put out on Tuesday morning. She had a lading of china clay and was bound for Malmo, but she was calling at Ipswich to pick up some other cargo. I learned that she took one or two passengers on board, and one of them was described to me as a big red-faced man of about forty, who looked like a pilot or a ship's officer. That sounded rather like Dan, and when I heard that he was carrying a biggish suitcase and had a yellow oilskin coat on his arm, I made pretty sure that it was."

"And how do you know that it was not Dan?"

"Why," replied Varney, "it turned out that this man had a woman with him."

"I see," said Margaret hastily, flushing scarlet and turning her head away. For a while she could think of nothing further to say. To her, of course, the alleged disproof of the passenger's identity was "confirmation strong as Holy Writ." But her pride would not allow her to confess this − at any rate to Varney − and she was in difficulties as to how to pursue the inquiry without making the admission. At length she ventured: "Do you think that is quite conclusive? I mean, is it certain that the woman belonged to the man? There is the possibility that she may have been merely a fellow-passenger whom he had casually accompanied to the ship. Or did you ascertain that they were actually − er − companions?"

"No, by Jove!" exclaimed Varney. "I never thought of any other possibilities. I heard that the man went on board with a woman, and at once decided that he couldn't be Dan. But you are quite right. They may have just met at the hotel or elsewhere and walked down to the ship together. I wonder if it's worth while to make any further inquiries about the ship − I mean at Ipswich, or, if necessary, at Malmo."

"Do you remember the ship's name?"

"Yes; the *Hedwig* of Hernosand. She left Falmouth early on Tuesday morning, so she will probably have got to Ipswich some time yesterday. She may be there now, or, of course, she may have picked up her stuff and gone to sea the same day. Would you like me to run down to Ipswich and see if I can find out anything?"

Margaret turned on him with a look that set his heart thumping and his pulses throbbing.

"Mr Varney," she said, in a low, unsteady voice, "you make me ashamed and proud − proud to have such a loyal, devoted friend, and ashamed to be such a tax on him."

"Not at all," he replied. "After all" – here his voice, too, became a little unsteady – "Dan was my pal, is my pal still," he added huskily. He paused for a moment, and then concluded: "I'll go down tonight and try to pick up the scent while it is fresh."

"It *is* good of you!" she exclaimed; and as she spoke her eyes filled, but she still looked at him frankly as she continued: "Your faithful friendship is no little compensation for" – she was going to say "his unfaithfulness," but altered the words to "the worry and anxiety of this horrid mystery. But I am ashamed to let you take so much trouble, though I must confess that it would be an immense relief to me to get *some* news of Dan. I don't hope for good news, but it is terrible to be so completely in the dark."

"Yes, that is the worst part of it," Varney agreed; and then, setting his cup on the table, he rose. "I had better be getting along now," he said, "so that I can catch the earliest possible train. Good-bye, Mrs Purcell, and good luck to us both."

The leave-taking almost shattered Varney's self-possession, for Margaret, in the excess of her gratitude, impulsively grasped both his hands and pressed them warmly as she poured out her thanks. Her touch made him tingle to the finger-ends. Heavens! how beautiful she looked, this lovely, unconscious young widow! And to think that she might in time be his own! A wild impulse surged through him to clasp her in his arms, to tell her that she was free and that he worshipped her. Of course, that was a mere impulse that interfered not at all with his decorous, deferential manner. And yet a sudden, almost insensible change in her made him suspect that his eyes had told her more than he had meant to disclose. Nevertheless, she followed him to the lobby to speed him on his errand, and when he looked back from the foot of the stairs, she was standing at the open door, smiling down on him.

The thoughts of these two persons, when each was alone, were strangely different. In Margaret's mind there was no doubt that the man on the steamer was her unworthy husband. But what did Varney think? That a man of the world should have failed to perceive that an unexplained disappearance was most probably an elopement seemed to her incredible. Varney could not be such an innocent as that. The only alternative was that he, like Mr Penfield, was trying to shield Dan; to hush up the disreputable elements of the escapade. But whereas the lawyer's obstinate reticence had aroused some slight resentment, she felt no resentment towards Varney. For he was Dan's friend first of all, and it was proper that he should try to shield his "pal." And he was really serving husband and wife equally. To hush things up would be the best for both. She wanted no scandal. Loyal and faithful wife as she had been, her feelings towards her husband were of that somewhat tepid quality that would have allowed her to receive him back without reproaches, and to accept the lamest explanations without question or comment. Varney's assumed policy was as much to her interest as to Dan's, and he was certainly playing the part of a devoted friend to them both.

One thing did, indeed, rather puzzle her. Her marriage had been, on her husband's side, undoubtedly a love-match. It was for no mercenary reasons that he had forced the marriage on her and her father, and up to the last he had seemed to be, in his rather brutal way, genuinely in love with her. Why, then, had he suddenly gone off with another woman? To her constant, faithful nature the thing was inexplicable.

Varney's reflections were more complex. A vague consciousness of the cumulative effects of actions was beginning to steal into his mind, a faint perception that he was being borne along on the current of circumstance. He had gone to Falmouth with the express purpose of losing Purcell. But it seemed necessary to pick up some trace of the imaginary fugitive; for the one essential to Varney's safety was that Purcell's disappearance must appear to date from the landing at Penzance. That landing must be taken as an established fact. There must be no inquiry into or discussion of the incidents of that tragic voyage. But to that end it was necessary that Purcell should make some reappearance on shore, must leave some traces for possible pursuers to follow. So Varney had gone to

Falmouth to find such traces – and to lose them. That was to have been the end of the business so far as he was concerned.

But it was not the end; and as he noted this, he noted, too, with a curious interest unmixed with any uneasiness, how one event generates others. He had invented Purcell's proposed visit to Falmouth to give a plausible colour to the disappearance and to carry the field of inquiry beyond the landing at Penzance. Then the Falmouth story had seemed to commit him to a visit to Falmouth to confirm it. That visit had committed him to the fabrication of the required confirmatory traces, which were to be found and then lost. But he had not quite succeeded in losing them. Margaret's question had seemed to commit him to tracing them further, and now he had got to find and lose Purcell at Ipswich. That, however, would be the end. From Ipswich Purcell would have to disappear for good.

The account that he had given Margaret was founded on facts. The ship that he had described was a real ship, which had sailed when he had said that she sailed and for the ports that he had named. Moreover, she had carried one or two passengers. But the red-faced man with the suitcase and his female companion were creatures of Varney's imagination.

Thus we see Varney already treading the well-worn trail left by multitudes of wrong-doers; weaving around him a defensive web of illusory appearances, laying down false tracks that lead always away from himself, never suspecting that the web may at last become as the fowler's snare, that the false tracks may point the way to the hounds of destiny. It is true that, as he fared on his way to Ipswich, he was conscious that the tide of circumstance was bearing him farther than he had meant to travel; but not yet did he recognize in this hardly perceived compulsion the abiding menace of accumulating consequences that encompasses the murderer.

CHAPTER FOUR

In Which Margaret Confers With Dr Thorndyke

The sun was shining pleasantly on the trees of King's Bench Walk, Inner Temple, when Margaret approached the handsome brick portico of No. 5A and read upon the jamb of the doorway the name of Dr John Thorndyke under the explanatory heading "First Pair." She was a little nervous of the coming interview, partly because she had met the famous criminal lawyer only twice before, but more especially by reason of a vague fear that her uneasy suspicions of her husband might presently be turned into something more definite and disagreeable.

Her nervousness on the first score was soon dispelled, for her gentle summons on the little brass knocker of the inner door – the "oak" was open – was answered by Dr Thorndyke himself, who greeted her as an old friend and led her into the sitting-room, where tea-things were set out on a small table between two armchairs. The homely informality of the reception, so different from the official stiffness of Mr Penfield, instantly put her at her ease; and when the teapot arrived in the custody of a small gentleman of archidiaconal aspect and surprising crinkliness of feature, she felt as if she were merely paying some rather unusual kind of afternoon call.

Dr Thorndyke had what would, in his medical capacity, have been called a fine bedside manner – pleasant, genial, sympathetic, but never losing touch with the business on hand. Insensibly a conversation of pleasing generality slipped into a consultation, and Margaret found herself stating her case, apparently of her own initiative. Having described her interview with Mr Penfield and commented on the old lawyer's very unhelpful attitude, she continued:

"It was Mr Rodney who advised me to consult you. As a civil lawyer with no experience of criminal practice, he felt hardly competent to deal with the case. That was what he said. It sounds rather ominous – as if he thought there might be some criminal element in the affair."

"Not necessarily," said Thorndyke. "But your husband is missing, and a missing man is certainly more in my province than in Rodney's. What did he suggest that you should ask me to do?"

"I should wish, of course," replied Margaret, "to get into communication with my husband. But if that is not possible, I should at least like to know what has become of him. Matters can't be left in their present uncertain state. There is the future to think of."

"Precisely," agreed Thorndyke, "and as the future must be based upon the present and the past, we had better begin by setting out what we actually know and can prove. First, I understand that on the 23rd of June your husband left Sennen, and was seen by several persons to leave, on a yacht in company with Mr Varney, and that there was no one else on board. The yacht reached Penzance at about half-past two in the afternoon, and your husband went ashore at once. He was seen by Mr Varney to land on the pier and go towards the town. Did anyone besides Mr Varney see him go ashore?"

"No – at least, I have not heard of anyone. Of course, he may have been seen by some fishermen or strangers on the pier. But does it matter? Mr Varney saw him land, and he certainly was not on the yacht when Mr Rodney arrived half an hour later. There can't be any possible doubt that he did land at Penzance."

"No," Thorndyke agreed; "but as that is the last time that he was certainly seen alive, and as the fact that he landed may have to be proved in a court of law, additional evidence would be worth securing."

"But that was not the last time that he was seen alive," said Margaret; and here she gave him an account of Varney's expedition to Falmouth, explaining why he went and giving full particulars respecting the steamer, all of which Thorndyke noted down on the note-block which lay by his side on the table.

"This is very important," said he, when she had finished. "But you see that it is on a different plane of certainty. It is hearsay at the best, and there is no real identification. What luck did Mr Varney have at Ipswich?"

"He went down there on the evening of the 27th, the day after his visit to Falmouth. He went straight to the quay-side and made inquiries about the steamer *Hedwig*, which he learned had left about noon, having come in about nine o'clock on the previous night. He talked to various quay-loafers, and from one of them ascertained that a single passenger had landed – a big man, carrying a large bag or portmanteau in his hand and a coat of some kind on his arm. The passenger landed alone. Nothing was seen of any woman."

"Did Mr Varney take the name and address of his informant at Ipswich or the one at Falmouth?"

"I am afraid not. He said nothing about it."

"That is unfortunate," said Thorndyke, "because these witnesses may be wanted, as they might be able to identify a photograph of your husband. We must find out from Mr Varney what he did in the matter."

Margaret looked at Dr Thorndyke with a slightly puzzled expression. "You speak of witnesses and evidence," said she, "as if you had something definite in your mind. Some legal proceedings, I mean."

"I have," he replied. "If your husband makes no sign and if he does not presently appear, certain legal proceedings will become inevitable." He paused for a few moments and then continued: "You must understand, Mrs Purcell, that when a man of any position – and especially a married man – disappears from 'his usual places of resort,' as the phrase goes, he upsets all the social adjustments that connect him with his surroundings, and, sooner or later, those adjustments have to be made good. If he disappears completely, it becomes uncertain whether he is alive or dead, and this uncertainty communicates itself to his property and to his dependents and relatives. If he is alive, his property is vested in himself; if he is dead, it is vested in his executors or in his heirs or next of kin. Should he be named as a beneficiary in a will, and the person who has made that will die after his disappearance, the question immediately arises whether he was dead or alive at the time of the testator's death – a vitally important question, since it affects not only himself and his heirs, but also the other persons who benefit under the will. And then there is the status of the wife, if the missing man is married: the question whether she is a married woman or a widow has, in justice to her, to be settled if and when possible. So you see that the disappearance of a man like your husband sets going a process that generates all sorts of legal problems. You cannot simply write him off and treat him as non-existent. His life must be properly wound up so that his estate may be disposed of, and this will involve the necessity of presuming his death; and presumption of death may raise difficult questions of survivorship, although these may arise at any moment."

"What is meant by a question of survivorship?" Margaret asked.

"It is a question which arises in respect of two persons, both of whom are dead and concerning one or both of whom the exact date of death is unknown. One of them must have died before the other, unless they both died at the same instant. The question is, Which survived the other? Which of them died first? It is a question on which may turn the succession to an estate, a title, or even a kingdom."

"Well," said Margaret, "it is not likely to arise in respect of Dan."

"On the contrary," Thorndyke dissented, "it may arise tomorrow. If some person who has left him a legacy should die today, that person's will could not be administered until it had been decided whether your husband was or was not alive at the time the testator died; that is, whether or not he survived the testator. But, as matters stand, we can give no answer to that question. We can prove that he was alive at half-past two on the 23rd of June. Thenceforward we have no knowledge of him."

"Excepting what Mr Varney has told us."

"Mr Varney's information is legally worthless unless he can produce the witnesses, and unless they can identify a photograph or otherwise prove that the man whom they saw was actually Mr Purcell. You must ask Mr Varney about it. However, at the moment you are more concerned to find out what has become of your husband. I suppose I may ask a few necessary questions?"

"Oh, certainly," she replied. "Pray don't have any scruples of delicacy. Ask anything you want to know."

"Thank you, Mrs Purcell," said Thorndyke. "And to begin with the inevitable question, Do you know of, or suspect, any kind of entanglement with any woman?"

The direct, straightforward question came rather as a relief to Margaret, and she answered without embarrassment:

"Naturally, I suspect, because I can think of no other reason for his leaving me in this way. But to be honest, I have never had the slightest grounds of complaint in regard to his behaviour with other women. He married me because he fell in love with me, and he has never seemed to change. Whatever he has been to other people, to me he has always appeared, in his rough, taciturn way, as devoted as his nature allowed him to be. This affair is an utter surprise to me."

Thorndyke made no comment on this, but, following the hint that Margaret had dropped, asked:

"As to his character in general, what sort of a man is he? Is he popular, for instance?"

"No," replied Margaret, "he is not very much liked – in fact, with the exception of Mr Varney he has no really intimate friends, and I have often wondered how poor Mr Varney put up with the way he treated him. The truth is that Dan is rather a bully; he is strong, big, and pugnacious, and used to having his own way and somewhat brutal, at times, in his manner of getting it. He is a very self-contained, taciturn, rather secretive man, and – well, perhaps he is not very scrupulous. I am not painting a very flattering picture, I am afraid."

"It sounds like a good portrait, though," said Thorndyke. "When you say that he is not very scrupulous, are you referring to his business transactions?"

"Well, yes, and to his dealings with people generally."

"By the way," asked Thorndyke, "what is his occupation?"

Margaret uttered a little apologetic laugh. "It sounds absurd, but I really don't quite know what his business is. He is so very uncommunicative. I have always understood that he is a financier, whatever that may be. I believe he negotiates loans and buys and sells stocks and shares, but he is not on the Stock Exchange. He has an office in Coleman Street, in the premises of a firm of outside brokers, and he keeps a clerk, a man named Levy. It seems to be quite a small establishment, though it appears to yield a fair income. That is all I can tell you, but I dare say Mr Levy could give you other particulars if you wanted them."

"I will make a note of the address, at any rate," said Thorndyke; and having done so, he asked: "As to your husband's banking account: do you happen to know if any considerable sum has been drawn out quite lately, or if any cheques have been presented since he disappeared?"

"His current account is intact," she replied. "I have an account at the same bank, and I saw the manager a couple of days ago. Of course, he was not very expansive, but he did tell me that no unusual amounts had been withdrawn, and that no cheque has been presented since the 21st of June, when Dan drew a cheque for me. It is really rather odd, especially as the balance is somewhat above the average. Don't you think so?"

"I do," he answered. "It suggests that your husband's disappearance was unpremeditated, and that extreme precautions are being taken to conceal his present whereabouts. But the mystery is what he is living on if he took no considerable sum with him and has drawn no cheques since. However, we had better finish with the general questions. You don't appear to know much about your husband's present affairs: what do you know of his past?"

"Not a great deal, and I can think of nothing that throws any light on his extraordinary conduct in taking himself off as he has done. I met him at Maidstone about six years ago. He was then employed in the office of a large paper mill – Whichboy's mill, I think it was – as a clerk or accountant. He had then recently come down from Cambridge, and seemed in rather low water. After a time, he left Whichboy's and went to London, and very shortly his circumstances began to improve in a remarkable way. It was then that he began his present business, which I know included the making of loans, because he lent my father money – in fact, it was through these transactions and his visits on business to my father that the intimacy grew which resulted finally in our marriage. He then seemed, as he always has, to be a keen business man, very attentive to the main chance, not at all sentimental in his dealings, and, as I have said, not over scrupulous as to his methods."

Thorndyke nodded gravely but made no comment. The association of loans to the father with marriage with an evidently not infatuated daughter seemed to throw a sufficiently suggestive light on Daniel Purcell's methods.

"And as to his personal habits and tastes?" he asked.

"He has always been reasonably temperate, though he likes good living and has a robust appetite; and he really has no vices beyond a rather unpleasant temper and excessive keenness on money. His principal interest is in boating, yachting, and fishing; he does not bet or gamble, and his relations with women have always seemed to be perfectly correct."

"You spoke of his exceptional intimacy with Mr Varney. Is the friendship of long standing?"

"Yes, quite. They were schoolfellows, they were at Cambridge together, and they both came down about the same time and for a similar reason. Both their fathers got suddenly into financial difficulties. Dan's father was a stockbroker, and he failed suddenly, either through some unlucky speculations or through the default of a client. Mr Varney's father was a clergyman, and he, too, lost all his money, and at about the same time. I have always suspected that there was some connection between the two failures, but I have never heard that there actually was. Dan is as close as an oyster, and, of course, Mr Varney has never referred to the affair."

"Mr Varney is not associated with your husband in business?"

"No. He is an artist, principally an etcher, and a very clever one, too. I think he is doing quite well now, but he had a hard struggle when he first came down from Cambridge. For a couple of years he worked for an engraver doing ordinary copperplate work for the trade, and I understand that he is remarkably skilful at engraving. But now he does nothing but etchings and mezzotints."

"Then his activities are entirely concerned with art?"

"I believe so – now, at any rate. After he left the engraver he went to a merchant in the City as a clerk. But he was only there quite a short time, and I fancy he left on account of some sort of unpleasantness, but I know nothing about it. After that he went abroad and travelled about for a time, making sketches and drawings of the towns to do his etchings from – in fact, he only came back from Belgium a couple of months ago. But I am afraid I am wasting your time with a lot of irrelevant gossip."

"It is my fault if you are," said Thorndyke, "since I put the questions. But the fact is that nothing is irrelevant. Your husband has vanished into space in a perfectly unaccountable manner, and we have to find, if we can, something in his known circumstances which may give us a clue to the motive and the manner of his disappearance and his probable whereabouts at present. Has he any favourite haunts abroad or at home?"

"He is very partial to the Eastern Counties, especially the Broads and rivers of Norfolk. You remember he was on his way to Oulton Broad when he disappeared?"

"Yes; and one must admit that the waterways of Norfolk and Suffolk, with all their endless communications, would form an admirable hiding-place. In a small yacht or covered boat a man might lose himself in that network of rivers and lakes and lie hidden for months, creeping from end to end of the county without leaving a trace. We must bear that possibility in mind. By the way, have you brought me a copy of that very cautious letter of Mr Penfield's?"

"I have brought the letter itself," she replied, producing it and laying it on the table.

"Thank you," said Thorndyke. "I will make a copy of it and let you have the original back. And there is another question: Has the letter which Mr Penfield ought to have received been returned to you?"

"No," replied Margaret.

"Ha!" said Thorndyke, "that is important, because it is undoubtedly a remarkable circumstance and rather significant. A letter in the wrong envelope practically always implies another letter in another wrong envelope. Now a letter was almost certainly written to Mr Penfield and almost certainly sent. It was presumably a business letter and of some importance. It ought certainly to have been returned to the sender, and under ordinary circumstances would have been. Why has it not been returned? The person to whom it was sent was the person to whom the mysterious communication that Mr Penfield received was addressed. That communication, we judge from Mr Penfield's letter, contained some highly confidential matter. But that implies some person who was in highly confidential relations with your husband. The suggestion seems to be that your husband discovered his mistake after he had posted the letter or letters, and that he went at once to this other person and informed him of what had happened."

"Informed her," Margaret corrected.

"I must admit," said Thorndyke, "that the circumstances give colour to your inference, but we must remember that they would apply equally to a man. They certainly point to an associate of some kind. The character of that associate and the nature of the association are questions that turn on the contents of that letter that Mr Penfield received."

"Do you think," asked Margaret, "that Mr Penfield would be more confidential with you than he was with me?"

"I doubt it," was the reply. "If the contents of that letter were of a secret nature, he will keep them to himself; and quite right, too. But I shall give him a trial all the same, and you had better let him know that you have consulted me."

This brought the conference to an end, and shortly afterwards Margaret went on her way, now more than ever convinced that the inevitable woman was at the bottom of the mystery. For some time after she had gone Thorndyke sat with his notes before him, wrapped in profound thought and deeply interested in the problem that he was called upon to solve. He did not share Margaret's suspicions, though he had not strongly contested them. To his experienced eye, the whole group of circumstances, with certain points which he had not thought fit to enlarge on, suggested something more sinister than a mere elopement.

There was Purcell's behaviour, for instance. It had all the appearances of an unpremeditated flight. No preparations seemed to have been made, no attempt to wind up his affairs. His banking account was left intact, though no one but he could touch it during his lifetime. He had left or sent no letter of farewell, explanation, or apology to his wife; and now that he was gone, he was maintaining a secrecy as to his whereabouts so profound that, apparently, he did not even dare to draw a cheque.

But even more significant was the conduct of Mr Penfield. Taking from its envelope the mysterious letter that had come to

Sennen and exploded the mine, Thorndyke spread it out and slowly read it though; and his interpretation of it now was the same as on the occasion when he heard Margaret's epitome of it at Sennen. It was a message to Purcell through his wife, telling him that something which had been discovered was not going to be divulged. What could that something be? The answer, in general terms, seemed to be given by Penfield's subsequent conduct. He had been absolutely uncommunicative to Margaret. Yet Margaret, as the missing man's wife, was a proper person to receive any information that could be given. Apparently, then, the information that Penfield possessed was of a kind that could not be imparted to anyone. Even its very nature could not be hinted at.

Now what kind of information could that be? The obvious inference was that the letter which had come to Penfield contained incriminating matter. That would explain everything. For if Penfield had thus stumbled on evidence of a crime, either committed or contemplated, he would have to choose between denouncing the criminal or keeping the matter to himself. But he was not entitled to keep it to himself; for, other considerations apart, this was not properly a client's secret. It had not been communicated to him: he had discovered it by accident. He was therefore not bound to secrecy, and he could not, consequently, claim a lawyer's privilege. In short, if he had discovered a crime and chose to suppress his discovery, he was, in effect, an accessory, before or after the fact, as the case might be; and he would necessarily keep the secret because he would not dare to divulge it.

This view was strongly supported by Purcell's conduct. The disappearance of the latter coincided exactly with the delivery of the mysterious letter to Penfield. The inference was that Purcell, having discovered his fatal mistake, and assuming that Penfield would immediately denounce him to the police, had fled instantly and was now in hiding. Purcell's and Penfield's conduct were both in complete agreement with this theory.

But there was a further consideration. If the contents of that letter were incriminating, they incriminated someone besides Purcell. The person for whom the letter was intended must have been a party to any unlawful proceedings referred to in it. He – or she – must, in fact, have been a confederate. Now, who could that confederate be? Someone, apparently, who was unknown to Margaret, unless it might be the somewhat shadowy Mr Levy. And that raised yet a further question: What was Purcell? How did he get his living? His wife evidently did not know, which was a striking and rather suspicious fact. He had been described as a financier. But that meant nothing. The word "financier" covered a multitude of sins; the question was, What sins did it cover in the present instance? And the answer to that question seemed to involve a visit of exploration to Coleman Street.

As Thorndyke collected his notes to form the nucleus of a dossier of the Purcell Case, he foresaw that his investigations might well unearth some very unlovely skeletons. But that was no fault of his, nor need the disclosures be unnecessarily paraded. But Margaret Purcell's position must be secured and made regular. Her missing husband must either be found and brought back, or he must be written off and disposed of in a proper and legal fashion.

CHAPTER FIVE

In Which Thorndyke Makes
a Few Inquiries

If Mr Penfield had been reluctant to arrange an interview with Margaret Purcell, he was yet more unwilling to accept one with Dr John Thorndyke. It is true that, as a lawyer of the old school, he regarded Thorndyke with a certain indulgent contempt, as a dabbler in law, an amateur, a mere doctor masquerading as a lawyer. But coupled with this contempt was an unacknowledged fear. For it was not unknown to him that this medico-legal hermaphrodite had strange and disconcerting methods; that he had a habit of driving his chariot through well-established legal conventions, and of using his eyes and ears in a fashion not recognized by orthodox legal precedents.

Accordingly, when he received a note from Thorndyke announcing the intention of the writer to call on him, he would have liked to decline the encounter. A less courageous man would have absented himself. But Mr Penfield was a sportsman to the backbone, and having got himself into difficulties by that very quality, elected to "face the music" like a man; and so it happened that when Thorndyke arrived in the clerks' office, he was informed that Mr Penfield was at liberty, and was duly announced and ushered into the sanctum.

The old solicitor received him with a sort of stiff cordiality, helped himself to a pinch of snuff, and awaited the opening of the offensive.

"You have heard from Mrs Purcell, I presume," said Thorndyke.

"Yes. I understand that you are commissioned by her to ascertain the whereabouts of her husband – a very desirable thing to do, and I wish you every success."

"I am sure you do," said Thorndyke, "and it is with that conviction that I have called on you to enable you to give effect to your good wishes."

Mr Penfield paused, with his snuff-box open and an infinitesimal particle between his finger and thumb, to steal a quick glance at Thorndyke.

"In what way?" he asked.

"You received a certain communication, concerning which you wrote to Mrs Purcell at – "

"I beg your pardon," interrupted Penfield," but I received no communication. A communication was no doubt dispatched by Mr Purcell, but it never reached me."

"I am referring to a letter which did reach you – a letter with certain enclosures, apparently put into the wrong envelope."

"And which," said Penfield, "is consequently no concern of mine, or, if you will pardon my saying so, of yours."

"Of that," said Thorndyke, "you are doubtless a better judge than I am, since you have read the letter and I have not. But I am instructed to investigate the disappearance of Mr Purcell, and as this letter appears to be connected with this disappearance, it naturally becomes an object of interest to me."

"Why do you assume that it is connected with the disappearance?" Penfield demanded.

"Because of the striking coincidence of the time of its arrival and the time of the disappearance" replied Thorndyke.

"That seems a very insufficient reason," said Penfield.

"Not, I think," rejoined Thorndyke, "if taken in conjunction with the terms of your own letter to Mrs Purcell. But do I understand you to say that there was no connection?"

"I did not say that. What I say is that I have inadvertently seen a letter which was not addressed to me and which I was not intended to see. You will agree with me that it would be entirely inadmissible for me to divulge or discuss its contents."

"I am not sure that I do agree with you, seeing that the writer of the letter is the husband of our client and the consignee is a person unknown to us both. But you will naturally act on your own convictions. Would it be admissible for you to indicate the nature of the enclosures?"

"It would be entirely inadmissible," replied Mr Penfield.

There was a short silence, during which Mr Penfield refreshed himself with a pinch of snuff and Thorndyke rapidly turned over the situation. Obviously, the old solicitor did not intend to give any information whatever, possibly for very good reasons. At any rate, his decision had to be accepted and this Thorndyke proceeded to acknowledge.

"Well, Mr Penfield," he said, "I mustn't urge you to act against your professional conscience. I am sure you would help me if you could. By the way, I assume that there would be no objection to my inspecting the envelope in which that letter was contained?"

"The envelope!" exclaimed Penfield, considerably startled. "Why, what information could you possibly gather from the envelope?"

"That is impossible to say until I have seen it," was the reply.

"However," said Penfield, "I am afraid that the same objection applies, sorry as I am to refuse."

"But," persisted Thorndyke, "why should you refuse? The letter, as you say, was not addressed to you, but the envelope was. It is your own envelope, and is entirely at your disposal."

Mr Penfield was cornered, and he had the wisdom to recognize the fact. Reluctant as he was to let Thorndyke examine even the envelope in which those incriminating blanks were enclosed, he saw that a refusal might arouse suspicion, and suspicion was what he must avoid at all costs. Nevertheless, he made a last effort to temporize.

"Was there any point on which I could enlighten you – in respect of the envelope? Can I give you any information?" he asked.

"I am afraid not," replied Thorndyke. "My experience has taught me always to examine the exteriors of letters closely. By doing so one often picks up unexpected crumbs of evidence; but, naturally, one cannot tell in advance what there may be to observe."

"No," agreed Penfield. "Quite so. It is like cross-examination. Well, I am afraid you won't pick up much this time, but if you really wish to inspect the envelope, I suppose, as you say, I need not scruple to place it in your hands."

With this he rose and walked over to the safe, opened it, opened an inner drawer, and, keeping his back towards Thorndyke, took out the envelope, which he carefully emptied of its contents. Thorndyke sat motionless, not looking at the lawyer's back but listening intently. Not a sound, however, reached his ears until the iron drawer slid back into its case, when Penfield turned and, without a word, laid the empty envelope on the table before him.

For a few moments Thorndyke looked at the envelope as it lay, noting that, although empty, it retained the bulge caused by its late contents, and that those contents must have been somewhat bulky. Then he picked it up and inspected it methodically, committing his observations to memory, since written notes seemed unadvisable under the circumstances. It was an oblong, "commercial" envelope, about six inches long by three and three-quarters wide. The address was written with a pen of medium width and unusually black ink in a rather small, fluent, legible hand, with elegant capitals of a distinctly uncial type. The postmark was that of Penzance, dated the 23rd of June, 8.30 p.m. But of more interest to Thorndyke than the date, which he already knew, was an impression which the postmark stamp had made by striking the corner of the enclosure and thus defining its position in the envelope. From this he was able to judge that the object enclosed was oblong in shape, about five inches long or a little more, and somewhat less than three inches wide, and that it consisted of some soft material, presumably folded paper, since the blow of the metal stamp had left but a blunt impression of the corner. He next examined the edge of the flap, first with the naked eye and then with his pocket lens, and finally, turning back the flap from the place where the envelope had been neatly cut open, he closely scrutinized its inner surface.

"Have you examined this envelope, Mr Penfield?" he asked.

"Not in that exhaustive and minute manner," replied the solicitor, who had been watching the process with profound disfavour. "Why do you ask?"

"Because there appears to me a suggestion of its having been opened by moistening the flap and then reclosed. Just look at it through the glass, especially at the inside, where the gum seems to have spread more than one would expect from a single closing, and where there is a slight cockling of the paper."

He handed the envelope and the lens to Penfield, who seemed to find some difficulty in managing the latter, and after a brief inspection returned both the articles to Thorndyke.

"I have not your experience and skill," he said. "You may be right, but all the probabilities are against your suggestion. If Purcell had reopened the letter, it would surely have been to correct an error rather than to make one. And the letter certainly belonged to the enclosures."

"On the other hand," said Thorndyke, "when an envelope has been steamed or damped open, it will be laid down flap uppermost, with the addressed side hidden, and a mistake might occur in that way. However, there is probably nothing in it. That, I gather, is your opinion?"

Unfortunately it was. Very glad would Penfield have been to believe that the envelope had been opened and the blanks put in by another hand. But he had read Purcell's letter, and knew its connection with the enclosures.

"May I ask if you were expecting a letter from Purcell?" Thorndyke asked.

"Yes. I had written to him, and was expecting a reply."

"And would that letter have contained enclosures of about the same size as those which were sent?"

"I have no reason to suppose that it would have contained any enclosures," Penfield replied. "None were asked for."

Thorndyke made a mental note of this reply and of the fact that Penfield did not seem to perceive its bearing, and rose to depart.

"I am sorry to have had to be so reticent," said Penfield, as they shook hands, "but I hope your visit has not been entirely unfruitful, and I speed you on your quest with hearty good wishes."

Thorndyke replied in similarly polite terms and went on his way, leaving Mr Penfield in a state of profound relief at having got rid of him, not entirely unmingled with twinges of apprehension lest some incriminating fact should have leaked out unnoticed by him. Meanwhile Thorndyke, as soon as he emerged into Lombard Street, halted and made a detailed memorandum in his pocket-book of the few facts that he had gleaned.

Having thus disposed of Mr Penfield, he turned his steps in the direction of Coleman Street with the purpose of calling on Mr Levy, not, indeed, with the expectation of extracting much information from him, but rather to ascertain, if possible, how Purcell got his living. Arrived at the number that Margaret had given him, he read through the list of occupants in the hall, but without finding among then the name of Purcell. There was, however, on the second floor a firm entitled Honeyball Brothers, who were described as "financial agents," and as this description was the only one that seemed to meet the case, he ascended the stairs and entered a small, well-furnished office bearing on its door the Honeyball superscription. The only occupant was a spectacled youth, who was busily directing envelopes.

"Is Mr Levy in?" Thorndyke inquired.

"I'll see," was the cautious reply. "What name?"

Thorndyke gave his name, and the youth crossed to a door marked "Private," which he opened, and having passed through closed it behind him. His investigations in the sanctum resulted in the discovery that Mr Levy was there, a fact which he announced when he reappeared, holding the door open and inviting Thorndyke to enter. The latter accordingly walked through into the private office, when the door immediately closed behind him, and a smartly dressed, middle-aged man rose from a writing-chair and received him with an outstretched hand.

"You are Mr Levy?" inquired Thorndyke.

"I am Mr Levy," was the answer, accompanied by an almost affectionate handshake and a smile of the most intense benevolence; "at your entire service, Dr Thorndyke. Won't you sit down? This is the more comfortable chair and is nearer to my desk, and so more convenient for conversation. Ahem. We are always delighted to meet members of your profession, Doctor. We do business with quite a number of them, and I may say that we find them peculiarly appreciative of the delicacy with which our transactions are conducted. Ahem. Now, in what way can I have the pleasure of being of service to you?"

"The fact is," replied Thorndyke, "I have just called to make one or two inquiries – "

"Quite so," interrupted Mr Levy. "You are perfectly right. The wisdom of our ancestors, Dr Thorndyke, expresses itself admirably in the old adage 'Look before you leap.' Don't be diffident, sir. The more inquiries you make the better we shall be pleased. Now, what is the first point?"

"Well," Thorndyke replied, "I suppose the first point to dispose of is whether I have or have not come to the right office. My business is concerned with Mr Daniel Purcell."

"Then," said Mr Levy, "I should say that you have come to the right office. Mr Purcell is not here at the moment, but that is of no consequence. I am his authorized deputy. What is the nature of your, business, Doctor?"

"I am acting for Mrs Purcell, who has asked me to ascertain her husband's whereabouts, if possible."

"I see," said Levy. "Family doctor, hey? Well, I hope you'll find out where he is, because then you can tell me. But isn't Mr Penfield looking into the matter?"

"Possibly. But Mr Penfield is not very communicative, and it is not clear that he is taking any steps to locate Purcell. May I take it that you are willing to help us, so far as you can?"

"Certainly," replied Levy; "I'm willing enough. But if you want information you are in the same position as myself. All I know is that I haven't got his present address, but I have no doubt I shall hear from him in due course. He is away on holiday, you must remember."

"You know of no reason for supposing that he has gone away for good?"

"Lord bless you! no," replied Levy. "The first I heard of anything unusual was when old Penfield came round to ask if he had been to the office. Of course he hadn't, but I gave Penfield his address at Oulton and I wrote to Oulton myself. Then it turned out that he hadn't gone to Oulton after all. I admit that it is queer he hasn't written, seeing how methodical he usually is; but there is nothing to make a fuss about. Purcell isn't the sort of man to go off on a jaunt that would involve his dropping money; I can tell you that."

"And meanwhile his absence is not causing any embarrassment in a business sense?"

Mr Levy rose with a somewhat foxy smile. "Do I look embarrassed?" he asked. "Try me. I should like to do a bit of business with you. No? Well, then, I will wish you good-morning and good luck; and don't worry too much about the lost sheep. He is very well able to take care of himself."

He shook hands once more with undiminished cordiality, and personally escorted Thorndyke out on to the landing.

There was one other matter that had to be looked into. Mr Varney's rather vague report of the voyage from Falmouth to Ipswich required to be brought into the region of ascertained fact. Accordingly, from Purcell's office Thorndyke took his way to Lloyd's, where a brief investigation put him in possession of the name and address of the owner of the steamship *Hedwig* of Hernosand. With this in his notebook he turned homewards to the Temple with the immediate purpose of writing to the owner and the captain of the ship asking for a list of the passengers from Falmouth and of those who disembarked at Ipswich, and further giving a description of Purcell in case he should have travelled, as was highly probable, under an assumed name.

With these particulars it would be possible at least to attempt to trace the missing man, while if it should turn out that Varney had been misinformed, the trouble and expense of a search in the wrong place would be avoided.

CHAPTER SIX

In Which Mr Varney
Prepares a Deception

Varney's domestic arrangements were of the simplest. Unlike the majority of those who engage in dishonest transactions, he was frugal, thrifty, and content with little. Of what he earned, honestly or otherwise, he saved as much as he could; and now that he was free of the parasite who had clung to him for so long and had a future to look forward to, he was more than ever encouraged to live providently well within his modest means. For residence he occupied a couple of furnished rooms in Ampthill Square, Camden Town; but he spent little of his time in them, for he had a little studio in a quiet turning off the High Street, which he held on lease, and which contained his few household gods and formed his actual home. Thither he usually repaired as soon as he had breakfasted, buying a newspaper on the way and sitting in the Windsor armchair by the gas fire – alight or not, according to the season – to smoke his morning pipe and glance over the news before beginning work.

Following his usual custom, on a bright, sunny morning near the end of October, he arrived at the studio with a copy of *The Times* under his arm, and, letting himself in with his latch-key, laid the paper on the work-bench, hung up his hat, and put a match to the gas fire. Then, having drawn a chair up to the fire, he drew forth his pipe and pouch and sauntered over to the bench, where he stood, filling his pipe and gazing absently at the bench whereon the paper lay, while his thoughts travelled along a well-worn if somewhat vague track into a pleasant and tranquil future. Not for him alone was that future pleasant and tranquil. It held another figure – a sweet and gracious figure that lived in all his countless daydreams. She should be happy, too, freed, like himself, from that bloated parasite who had fastened upon her. Indeed, she was free now, if only she could be made to know it.

Again, for the thousandth time, he wondered, did she care for him? It was impossible to guess. She seemed always pleased to see him; she was warmly appreciative of his attentiveness and his efforts to help her, and her manner towards him was cordial and friendly. There was no doubt that she liked him, and what more could he ask until such time as the veil should be lifted and her freedom revealed to her? For Maggie Purcell was not only a pure-minded and innocent woman: she was the very soul of loyalty, even to the surly brute who had intruded unbidden into her life. And for this Varney loved her the more. But it left his question un-answered and unanswerable. For while her husband lived, in her belief, no thought of love for any other could be consciously admitted to that loyal heart.

He had filled his pipe, and taken a matchbox from his pocket, and was in the act of striking a match when, in an instant, his movement was arrested, and he stood, rigid and still, with the match poised in his hand and his eyes fixed on the newspaper. But no longer absently, for his wandering glance, travelling unheedingly over the printed page, had lighted by chance upon the name Purcell, printed in small capitals. For a few moments he stood with his eyes riveted on the familiar name; then he picked up the paper and read eagerly.

It was an advertisement in the "Personal" column, and read thus: "Purcell (D) is requested to communicate at once with Mr J Penfield, who has important information to impart to him *in re* Catford, deceased. The matter is urgent, as the will has been proved and must now be administered."

Varney read the advertisement through twice, and as he read it he smiled grimly, not, however, without a certain vague discomfort. There was nothing in the paragraph which affected him, but yet he found it, in some indefinable way, disquieting. And the more he reflected on the matter the more disturbing did it appear. Confound Purcell! The fellow was dead, and there was an end of it — at least, that was what he had intended and what he wished. But it seemed that it was not the end of it. Ever since that tragic voyage, when he had boldly cut the Gordian knot of his entanglements, Purcell had continued to reappear in one way or another, still, as ever, seeming to dominate his life. From his unknown and unsuspected grave, fathoms deep in the ocean, mysterious and disturbing influences seemed to issue, as though, even in death, his malice was still active. When would it be possible to shake him off for good?

Varney laid down the paper, and, flinging himself into the chair, set himself to consider the bearings of this new incident. How did it affect him? At the first glance it appeared not to affect him at all. Penfield would get no reply, and after one or two more trials he would have to give it up. That was all. The affair was no concern of his.

But was that all? And was it no concern of his? Reflection did not by any means confirm these assumptions. Varney knew little about the law, but he realized that a will which had been proved was a thing that had to be dealt with in some conclusive manner. When Penfield failed to get into touch with Purcell, what would he do? The matter, as he had said, was urgent. Something would have to be done. Quite probably Penfield would set some inquiries on foot. He would learn from Maggie, if he did not already know, of Purcell's supposed visit to Falmouth and the mythical voyage to Ipswich. Supposing he followed up those false tracks systematically? That might lead to complications. Those inventions had been improvised rather hastily, principally for Maggie's benefit. They might not stand such investigation as a lawyer might bring to bear on them. There was the ship, for instance. It would be possible to ascertain definitely what passengers she carried from Falmouth. And when it became certain that Purcell was not one of them, at the best the inquiry would draw a blank, at the worst there might be some suspicion of a fabrication of evidence on his part. In any case, the inquiry would be brought back to Penzance.

That would not do at all. Inquiries must be kept away from Penzance. He was the only witness of that mythical landing on the pier, and hitherto no one had thought of questioning his testimony. He believed that his own arrival on the pier had been unnoticed. But who could say? A vessel entering a harbour is always an object of interest to every nautical eye that beholds her. Who could say that some unseen watcher had not observed the yacht's arrival and noted that she was worked single-handed, and that one man only had gone ashore? It was quite possible, though he had seen no such watcher, and the risk was too great to be thought of. At all costs the inquiry must be kept away from Penzance.

How was that to be managed? The obvious way was to fabricate some sort of reply to the advertisement purporting to come from Purcell – a telegram, for instance, from France or Belgium, or even from some place in the Eastern Counties. The former was hardly possible, however. He could not afford the time or expense of a journey abroad, and, moreover, his absence from England would be known, and its coincidence with the arrival of the telegram might easily be noticed. Coincidences of that kind were much better avoided.

On reflection, the telegram did not commend itself. Penfield would naturally ask himself: "Why a telegram when a letter would have been equally safe and so much more efficient?" For both would reveal, approximately, the whereabouts of the sender. No, a telegram would not answer the purpose. It would not be quite safe, for telegrams, like typewritten letters, are always open to suspicion as to their genuineness. Such suspicions may lead to inquiries at the telegraph office. On the other hand, a letter, if it could be properly managed, would have quite the contrary effect. It would be accepted as convincing evidence, not only of the existence of the writer, but of his whereabouts at the time of writing – if only it could be properly managed. But could it be?

He struck a match and lit his pipe – to little purpose, for it went out and was forgotten in the course of a minute. Could he produce a letter from Purcell – a practicable letter which would pass without suspicion the scrutiny, not only of Penfield himself, who was familiar with Purcell's handwriting, but also of Maggie, to whom it would almost certainly be shown? It was a serious question, and he gave it very serious consideration, balancing the chances of detection against the chances of success, and especially dwelling upon the improbability of any question arising as to its authenticity.

Now, Varney was endowed in a remarkable degree with the dangerous gift of imitating handwriting; indeed, it was this gift, and its untimely exercise, that had been the cause of all his troubles. And the natural facility in this respect had been reinforced by the steadiness of hand and perfect control of line that had come from his years of practice as a copperplate engraver. In that craft his work had largely consisted of minute and accurate imitation of writing and other linear forms, and he was now capable of reproducing his "copy" with microscopic precision and fidelity. Reflecting on this, and, further, that he was in possession of Purcell's own fountain pen with its distinctive ink, he decided confidently that he could produce a letter which would not merely pass muster but would even defy critical examination, to which it was not likely to be subjected.

Having decided that the letter could be produced, the next question was that of ways and means. It would have been best for it to be sent from some place abroad, but that could not very well be managed. However, it would answer quite well if it could be sent from one of the towns or villages of East Anglia – in fact, that would perhaps be the best plan, as it would tend to confirm the Falmouth and Ipswich stories and be, in its turn, supported by them. But there was the problem of getting the letter posted. That would involve a journey down to Suffolk or Norfolk, and to this there were several objections. In the first place, he could ill spare the time, for he had a good deal of work on hand: he had an engagement with a dealer on the present evening, he had to arrange about an exhibition on the following day, and in the evening he was to dine with Maggie and Philip Rodney. None of these engagements, but especially the last, was he willing to cancel; and yet, if the letter was to be sent, there ought not to be much delay. But the most serious objection was the one that had occurred to him in relation to the telegram. His absence from town would probably be known and he might even be seen, either at his East Anglian destination or on his way thither or returning, and the coincidence of those movements with the arrival of the letter could hardly fail to be noticed. Indeed, if he were seen in the locality from whence the letter came, or going or returning, that would be a perilously striking coincidence.

What, then, was the alternative? He reflected awhile, and presently he had an idea. How would it answer if he should not post the letter at all, but simply drop it into Penfield's letter-box? There was something to be said for that. It would go to prove that Purcell must be lurking somewhere in London – not an unlikely thing in itself, for London is so large that it is hardly a locality at all, and it is admittedly one of the safest of hiding-places. But, for that matter, why not post the letter, say, in Limehouse or Ratcliff, and thus suggest a lurking-place in the squalid and nautical east? That did not seem a bad idea. But still his preferences leaned towards the Eastern Counties – somewhere in the neighbourhood of Ipswich, which would give consistency to the account of the voyage from Falmouth. It was something of a dilemma, and he turned over the alternative plans for some time without coming to any conclusion.

As he sat thus meditating, his eye roamed idly about the bare but homely studio, and presently it encountered an object that started a new and interesting train of thought. Pushed away in a corner was a small lithographic press, now mostly disused, for the little "auto-lithographs" that he used to produce had ceased to be profitable now that there was a fair demand for his etchings and mezzotints. But the press was in going order, and he was a moderately expert lithographer – quite expert enough to produce a perfectly convincing post-mark on a forged letter, especially if that post-mark were carefully indented after printing, to disguise the process by which it had been produced.

It was a brilliant idea. In his pleased excitement he started up from his chair and began rapidly to pace up and down the studio. A most admirable plan! For it not only disposed of all the difficulties but actually turned them into advantages. He would get the letter prepared; he would keep his engagement with Maggie; then, after leaving her, he would make his way to George Yard and there drop the letter into Penfield's letter-box. It would be found on the following morning, and would appear to have been posted the previous evening and delivered by the first post. He would actually be present in Maggie's flat at the very moment when the letter was (apparently) being posted in Suffolk. A most excellent scheme!

Chuckling with satisfaction, he set himself forthwith to carry it out. The means and appliances were in a cupboard that filled a recess – just a plain wall cupboard, but fitted with a Chubb lock of the highest class. Unlocking this, he cast his eye over the orderly shelves. Here, standing upright in an empty ink-bottle, was the thick-barrelled fountain pen that had once been Purcell's. Varney took out the pen in its container and stood it on the table. Next, from the back of the cupboard, he reached out an expanding letter-file, and, opening it, took from the compartment marked "P" a small bundle of letters docketed "Purcell," which he also laid on the table. They were all harmless unimportant letters (saved for that very reason), and if one should have asked why Varney had kept them, the answer, applicable to most of the other contents of the file, would have been that they had been preserved in obedience to the forger's instinct to keep a few originals in stock on the chance that they might come in handy one day.

He drew a chair up to the table and began methodically to look through the letters, underlining with a lead pencil the words that he would probably want to copy. In the third letter that he read he had an unexpected stroke of luck, for it contained a reference to Mr Penfield, to whom some enclosed document was to be sent, and it actually gave his full name and address. This was a windfall indeed! As he encircled the address with a pencil mark, Varney smiled complacently, and felt that Fortune was backing him up handsomely.

Having secured the "copy" for the handwriting, the next thing was to get the post-mark drawn and printed. The letters in the file had no envelopes, but he had in his pocket a letter that he had received that morning from an innkeeper at Tenterden, to whom he had written for particulars as to accommodation. It was probably a typical country letter, and its post-mark would serve as well as any other. He took it from his pocket, and, laying it on a small drawing board, pinned a piece of tracing paper over it and made a very careful tracing of the post-mark. Then he drew away the letter, and slipped in its place a small piece of lithographic transfer paper with a piece of black lead transfer paper over it, and went over the tracing carefully with a hard pencil. He now had a complete tracing of the post-mark on the lithographic paper, including the name "Tenterden" and the date and time, which he had included to give the dimensions and style of the lettering. But he now partially erased them, excepting the year date, and replaced them, in the same style and size, with the inscription "Woodbridge, Oct. 28, 4.30 p.m.," drawn firmly with a rather soft pencil.

He now fetched his lithographic ink and pens from the cupboard, and, with the original before him, inked in the tracing, being careful to imitate all the accidental characters of the actual postmark, such as the unequal thickness of the lines due to the uneven pressure of the marking stamp. When he had finished, he turned the envelope over and repeated the procedure with the London postmark, only here he made an exact facsimile excepting as to the date and time, which he altered to "Oct. 29, 11.20 p.m."

The next proceeding was to transfer the inked tracings to a lithographic stone. He used a smallish stone, placing the two post-marks a convenient distance apart, so that they could be printed separately. When the transfer and the subsequent "etching" processes were completed and the stone was ready for printing, he inked up and took a trial proof of the two post-marks on a sheet of paper. The result was perfectly convincing. Ridiculously so. As he held the paper in his hand and looked at those absurd post-marks, he chuckled aloud. With a little ingenuity, how easy it was to sprinkle salt on the forensic tail of the inscrutable Penfield! He was disposed to linger and picture to himself the probable proceedings of that astute gentleman when he received the letter. But there was a good deal to do yet, and he must not waste time. There was the problem of printing the Woodbridge post-mark fairly on the stamp, and then there was the addressing and writing of the letter.

The first problem he solved by tracing the outline of an envelope on the sheet that he had printed, with the post-mark in the correct place for the stamp, cutting this piece out and using it to make register marks on the stone. Then he affixed a stamp exactly to the correct spot on the envelope, inked up the stone, laid the envelope against the register marks, and passed the stone under the roller. When he picked up the envelope, the stamp bore the Woodbridge post-mark with just that slight inaccuracy of imposition that made it perfectly convincing. The London post-mark presented no difficulty, as it did not matter to half an inch where it was placed. Another ink-up and another turn of the crank-handle, and the envelope was ready for the penmanship.

Although Varney was so expert a copyist, he decided to take no unnecessary risks. Accordingly, he made a careful tracing of Penfield's name and address from the original letter and transferred this in black lead to the envelope. Then with Purcell's pen, charged with its special black ink, and with the original before him, he inked in the tracing with a free and steady hand and quickly enough to avoid any tell-tale wavering or tremor of the line. It was certainly a masterly performance, and when it was done it would have puzzled a much greater expert than Penfield to distinguish between the copy and the original.

Varney regarded it with deep satisfaction. He was about to put it aside to dry, before he should rub out the tracing marks, when it occurred to him that Purcell would almost certainly have marked it "confidential" or "personal." It was, in fact, rather desirable that this missive should be opened by Penfield himself. The fewer hands it passed through the better; and then, of course, it was not worth while to let any of the clerks into the secret of Purcell's disappearance. Accordingly, with the original letter still before him, he wrote at the top of the envelope, in bold and rather large characters, the word "personal." That ought to make it safe.

He put the envelope aside and began to think out the text of the letter that he was going to write. As he did so, his eyes rested gloatingly on the work that he had done, and done to such a perfect finish. It was really a masterpiece of deception. Even a post-office sorter would have been taken in by it. He took it up and again regarded it admiringly. Then he began to consider whether "confidential" would not have been better than "personal." It was certainly most desirable that this letter should not be opened even by the chief clerk, for it would let the cat out of the bag rather completely. He held the envelope irresolutely for a full minute, turning the question over. Finally, he picked up the pen, and, laying the envelope before him, turned the full stop into an "and" and followed this with the word "confidential." There was not as much space as he would have liked, and in his anxiety to preserve the character of the handwriting while compressing the letters the tail of the final *l* strayed on to the edge of the stamp, which to his critical eye looked a little untidy; but that was of no consequence – in fact, it was rather an additional realistic touch.

He now set to work upon the letter itself. It was to be but a short letter, and it took him only a few minutes to draft out the matter in pencil. Then, spreading Purcell's letter before him, he studied it word by word and letter by letter. When he had got the character of the writing well into his mind, he took a sheet of notepaper, and with a well-sharpened H pencil made a very careful copy of his draft, constantly referring to Purcell's original and even making tracings of important words and of the signature. Having compared the lightly pencilled copy with Purcell's letter and made one or two corrections, he picked up the pen and traced over the pencil writing with the sureness and steadiness that his training as an engraver made possible.

The letter being finished with a perfect facsimile of the signature, he made a final comparison of the handwriting with Purcell's, and, finding it beyond criticism, read through the letter again, speculating on Mr Penfield's probable proceedings when he received it. The text of the letter ran thus:

"Dear Mr Penfield,

"I have just seen your advertisement in *The Times*, and am writing to let you know that circumstances render it impossible for me to call on you, and for the same reason I am unable to give you my present address. If there is anything connected with the Catford business that you wish me to know, perhaps you could put it briefly in another advertisement, to which I could reply if necessary. Sorry to give you this trouble.

Yours sincerely,

Daniel Purcell."

Laying down the letter, Varney once more turned to the envelope. First, with a piece of artist's soft rubber he removed the pencil marks of the tracing. Then, placing the envelope on a sheet of blotting-paper, he carefully traced over the post-marks with an agate tracing-style, following the two concentric circles of each with their enclosed letters and figures with minute accuracy and pressing somewhat firmly. The result was that each of the two post-marks was visibly indented, as if made by a sharply-struck marking stamp. It only remained to erase the pencil marks from the letter, to place it in the envelope, and close the latter; and when this was done, Varney rose and, having once more lit his pipe, began to replace the materials in the cupboard, where also he bestowed the letter for the present.

He was in the act of closing the cupboard door, when his glance fell on a small deed-box on the top shelf. He looked at it thoughtfully for a few moments, then lifted it down, placed it on the table, and unlocked it. The contents were three paper packets, each sealed with his ring-seal. He broke the seals of all three and opened the packets. Two of them contained engraved copper plates, of a twenty-pound and a five-pound note respectively. The third contained a sheaf of paper blanks. Varney took out the latter and counted them, holding each one up to the light to examine the water-mark. There were twelve of them, all five-pound notes. He laid them down and cogitated profoundly; and unconsciously his eyes turned to the etching press at the end of the bench. A few minutes' work, a smear of ink, and a turn of the press, would convert those blanks into actual notes, so good that they could be passed with perfect safety. Twelve fives − sixty pounds. It was handsome pay for half an hour's work, and five-pound notes were so easy to get rid of.

It was a severe temptation to a comparatively poor man whose ethical standards were none of the highest. Prosperous as he now thought himself with the growing demand for his etchings, sixty pounds represented the product of nearly two months' legitimate work. It was a great temptation. There were the blanks, all ready for the magic change. It seemed a pity to waste them. There were only a dozen, and there would be no more. This would really be the end of the lay. After this he could go straight and live a perfectly reputable life.

The gambler's lure, the attraction of easily won wealth, was beginning to take effect. He had actually picked up the five-pound plate, and was moving towards the bench, when something in his mind brought him suddenly to a stop. In that moment there had risen before his mental vision the sweet and gracious figure of

Margaret Purcell. Instantly his feelings underwent a revulsion. That which, but a minute ago, had seemed natural and reasonable now looked unspeakably sordid and base. No compulsion now urged him on unwillingly to crime. It would be his own choice – the choice of mere greed. Was it for this that he had set her and himself free? Could he stand in her presence and cherish thoughts of honourable love with this mean crime, committed of his own free-will, on his conscience? Assuredly not. The very corpse of Purcell cried out from its dark tomb beneath the Wolf on this voluntary resumption of the chains which he had broken at the cost of murder.

Once more he turned towards the bench, but now with a different purpose. Hurriedly, as if fearful of another backsliding, he caught up a large graver and drove its point across the plate from corner to corner, ploughing up the copper in a deep score. That finished the matter. Never again could that plate be printed from. But he did not leave it at that. With a shaving scraper he pared off the surface of the plate until the engraving on it was totally obliterated. He fetched the other plate and treated it in a similar manner. Then he flung both plates into a porcelain dish and filled it with strong nitric acid mordant. Finally, as the malodorous red fumes began to rise from the dish, he took up the sheaf of blanks and held them in the flame of the gas-stove. When the last blackened fragments had fallen to the hearth, he drew a deep breath. Now at last he was free. Really free. Free even from the peril of his own weakness.

His labours had consumed the best part of the morning, but, in any case, he was in no mood for his ordinary work. Opening the window a little wider to let the fumes escape, he took his hat from the peg and went forth, turning his steps in the direction of Regent's Park.

CHAPTER SEVEN

The Flash Note Factory

To the lover of quiet and the admirer of urban comeliness, the ever-increasing noise and turmoil of London and its ever-decreasing architectural interest and charm give daily an added value to the Inns of Court, in whose peaceful precincts quiet and comeliness yet survive. And of the Inns of Court, if we except Old Buildings, Lincoln's Inn, the Temple with its cloisters, its fountain, and its ancient church, makes the strongest appeal to the affections of that almost extinct creature the Londoner; of which class the last surviving genuine specimens are to be found in its obsolete chambers, living on amidst the amenities of a bygone age.

But it was neither the quiet nor the architectural charm of the old domestic buildings that had caused Mr Superintendent Miller, of the Criminal Investigation Department, to take the Temple on his way from Scotland Yard to Fleet Street (though it was as short a way as any); nor was it a desire to contemplate the houses attributed to Wren that made him slow down when he reached King's Bench Walk and glance hesitatingly up and down that pleasant thoroughfare – if a thoroughfare it can be called. The fact is that Mr Miller was engaged in certain investigations, which had led him, as investigations sometimes do, into a blind alley; and it was in his mind to see if the keen vision of Dr John Thorndyke could detect a way out. But he did not want a formal consultation.

Rather, he desired to let the matter arise, as it were, by chance, and he did not quite see how to manage it.

Here, as he stood hesitating opposite Thorndyke's chambers, Providence came to his aid; for at this moment a tall figure emerged from the shadow of the covered passage from Mitre Court and came with an easy, long-legged swing down the tree-shaded footway. Instantly the Superintendent strode forward to intercept the newcomer, and the two met halfway up the Walk.

"You were not coming to see me, by any chance?" Thorndyke asked, when the preliminary greetings had been exchanged.

"No," replied Miller, "though I had half a mind to look in on you, just to pass the time of day. I am on my way to Clifford's Inn to look into a rather queer discovery that has been made there."

Here the Superintendent paused with an attentive eye on Thorndyke's face, though experience should have told him that he might as well study the expression of a wigmaker's block. As Thorndyke showed no sign of rising to the bait, he continued:

"A remarkably queer affair. Mysterious, in fact. Our people are rather stuck, so I am going to have a look round the chambers to see if I can pick up any traces."

"That is always a useful thing to do," said Thorndyke. "Rooms, like clothes, tend to take certain impressions from those who live in them. Careful inspection, eked out by some imagination, will usually yield something of interest."

"Precisely," agreed Miller. "I realized that long ago from watching your own methods. You were always rather fond of poking about in empty houses and abandoned premises. By the way," he added, forced into the open by Thorndyke's impassiveness, "I wonder if you would care to stroll up with me and have a look at these chambers?"

"Are the facts of the case available?" asked Thorndyke.

"Certainly," replied Miller, "to you — so far as they are known. If you care to walk up with me, I'll tell you about the case as we go along."

Thereupon Thorndyke (to whom the insoluble mystery and especially the untenanted chambers were as a hot scent to an eager fox-hound) turned and retraced his steps in company with the Superintendent.

"The history of the affair," the latter began, "is this: At No. 92, Clifford's Inn a man named Bromeswell had chambers on the second floor. He had been there several years, and was an excellent tenant, paying his rent and other liabilities with clockwork regularity on, or immediately after, quarter day. He had never been known to be even a week in arrear with rent, gas, or anything else. But at Midsummer he failed to pay up in his usual prompt manner, and, after a fortnight had passed, a polite reminder was dropped into his letter-box. But still he made no sign. However, as he was an old tenant and his character was so excellent, nothing was done beyond dropping in another reminder. Once or twice the porter went to the door of the chambers but he always found the "oak" shut, and when he hammered on it with a stick, he got no answer.

"Well, the time ran on, and the porter began to think that things looked a bit queer, but still nothing was done. Then one day the postman brought a batch of letters, or, rather, circulars, to the lodge addressed to Bromeswell. He had tried to get them into Bromeswell's letter-box, but couldn't get them in, as the box was chokefull. Now this made pretty clear that Bromeswell had not been in his chambers for some considerable time, unless he was dead and his body shut up in them, so the porter acquainted the treasurer with the state of affairs and consulted with him as to what was to be done. There were no means of getting into the chambers without breaking in, for the tenant had at some time fixed a new patent lock on the outer door, and the porter had no duplicate key. But the chambers couldn't be left indefinitely, especially as there was possibly a dead man inside, so the treasurer decided to send a man up a ladder to break a window and let himself in. As a matter of fact, the porter went up himself, and as soon as he got into the chambers and had a look round, he began to smell a rat.

"The appearance of the place, and especially the even coating of dust that covered everything, showed that no one had been in those rooms for two or three months at least; but what particularly attracted the attention of the porter, who is a retired police sergeant, was a rather queer-looking set of apparatus that suggested to him the outfit of a maker of flash notes. On this he began to make some inquiries, and then it transpired that nobody knew anything about Bromeswell. Mr Duskin, the late porter, must have known him, since he must have let him the chambers; but Duskin left the Inn some years ago, and the present porter has never met this tenant. It seems an incredible thing, but it appears to be a fact that no one even knows Bromeswell by sight."

"That does really seem incredible," said Thorndyke, "in the case of a man living in a place like Clifford's Inn."

"Ah, but he wasn't really living there. That was known, because no milk or bread was ever left there and no laundress ever called for washing. There are no resident chambers in No. 92. The porter had an idea that Bromeswell was a press artist or something of that kind, and used the premises to work in. But of course it wasn't any concern of his."

"How was the rent paid?"

"By post, in notes and cash. And the gas was paid in the same way; never by cheque. But to go on with the history: The porter's suspicions were aroused, and he communicated them to the treasurer, who agreed with him that the police ought to be informed. Accordingly, they sent us a note, and we instructed Inspector Monk, who is a first-class expert on flash notes, to go to Clifford's Inn and investigate, but to leave things undisturbed as far as possible. So Monk went to the chambers and had a look at the apparatus, and what he saw made him pretty certain that the porter was right. The apparatus was a complete paper-maker's plant in miniature, all except the moulds. There were no moulds to be seen, and until they were found it was impossible to say that the paper was not being made for some lawful purpose, though the size of the pressing plates – eighteen inches by seven – gave a pretty broad hint. However, there was an iron safe in the room, one of Wilkins' make, and Monk decided that the moulds were probably locked up in it. He also guessed what the moulds were like. You may have heard of a long series of most excellent forgeries of Bank of England notes."

"I have," said Thorndyke. "They were five-pound and twenty-pound notes, mostly passed in France, Belgium, Switzerland and Holland."

"That's the lot," said Miller, "and first-class forgeries they were; and for a very good reason. They were made with the genuine moulds. Some six years ago two moulds were lost or stolen from the works at Maidstone, where the Bank of England makes its paper. They were the moulds for five-pound and twenty-pound notes respectively, and each mould would make a sheet that would cut into two notes – a long narrow sheet sixteen and three-quarter inches by five and five thirty-seconds in the case of a five-pound note. Well, we have been on the lookout for those forgers for years, but, naturally, they were difficult to trace, for the forgeries were so good that no one could tell them from the real thing but the experts at the Bank. You see, it is the paper that the forger usually comes a cropper over. The engraving is much easier to imitate. But this paper was not only made in the proper moulds with all the proper water-marks, but it seemed to be made by a man who knew his job. So you can reckon that Monk was as keen as mustard on getting those moulds.

"And get them he did. On our authority Wilkins made him a duplicate key – as we didn't want to blow the safe open – and sure enough, as soon as he opened the door, there were the two moulds. So that's that. There is an end of those forgeries. But the question is, Who and where the devil is this fellow Bromeswell? And there is another question. This only accounts for the paper. The engraving and printing were done somewhere else and by some other artist. We should like to find out who he is. But, for the present, he is a bird in the bush. Bromeswell is our immediate quarry."

"He seems to be pretty much in the bush, too," remarked Thorndyke. "Is there no trace of him at all? What about his agreement and his references?"

"Gone," replied Miller. "When the Inn was sold most of the old papers were destroyed. They were of no use."

"It is astonishing," said Thorndyke, "that a man should have been in occupation of those chambers for years and remain completely unknown. And yet one sees how it can have happened with the change of porters. Duskin was the only link that we have with Bromeswell, and Duskin is gone. As to his not being known by sight, he probably came to the chambers only occasionally to make a batch of paper, and if there were no residents in his block, no one would be likely to notice him."

"No," Miller agreed; "Londoners are not inquisitive about their neighbours, especially in a business quarter. This is the place, and those are his rooms on the second floor."

As he paused by an ancient lamp-post near the postern gate that opens on Fetter Lane, the Superintendent indicated a small, dark entry, and then nodded at a range of dull windows at the top of the old house. Then he crossed a tiny courtyard, plunged into the dark entry, and led the way up the narrow stairs, groping with his hands along the unseen handrail, and closely followed by Thorndyke.

At the first floor they emerged for a moment into modified daylight, and then ascended another flight of dark and narrow stairs, which opened on a grimy landing, whose only ornaments were an iron dust-bin and a gas-meter, and which displayed a single ironbound door, above which appeared in faded white lettering the inscription "Mr Bromeswell."

The Superintendent unlocked the massive outer door, which opened with a rusty creak, revealing an inner door fitted with a knocker. This Miller pushed open, and the two men entered the outer room of the "set" of chambers, halting just inside the door to make a general survey of the room, of which the most striking feature was its bareness. And this was really a remarkable feature when the duration of the tenancy was considered. In the course of some years of occupation the mysterious tenant had accumulated no more furniture than a small kitchen table, a Windsor chair, a canvas-seated camp armchair, a military camp bedstead with a sleeping-bag, and a couple of rugs and a small iron safe.

"It is obvious," said Thorndyke, "that Bromeswell never lived here. Apparently he visited the place only at intervals, but when he came he stayed until he had finished what he had come to do. Probably he brought a supply of food, and never went out between his arrival and departure."

He strolled into the tiny kitchen, where a gas ring, a teapot, a cup and saucer, one or two plates, a tin of milk-powder, one of sugar, another of tea, and a biscuit-tin containing an unrecognizable mildewy mass, bore out his suggestion. With a glance at the loaded letter-box, he crossed the room, and, opening the door, entered what was intended to be the bedroom, but had been made into a workshop. And very complete it was, being fitted with a roomy sink and tap, a small boiler – apparently a dentist's vulcanizer – and a mixer or beater worked by a little electric motor, driven by a bichromate battery, there being no electric light in the premises. By the window was a strong bench, on which was a powerful office press, a stack of long, narrow copper plates, and a pile of pieces of felt of a similar shape but somewhat larger. Close to the bench was a trough made from a stout wooden box, lined with zinc and mounted on four legs, in which was a folded newspaper containing a number of neat coils of cow-hair cord, each coil having an eye-splice at either end, evidently to fit on the hooks which had been fixed in the walls.

"Those cords," Miller explained, as Thorndyke took them from the paper to examine them, "were used as drying lines to hang the damp sheets of paper on. They are always made of cow hair, because that is the only material that doesn't mark the paper. But I expect you know all about that. Is there anything that catches your eye in particular? You seem interested in those cords."

"I was looking at these two," said Thorndyke, holding out two cords which he had uncoiled. "This one, you see, was too long; it had been cut the wrong length, or, more probably, was the remainder of a long piece. But instead of cutting off the excess, our friend has thriftily shortened this rather expensive cord by working a sheep-shank on it. Now it isn't everyone who knows how to make a sheep-shank, and the persons who do are not usually papermakers."

"That's perfectly true, Doctor," assented Miller. "I'm one of the people who don't know how to make that particular kind of knot. What is the other point?"

"This other cord," replied Thorndyke, "which looks new, has an eye-splice at one end only, but it is, as you see, about five inches longer than the other; just about the amount that would be taken up by working the eye-splice. That looks as if Bromeswell had worked the splices himself, and if you consider the matter you will see that is probably the case. The length of these cords is roughly the width of this room. They have been cut to a particular measure, but the cord was most probably bought in a single length, as this extra long piece suggests."

"Yes," agreed Miller. "They wouldn't have been sold with the eye-splices worked on them, and, in fact, I don't see what he wanted with the eye-splices at all. A simple knotted loop would have answered the purpose quite as well."

"Exactly," said Thorndyke. "They were not necessary. They were a luxury, a refinement; and that emphasizes the point that they suggest, which is that Bromeswell is a man who has some technical knowledge of cordage, is probably a sailor, or in some way connected with the sea. As you say, a common knotted loop, such as a bowline knot, would have answered the purpose perfectly. But that is true of most of the cases in which a sailor uses an eye-splice. Then why does he take the trouble to work the splice? Principally for the sake of neatness of appearance, because, to an expert eye, a tied loop with its projecting end looks slovenly.

"Now this man will have had quite a lot of time on his hands. He will have had to wait about for hours while the pulp was boiling and while it was being beaten up. A sailor would very naturally spend a part of his idle time in tidying up the cordage."

The Superintendent nodded reflectively. "Yes," he said, "I think you are right, Doctor, and it is an important point. This fellow was a fairly expert papermaker. He wasn't a mere amateur, like most of the note forgers. If he was some kind of sailor man as well, that would make him a lot easier to identify if we should get on his track. But that is just what we can't do. There is nothing to start from. He is a mere name, and pretty certainly a false name at that."

As he spoke, Miller looked about him discontentedly, running his eye over the bench and its contents. Suddenly he stepped over to the press, and, diving into the shadowed space between it and the wall, brought up his hand grasping a silver-mounted briar pipe.

"Now, Doctor," he said with a grin, handing it to Thorndyke when he had inspected it, "here is something in your line. Just run your eye over that pipe and tell me what the man is like."

Thorndyke laughed as he took the pipe in his hand. "You are thinking of the mythical anatomist and the fossil bone," said he. "I am afraid this relic will not tell us much. It is a good pipe; it must have cost half a guinea, which would have meant more if its owner had been honest. The maker's name tells us that it was bought in Cheap-side, near the Bank, its weight and the marks on the mouthpiece tell us that the owner has a strong jaw and a good set of teeth; its good condition suggests a careful, orderly man, and its presence here makes it likely that the owner was Mr Bromeswell. That isn't much, but it confirms the other appearances."

"What other appearances?" demanded Miller.

"Those of the bed, the chair, the bench, the hooks, and the trough. They all point to a big, heavy man. The bedstead is about six feet six inches long, but the heel-marks are near the foot and the pillow is right at the head. This bench and the trough have been put up for this man's use – they were apparently knocked up by himself – and they are both of a suitable height for you or me.

A short man couldn't work at either. The hooks are over seven feet from the floor. The canvas seat of the chair is deeply sagged, although the woodwork looks in nearly new condition, and the canvas of the bed is in the same condition. Add this massive, hard-bitten pipe to those indications, and you have the picture of a tall, burly, powerful man. We must have a look at his pillow and rugs to see if we can pick up a stray hair or two and get an idea of his complexion. What did he make the pulp from? I don't see any traces of rags."

"He didn't use rags. He used Whatman's water-colour paper, which is a pure linen paper. Apparently he tore it up into tiny fragments and boiled it in soda lye until it was ready to go into the beater. Monk found a supply of the paper in a cupboard and some half-cooked stuff in the boiler." As he spoke, Miller unscrewed and raised the lid of the boiler, which was then seen to be half filled with a clear liquid, at the bottom of which was a mass of sodden fragments of shredded paper. From the boiler he turned to a small cupboard and opened the door. "That seems to be his stock of material," he said, indicating a large roll of thick white paper. He took out a sheet and handed it to Thorndyke, who held it up to the light and read the name "Whatman," which formed the water-mark.

"Yes," said Thorndyke, as he returned the sheet. "His method of work seems clear enough, but that is not of much interest, as you have the moulds. What we want is the man himself. You have no description of him, I suppose?"

"Not if your description of him is correct," replied Miller. "The suspected person, according to the Belgian police, is a smallish, slight, dark man. They may be on the wrong track, or there may be a confederate. There must have been a confederate, perhaps more than one. But Bromeswell only made the paper. Someone else must have done the engraving and printing. As to planting the notes, that may have been done by some other parties, or by either or both of these two artists. I should think they probably kept the game to themselves, judging by what we have seen here. This seems to be a one man show, and it looks as if even the engraver didn't know where the paper was made, or the moulds wouldn't have been left in this way. Shall we go and look for those hairs that you spoke of?"

They returned to the outer room, where they both subjected the little pillow of the camp bed to a searching scrutiny. But though they examined both sides and even took off the dusty pillow-case, not a single hair was to be found. Then they turned their attention to the rugs, which had been folded neatly and placed on the canvas – there was no mattress – unfolding them carefully and going over them inch by inch. Here, too, they seemed to have drawn a blank, for they had almost completed their examination, when the Superintendent uttered an exclamation, and delicately picked a small object from near the edge of the rug.

"This seems to be a hair, Doctor," said he, holding it up between his finger and thumb. "Looks like a moustache hair, but it's a mighty short one."

Thorndyke produced his pocket lens and a sheet of notepaper, and holding the latter while Miller cautiously dropped the hair on it, he inspected the find through his lens.

"Yes," he said, "it is a moustache hair, about half an inch long, decidedly thick, cleanly cut, and of a lightish red-brown colour. Somehow it seems to fit the other characters. A closely-cropped, bristly, sandy moustache appears to go appropriately with the stature and weight of the man and that massive pipe. There is a tendency for racial characters to go together, and the blond races run to height and weight. Well, we have a fairly complete picture of the man, unless we have made some erroneous inferences, and we seem to have finished our inspection. Have you been through the stuff in the letterbox?"

"Monk went through it, but we may as well have a look at it to make sure that he hasn't missed anything. I'll hand the things out if you will put them on the table and check them."

As Miller took out the letters in handfuls, Thorndyke received them from him and laid them out on the table. Then he and Miller examined the collection systematically.

"You see, Doctor," said the latter, "they are all circulars; not a private letter among them excepting the two notes from the treasurer about the rent. And they are quite a miscellaneous lot. None of these people knew anything about Bromeswell, apparently; they just copied the address out of the directory. Here's one from a money-lender. Bromeswell could have given him a tip or two. The earliest post-mark is the eleventh of June, so we may take it that he wasn't here after the tenth or the morning of the eleventh."

"There is a slight suggestion that he left at night," said Thorndyke, as he made a note of the date. "The place where you found the pipe would be in deep shadow by gaslight, but not by daylight. Certainly the blind was up, but he would probably have drawn it up after he had turned the gas out, as its being down during the day might attract attention."

"Yes," said Miller, "you are probably right about the time; and that reminds me that Monk found a small piece of paper under the bench — I've got it in my pocket — which seems to bear out your suggestion." He took from his pocket a bulky letter-case, from an inner recess of which he extracted a little scrap of Whatman paper. "Here it is," he said, handing it to Thorndyke. "He seems to have just jotted down the times of two trains, and, as you say, they were probably night trains."

Thorndyke looked with deep attention at the fragment, on which was written, hastily but legibly in very black ink, "8.15 and 11.1 P," and remarked:

"Quite a valuable find in its way. The writing is very characteristic, and so is the ink. Probably it would be more so when seen through the microscope. Magnification brings out shades of colour that are invisible to the naked eye."

"Well, Doctor," said Miller, "if you can spare the time to have a look at it through the microscope, I wish you would, and let us know if you discover anything worth noting. And perhaps you wouldn't mind taking a glance at the hair, too, to settle the colour more exactly."

He transferred the latter, which he had carefully folded in paper and put in his pocket-book, to Thorndyke, who deposited it, with the scrap of paper, in his letter-case, after pencilling on the wrapper a note of the nature and source of the object.

"And that," said the Superintendent, "seems to be the lot. We haven't done so badly, after all. If you are right – and I expect you are – we have got quite a serviceable description of the man Bromeswell. But it is a most mysterious affair. I can't imagine what the deuce can have happened. It is pretty clear that he came here about the tenth of June, and probably made a batch of paper, which we shall hear of later. But what can have happened to the man? Something out of the common, evidently. He would never have stayed away voluntarily with the certainty that the premises would be entered, his precious moulds found, and the whole thing blown upon. If he had intended to clear out he would certainly have taken the moulds with him, or at least destroyed them if he thought that the game was up. What do you think, Doctor?"

"It seems to me," replied Thorndyke, "that there are three possibilities. He may be dead, and if so he probably died suddenly, before he was able to make any arrangements; he may be in prison on some other charge; or he may have got a scare that we know nothing of and had to keep out of sight. You said that the Belgian police were taking some action."

"Yes, they have got an officer over here, by agreement with us, who is making inquiries about the man who planted the notes in Belgium. But he isn't after Bromeswell. He is looking for quite a different man, as I told you. But he doesn't pretend that he could recognize him."

"It doesn't follow that Bromeswell knows that. If the confederate has discovered that inquiries are being made, he may have given his friend a hint and the pair of them may have absconded. But that is a mere speculation. As you say, something extraordinary must have happened, and it must have been something sudden and unforeseen. And that is all that we can say at present."

By the time that this conclusion was reached, they had emerged from Clifford's Inn Passage, into Fleet Street; and here they parted, the Superintendent setting a course westward and Thorndyke crossing the road to the gateway of Inner Temple Lane.

Chapter Eight

In Which Thorndyke Tries
Over the Moves

It was in a deeply meditative frame of mind that Thorndyke pursued his way towards his chambers after parting with the Superintendent. For the inspection which he had just made had developed points of interest other than those which he had discussed with the detective officer. To his acute mind, habituated to rapid inference, the case of the mysterious Mr Bromeswell had inevitably presented a parallelism with that of Daniel Purcell. Bromeswell had disappeared without leaving a trace. If he had absconded, he had done so without premeditation or preparation, apparently under the compulsion of some unforeseen but imperative necessity. But that was precisely Purcell's case; and the instant the mere comparison was made, other points of agreement began to appear and multiply in the most startling manner.

The physical resemblance between Purcell and the hypothetical Bromeswell was striking but not conclusive. Both were big, heavy men; but such men are not uncommon, and the resemblance in the matter of the moustache had to be verified – or disproved. But the other points of agreement were very impressive – impressive alike by their completeness and by their number. Both men were connected with the making of paper and of the same kind – handmade paper. The banknote moulds had been stolen or lost at Maidstone about six years ago. But at that very time Purcell was at

Maidstone, and was then engaged in the paper industry. Bromeswell appeared to have a sailor's knowledge and skill in respect of cordage. But Purcell was a yachtsman and had such knowledge and skill. Then the dates of the two disappearances coincided very strikingly. Bromeswell disappeared from London about the tenth of June; Purcell disappeared from Penzance on the twenty-third of June. Even in trivial circumstances there was curious agreement. For instance, it was a noticeable coincidence that Bromeswell's pipe should have been bought at a shop within a minute's walk of Purcell's office.

But there was another coincidence that Thorndyke had noted even while he was examining the premises at Clifford's Inn. Those premises were concerned exclusively with the making of the paper blanks on which the notes would later be printed. Of the engraving and printing activities there was no trace. Bromeswell was a papermaker pure and simple; but somewhere in the background there must have been a confederate, who was an engraver and a printer, to whom Bromeswell supplied the paper blanks and who engraved the plates and printed the notes. But Purcell had one intimate friend; and that friend was a skilful engraver, who was able to print from engraved plates. Moreover, the rather vague description given by the Belgian police of the man who uttered the forged notes, while it obviously could not apply to Purcell, agreed very completely with Purcell's intimate friend.

And there was yet another agreement, perhaps more striking than any. If it were assumed that Bromeswell and Purcell were one and the same person, the whole of the mystery connected with Mr Penfield's letter was resolved. Everything became consistent and intelligible – up to a certain point. If the mysterious "enclosures" were a batch of paper blanks with the Bank of England watermark on them, it was easy to understand Mr Penfield's reticence; for he had made himself an accessory to a felony, to say nothing of the offence that he was committing by having these things in his possession. It would also account completely for Purcell's sudden flight and his silence as to his whereabouts; for he would, naturally, assume that no lawyer would be such an imbecile as to accept the position of an accessory to a crime that he had no connection with. He would take it for granted that Penfield would forthwith hand the letter and the enclosures to the police.

But there were one or two difficulties. In the first place, the theory implied an incredible lack of caution on the part of Penfield, who was a lawyer of experience, and would fully appreciate the risk he was running. Then it assumed an equally amazing lack of care and caution in the case of Purcell – a carelessness quite at variance with the scrupulous caution and well-maintained secrecy of the establishment at Clifford's Inn. But the most serious discrepancy was the presence of the paper blanks in a letter. The letter into which they ought to have been put would be addressed to the confederate, and that confederate was assumed to be Varney. But why should they have been sent in a letter to Varney? On the very day on which the letter was posted, Varney and Purcell had been alone together for some hours on the yacht. The blanks could have been handed to Varney then, and naturally would have been. The discrepancy seemed to render the hypothesis untenable, or at any rate to rule out Varney as the possible confederate.

But it was impossible to dismiss the hypothesis as untenable. The agreement with the observed facts were too numerous; and as soon as the inquiry was transferred to a new field, a fresh set of agreements came into view. Very methodically Thorndyke considered the theory of the identity of Purcell with Bromeswell in connection with his interviews with Mr Penfield and Mr Levy.

Taking the latter first, what had it disclosed? It had shown that Purcell was a common moneylender; not an incriminating fact, for the business of a moneylender is not in itself unlawful. But it is a vocation to which little credit attaches, and its practice is frequently associated with very unethical conduct. It is rather on the outside edge of lawful industry.

But what of Levy? Apparently he was not a mere employee. He appeared to be able to get on quite well without Purcell, and seemed to have the status of a partner. Was it possible that he was a partner in the other concern, too? It was not impossible. A moneylender has excellent opportunities for getting rid of good flash notes. His customers usually want notes in preference to cheques, and he could even get batches of notes from the Bank and number his forgeries to correspond, thus protecting himself in case of discovery. But even if Levy were a confederate he would not exclude Varney, for there was no reason to suppose that he was an engraver, whereas Varney was both an engraver and an old and constant associate of Purcell's. In short, Levy was not very obviously in the picture at all, and, for the time being, Thorndyke dismissed him and passed on to the other case. Taking now the interview with Penfield, there were the facts elicited by the examination of the envelope. That envelope had contained a rather bulky mass, apparently of folded paper, about five inches long or a little more, and somewhat less than three inches wide. Thorndyke rose, and, taking from the bookshelves a manuscript book labelled "Dimensions," found in the index the entry "Banknotes" and turned to the page indicated. Here the dimensions of a five-pound note were given as eight inches and three-eighths long by five inches and five thirty-seconds wide. Folded lengthwise into three, it would thus be five inches and five thirty-seconds, or say five and an eighth long by two and three-quarters wide, if folded quite accurately, or a fraction more if folded less exactly. The enclosure in Penfield's envelope was therefore exactly the size of a small batch of notes folded into three. It did not follow that the enclosures actually were banknotes. They might have been papers of some other kind but of similar size. But the observed facts were in complete agreement with the supposition that they were banknotes, and taken in conjunction with Penfield's extraordinary secrecy and the wording of his letter to Margaret Purcell, they strongly supported that supposition.

Then there was the suggestion that the envelope had been steamed open and reclosed. It was only a suggestion, not a certainty. The appearance might be misleading. But to Thorndyke's expert eye the suggestion had been very strong. The gum had smeared upwards on the inside, which seemed impossible if the envelope had been closed once for all; and the paper showed traces of cockling, as if it had been damped. Mr Penfield had rejected the suggestion, partly for the excellent reasons that he had given, but also, perhaps, because Purcell's flight implied that he had discovered the mistake, and that therefore the mistake was presumably his own.

But there was one important point that Penfield seemed to have overlooked. The letter that he expected to receive would (presumably) have contained no enclosures. The letter that he did receive contained a bulky enclosure which bulged the envelope. The two letters must therefore have been very different in appearance. Now, ordinarily, when two letters are put each into the envelope of the other, when once the envelopes are closed the mistake is covered up. There is nothing in their exterior to suggest that any mistake has occurred. But in the present case the error was blatantly advertised by the appearance of the closed letters. Penfield's envelope, which should have been flat, bulged with its contents. The other envelope – if there was one, as there almost certainly must have been – which should have bulged, was conspicuously flat. Of course, Penfield may have been wrong in assuming that no enclosures were to be sent to him. Both letters may have held enclosures. But taking the evidence as it was presented, it was to the effect that there were enclosures in only one of the letters. And if that were the case, the mistake appeared incredible. It became impossible to understand how Purcell could have handled the two letters and finally put them into the post without seeing that the enclosures were in the wrong envelope.

What was the significance of the point? Well, it raised the question whether Purcell could possibly have posted this letter himself; and this question involved the further question whether the envelope had been opened and reclosed. For if it had, the transposition of the contents must have taken place after the letters left Purcell's hands. Against this was the fact of Purcell's flight, which made it practically certain that he had become aware of the transposition. But it was not conclusive, and having noted the objection, Thorndyke proceeded to follow out the alternative theory. Accepting, for the moment, the hypothesis that the letter had been opened and the transposition made intentionally, certain other questions arose. First, who had the opportunity? Second, what could have been the purpose of the act? And, third, who could have had such a purpose? Thorndyke considered these questions in the same methodical fashion, taking them one by one and in the order stated.

Who had the opportunity? That depended, among other things, on the time at which the letter was posted. Penfield had stated that the letter had been posted at 8.30 p.m. If that were true, it put Varney out of the problem, for he had left Penzance some hours before that time. But it was not true. The time shown by the post-mark was not the time at which the letter was posted, but that at which it was sorted at the post office. It might have been posted at a pillar-box some hours previously. It was therefore not impossible that it might have been posted by Varney. And if it was physically possible, it at once became the most probable assumption, since there was no reasonable alternative. It was inconceivable that Purcell should have handed the letters to a stranger to post; and if he had, it was inconceivable that that stranger should have opened the letters and transposed their contents. There was, indeed, the possibility that Purcell had met a confederate at Penzance and had handed him the letters – one of which would be addressed to himself – to post, and that this confederate might have made the transposition. But this was pure speculation, without a particle of evidence to support it; whereas Varney, as an intimate friend, even if not a confederate, might conceivably have had the letters handed to him to post, though this was profoundly improbable, seeing that Purcell was going ashore and Varney was in charge of the yacht. In effect, there was no positive evidence that anybody had had the opportunity to make the transposition; but if it had not been done by Purcell, himself, then Varney appeared to be the only possible agent.

From this vague and unsatisfactory conclusion Thorndyke proceeded to the second question: Assuming the transposition to have been made intentionally, what could have been the purpose of the act? To this question, so far as the immediate purpose was concerned, the answer was obvious enough, since only one was possible. The blanks must have been put into Mr Penfield's envelope for the express purpose of notifying the solicitor that Purcell was a banknote forger – in short, for the purpose of exposing Purcell. This led at once to the third question: Who could have had such a purpose? But to this also the answer was obvious. The only person who could have had such a purpose would be a confederate, for no one else would have been in possession of the knowledge that would make such a purpose possible. The transposition could have been made only by someone who knew what the contents of the envelope were.

But why should any confederate have done this? The exposure of Purcell involved at least a risk of the exposure of his confederate; and it could be assumed that if Purcell suspected that he had been betrayed, he would certainly denounce his betrayer. The object, therefore, could not have been to secure the arrest of Purcell – a conclusion that was confirmed by the fact that Purcell had become aware of the transposition, and, if he had not done it himself, must apparently have been informed in time to allow of his escaping.

But what other object could there be? Was it possible that the confederate wished to get rid of Purcell, and made this exposure with the express purpose of compelling him to disappear? That raised the question: When did Purcell become aware that the transposition had been made? And the answer was somewhat perplexing. He could not have become aware of it immediately, or he would have telegraphed to Penfield and stopped the letter; and yet he seemed to have absconded at once, before the letter could have been delivered to Penfield. He was due at Oulton the following day, and he never arrived there. He was stated to have gone from Penzance to Falmouth. That might or might not be true, but the voyage to Ipswich was evidently a myth. The answer that he had received from the owners of the *Hedwig*, enclosing a report from the captain of the ship, showed that the only passengers who embarked at Falmouth were three distressed Swedish sailors, who travelled with the ship to Malmo, and that no one went ashore at Ipswich. It followed that Varney had either been misinformed or had invented the incidents; but when it was considered that he must, if he was telling the truth, have been misinformed in the same manner on both separate occasions, it seemed more probable that the story of the voyage was a fabrication. In that case the journey to Falmouth, of which no one but Varney had heard, was probably a fabrication, too. This left Penzance as the apparent starting-point of the flight. Purcell had certainly landed at Penzance and had forthwith disappeared from view. What became of him thereafter it was impossible to guess. He seemed to have vanished into thin air.

Arrived at this point, Thorndyke's quietly reflective attitude suddenly gave place to one of intense attention. For a new and somewhat startling question had presented itself. With an expression of deep concentration he set himself to consider it.

Hitherto he had accepted Purcell's landing at Penzance as an undeniable fact, from which a secure departure could be taken. But was it an undeniable fact? The only witness of that landing was Varney, and Varney had shown himself a very unreliable witness. Apparently he had lied about the Ipswich voyage, probably, too, about the visit to Falmouth. What if the landing at Penzance were a fabrication, too? It seemed a wild suggestion, but it was a possibility; and Thorndyke proceeded carefully to develop the consequences that would follow if it were true.

Suppose that Purcell had never landed at Penzance at all. Then several circumstances hitherto incomprehensible became understandable. The fables of Purcell's appearance at Falmouth and Ipswich, which had seemed to be motiveless falsehoods, now showed a clear purpose; which was to create a certainty that Purcell had landed from the yacht as stated and to shift the search for the missing man from Penzance to Ipswich. Again, if Purcell had never landed at Penzance, the letter could not have been posted by him, and it became practically certain that it must have been posted there by Varney and the transposition made by him. And this made the transposition understandable by developing a very evident purpose. When Penfield opened the letter, and when, later, he heard of Purcell's disappearance, he would at once assume that Purcell had absconded to avoid being arrested. The purpose of the transposition, then, was to furnish a reasonable explanation of a disappearance that had already occurred.

But what had become of Purcell? If he had not landed at Penzance he certainly had not landed anywhere else, for there had not been time for the yacht to touch at any other port. Nor could it be supposed that he had trans-shipped on to another vessel during the voyage. There was no reason why he should. The letter had not been posted, and until it had been posted there was no reason for flight. The only reasonable inference from the facts, including Varney's false statements, was that something had happened during the voyage from Sennen; that Purcell had disappeared, presumably overboard; and that Varney had reasons for concealing the circumstances of his disappearance. In short, that Purcell was dead, and that Varney was responsible for his death.

It was an appalling theory. Thorndyke hardly dared even to propound it to himself. But there was no denying that it fitted the facts with the most surprising completeness. Once assume it to be true, and all the perplexing features of the case became consistent and understandable. Not only did it explain Varney's otherwise inexplicable anxiety to prove that Purcell had been seen alive at a date subsequent to that of the alleged landing at Penzance; it accounted for the facts that Purcell had taken no measures to provide himself with a stock of cash before disappearing, and that he had made no communication of any sort to his wife since his departure, though he could have done so with perfect safety. It was in perfect agreement with all the known facts and in disagreement with none. It was a complete solution of the mystery; and there was no other.

When Thorndyke reached this conclusion, he roused himself from his reverie, and, filling his pipe, took an impartial survey of the scheme of circumstantial evidence that he had been engaged in constructing. It was all very complete and consistent. There were, so far, no discrepancies or contradictions. All the evidence pointed in the one direction. The assumed actions of Varney were in complete agreement with the circumstances that were known and the others that were inferred, as well as with the assumed motives. But it was largely hypothetical, and might turn out to be entirely illusory. If only one of the assumed facts should prove to be untrue, the whole structure of inference would come tumbling down. He took out of his pocket-book the folded paper containing the single moustache hair that the Superintendent had found in the Clifford's Inn rooms. Laying it on a sheet of white paper, he once more examined it, first through his lens, then under the microscope, noting the length, thickness, and colour, and mentally visualizing the kind of moustache from which it had come. Here was an indispensable link in the chain of evidence. If Purcell had had such a moustache, that would not prove that he and Bromeswell were one and the same person, but it would be consistent with their identity. But if Purcell had no such moustache, then it was probable – indeed, nearly certain – that he and Bromeswell were different persons. And if they were, the whole hypothetical scheme that he had been working out collapsed. Both Purcell and Varney ceased to have any connection with the forged notes, the mysterious "enclosures" could not be of the nature that he had assumed, and all the deductions from those assumed facts ceased to be valid. It was necessary without delay to test this essential link, to ascertain whether this derelict hair could have been derived from Daniel Purcell.

Enclosed with it was the slip of paper with the notes of the trains, which he had, for the moment, forgotten. He now examined it minutely, and was once more struck by the intense blackness of the ink; and he recalled that a similar intensity of blackness had been noticeable in the address on Mr Penfield's envelope. It had appeared almost like the black of a carbon ink, but he had decided that it was not. So it was with the present specimen, but now he had the means of deciding definitely. Fetching the microscope, he laid the paper on the stage and examined it, first by reflected, then by transmitted, light. The examination made it clear that this was an iron-tannin ink of unusual concentration, with a "provisional" blue pigment, probably methyl blue. There was only one letter, *P*, and this he tried to compare with the *P* on Mr Penfield's envelope, so far as he could remember it; but he could not get beyond a belief that there was a resemblance – a belief that would have to be tested by a specimen of Purcell's handwriting.

Having finished with the paper he returned to the hair. He decided to write to Margaret, asking for a description of her missing husband, and had just reached out to the stationery case, when an elaborate and formal tattoo on the small brass knocker of the inner door arrested him. Rising, he crossed the room and threw the door open, thereby disclosing the dorsal aspect of a small elderly gentleman. As the door opened the visitor turned about, and Thorndyke immediately, not without surprise, recognized him. It was Mr Penfield.

Chapter Nine

In Which Mr Penfield
Receives a Shock

Mr Penfield greeted Thorndyke with a little stiff bow, and bestowed upon the extended hand a formal and somewhat rheumatic shake.

"I must apologize," he said, as his host ushered him into the room, "for disturbing you by this visit, but I had a little matter to communicate to you, and thought it better to make that communication personally rather than by correspondence."

"You are not disturbing me at all," Thorndyke replied. "On the contrary, I expect that your visit will save me the necessity of writing a letter."

"To me?" asked Penfield.

"No; to Mrs Purcell. I was on the point of writing to her to ask for a description of her husband. As I have never met him I thought it as well that I should get from her such details of his appearance as might be necessary for purposes of identification."

"Quite so," said Mr Penfield. "Very desirable indeed. Well, I think I can tell you all you want to know, unless you want very minute details. And it happens that your inquiry comes rather opportunely in respect of the matter that I have to communicate. Shall we dispose of your question first?"

"If you please," replied Thorndyke. He took from a drawer a pad of ruled paper, and, uncapping his fountain pen, looked at Mr

Penfield, whom he had inducted into an easy chair. "May I offer you a cigar, Mr Penfield?" he asked.

"I thank you," was the reply, "but I am not a smoker. "Perhaps – " Here he held out his snuff-box tentatively. "No? Well, it is an obsolete vice, but I am a survivor from an obsolete age." He refreshed himself with a substantial pinch, and continued: "With regard to Purcell: his person is easy to describe and should be easy to identify. He is a big lump of a man, about six feet or a fraction over. Massive, heavy, but not fat; just elephantine. Rather slow in his movements, but strong, active, and not at all clumsy. As to his face, I would call it beefy – a full red face with thick, bright-red, crinkly ears and full lips. Eyes, pale blue; hair, yellowish or light brown, cropped short. No beard or whiskers, but a little, bristly, pale-reddish moustache, cut short like a sandy toothbrush. Expression, surly; manner, short, brusque, taciturn, and rather morose. Big, thick, purple hands that look, in spite of their size, capable, neat, and useful hands. In fact, the hands are an epitome of Purcell: a combination of massive strength and weight with remarkable bodily efficiency. How will that do for you?"

"Admirably," replied Thorndyke, inwardly somewhat surprised at the old solicitor's powers of observation. "It is a very distinctive picture, and quite enough for what we may call prima facie identification. I take it that you know him pretty well?"

"I have seen a good deal of him since his marriage, when his wife introduced him to me, and I have managed his legal business for some years. But I know very little of his private affairs. Very few people do, I imagine. I never met a less communicative man. And now, if we have done with his appearance, let us come to the question of his present whereabouts. Have you any information on the subject?"

"There is a vague report that he was seen some months ago at Ipswich. It is quite unconfirmed, and I attach no importance to it."

"It is probably correct, though," said Penfield. "I have just had a letter from him, and the postmark shows that it came from that very locality."

"There is no address on the letter, then?"

"No; and I am invited to reply by advertisement. The occasion of the letter was this: a client of mine, a Mrs Catford, who is a relative of Mrs Purcell's, had recently died, leaving a will of which I am the executor and residuary legatee. By the terms of that will Mrs Purcell and her husband each benefits to the extent of a thousand pounds. Now, as Mrs Catford's death occurred subsequently to Purcell's disappearance, it became necessary to establish his survival of the testatrix or the contrary – in order that the will might be administered. As his whereabouts were unknown, the only method that I could think of was to put an advertisement in the 'Personal' column of *The Times*, on the bare chance that he might see it, asking him to communicate with me. By a lucky chance he did see it and did communicate with me. But he gave no address, and any further communication from me will have to be by advertisement, as he suggests. That, however, is of no importance to me. His letter tells me all I want to know; that he is alive at a date subsequent to the death of the testatrix, and that the bequest in his favour can consequently take effect. I am not concerned with his exact whereabouts. That matter is in your province."

As he concluded, punctuating his conclusion with a pinch of snuff, the old lawyer looked at Thorndyke with a sly and slightly ironical smile.

Thorndyke reflected rapidly on Mr Penfield's statement. The appearance of this letter was very remarkable, and the more so coming as it did on top of the confirmatory evidence respecting the moustache hair. It was now highly probable – almost certain – that Bromeswell and Purcell were one and the same person. But if that were so, all the probabilities went to show that Purcell must be dead. And yet here was a letter from him, not to a stranger, but to one who knew his handwriting well. It was very remarkable.

Again, the report of Purcell's voyage from Falmouth to Ipswich was certainly untrue. But if it was untrue there was no reason for supposing that Purcell had ever been at Ipswich at all. Yet here was a letter sent by Purcell from that very locality. That was very remarkable, too. Clearly, the matter called for further investigation, and that involved, in the first place, an examination of this letter that had come so mysteriously to confirm a report that was certainly untrue. He returned Mr Penfield's smile, and then asked:

"You accept this letter, then, as evidence of survival?"

Mr Penfield looked astonished. "But, my dear sir, what else could I do? I may be insufficiently critical, and I have not your great special knowledge of this subject, but to my untrained intelligence it would appear that the circumstance of a man's having written a letter affords good presumptive evidence that he was alive at the date when it was written. That is my own view, and I propose to administer the will in accordance with it. Do I understand that you dissent from it?"

Thorndyke smiled blandly. He was beginning rather to like Mr Penfield.

"As you state the problem," said he, "you are probably right. At any rate, the administration of the will is your concern and not mine. As you were good enough to remark, my concern is with the person and the whereabouts of Mr Purcell and not with his affairs. Were you proposing to allow me to inspect the envelope of this letter?"

"It was for that very purpose that I came," replied Penfield, with a smile and a twinkle of mischief in his eyes; "but I will not restrict you to the envelope this time. You shall inspect the letter as well, if a mere letter will not be superfluous when the envelope has given up its secrets."

He produced a wallet from his pocket and, opening it, took out a letter, which he gravely handed to Thorndyke. The latter took it from him, and as he glanced at the jet-black writing of the address said:

"I take it that you are satisfied that the handwriting is Purcell's?"

"Certainly," was the reply. "But whose else should it be? The question does not seem to arise. However, I may assure you that it is undoubtedly Purcell's writing and also Purcell's ink, though that is less conclusive. Still, it is a peculiar ink. I have never seen any quite like it. My impression is that he prepares it himself."

As Penfield was speaking, Thorndyke examined the envelope narrowly. Presently he rose, and, taking a reading-glass from the mantelshelf, went over to the window, where, with the aid of the glass, he scrutinized the envelope inch by inch on both sides. Then, laying down the reading-glass, he took from his pocket a powerful doublet lens, through which he examined certain parts of the envelope, particularly the stamp and the London post-mark. Finally, he took out the letter, opened the envelope, and carefully examined its interior, and then inspected the letter itself before unfolding it, holding it so that the light fell on it obliquely and scrutinizing each of the four corners in succession. At length he opened the letter, read it through, again examined the corners, and compared some portions of the writing with that on the envelope.

These proceedings were closely observed by Mr Penfield, who watched them with an indulgent smile. He was better able than on the last occasion to appreciate the humour of Thorndyke's methods. There was nothing about this letter that he had need to conceal. He could afford to let the expert find out what he could this time; and Mr Penfield, from a large and unfavourable experience of expert witnesses, suspected that the discovery would probably take the form of a mare's nest.

"Well," he said, as Thorndyke returned to his chair with the letter in his hand, "has the oracle spoken? Have we made any startling discoveries?"

"I wouldn't use the word 'discoveries,'" replied Thorndyke, "which seems to imply facts definitely ascertained, but there are certain appearances which suggest a rather startling inference."

"Indeed!" said Mr Penfield, taking snuff with great enjoyment. "I somehow expected that they would when I decided to show you the letter. What is the inference that is suggested?"

"The inference is," replied Thorndyke, "that this letter has never been through the post."

Mr Penfield paused with his hand uplifted, holding a minute pinch of snuff, and regarded Thorndyke in silent astonishment.

"That," he said, at length, "is certainly a startling inference, and it would be still more startling if there were any possibility that it could be true. Unfortunately, the letter bears a post-mark showing that it was posted at Woodbridge, and another showing that it was sorted at the London office. But no doubt you have observed and allowed for those facts."

"The appearances," said Thorndyke, "suggest that when the post-marks were made the envelope was empty and probably unaddressed."

"But, my dear sir," protested Penfield, "that is a manifest impossibility. You must see that for yourself. How could such a thing possibly have happened?"

"That is a separate question," replied Thorndyke. "I am now dealing only with the appearances. Let me point them out to you. First, you will notice that the words 'personal and confidential' have been written at the top of the envelope. Apparently the word 'personal' was first written alone and the words 'and confidential' added as an afterthought. That is suggested by the change in the writing and the increasingly condensed form of the letters towards the end, due to the want of space. But in spite of the squeezing up of the letters the tail of the final *l* has been forced on to the stamp, and actually touches the circle of the post-mark; and if you examine it through this lens you can see plainly that the written line is on top of the postmark. Therefore the post-mark was already there when that word was written."

He handed the envelope and the lens to Mr Penfield, who, after some ineffectual struggles, rejected the lens and had recourse to his spectacles.

"It has somewhat the appearance that you suggest," he said at length; "but I have not your expert eye, and therefore not your confidence. I should suppose it to be impossible to say with certainty whether one written mark was on top of or underneath another."

"Very well," said Thorndyke; "then we will proceed to the next point. You will notice that both of the post-marks are deeply indented; unusually so. As a matter of fact, post-marks are usually not visibly indented at all, and it is a noticeable coincidence that this envelope should bear two different post-marks, each unusually indented."

"Still," said Penfield, "that might easily have happened. The laws of chance are not applicable to individual cases."

"Quite so," Thorndyke agreed. "But now observe another point. These post-marks are so deeply indented that, in both cases, the impression is clearly visible on the opposite side of the envelope, especially inside. That is rather remarkable, seeing that, if the letter was inside, the impression must have penetrated four thicknesses of paper."

"Still," said Penfield, "it is not impossible."

"Perhaps not," Thorndyke admitted. "But what does seem impossible is that it should have done so without leaving any trace on the letter itself. But that is what has happened. If you will examine the letter you will see that there is not a vestige of an indentation on any part of it. From which you must agree with me that the only reasonable inference is that when the indentations were made the letter was not in the envelope."

Mr Penfield took the letter and the envelope and compared them carefully. There was no denying the obvious facts. There was the envelope with the deeply indented post-marks showing plainly on the reverse sides, and there was the letter with never a sign of any mark at all. It was certainly very odd. Mr Penfield was a good deal puzzled and slightly annoyed. To his orthodox legal mind this prying into concrete facts and physical properties was rather distasteful. He was accustomed to sworn testimony, which might be true or might be untrue (but that was the witnesses' lookout), but which could be accepted as admitted evidence. He could not deny that the facts were apparently as Thorndyke had stated. But that unwilling admission produced no conviction. He was a lawyer, not a scientific observer.

"Yes," he agreed reluctantly, "the appearances are as you say. But they must be in some way illusory. Perhaps some difference in the properties of the paper may be the explanation. At any rate, I cannot accept your inference, for the simple reason that it predicates an impossibility. It assumes that this man, or some other, posted a blank, empty envelope, got it back, put a letter in it, addressed it, and then delivered it by hand, having travelled up from Woodbridge to do so. That would be an impossibility, unless the person were a post office official; and then, what on earth could be the object of such an insane proceeding? Have you asked yourself that question?"

As a matter of fact, Thorndyke had, and he had deduced a completely sufficient answer. But he did not feel called upon to explain this. It was not his concern to convince Mr Penfield. That gentleman's beliefs were a matter of perfect indifference to him. He had considered it fair to draw Mr Penfield's attention to the observed facts and even to point out the inferences that they suggested. But if Mr Penfield chose to shut his eyes to the facts, or to reject the obvious inferences, that was his affair.

"At the moment," he replied, "I am concerned with the appearances and the immediate inferences from them. When I am sure of my facts I shall go on to consider their bearing – those questions of motive, for instance, to which you have referred. That would be premature until I have verified the facts by a more searching examination. Would it be convenient for you to leave this letter with me for a few hours, that I might examine it more completely?"

Mr Penfield would have liked to refuse. But there was no pretext for such refusal. He therefore made a virtue of necessity, and replied graciously:

"Certainly, certainly. By all means. I will just take a copy, and then you can do as you please with the original, short of destroying it. But don't, pray don't let it lead you astray."

"In what respect?"

"Well," said Mr Penfield, taking a deprecating pinch of snuff, "it has sometimes seemed to me that the specialist has a tendency – just a tendency, mark you – to mislead himself. He looks for a certain thing, which might be there, and – well, he finds it. I cannot but remark your own unexpected successes in your search for the – ha – the unusual, shall we say. On two occasions I have shown you an envelope. On both occasions you have made most surprising discoveries, involving the strangest aberrations of conduct on the part of Purcell and others. Today you have found unheard-of anomalies in the post-marks, from which you infer that Purcell or another has exerted immense ingenuity and overcome insuperable obstacles in order to behave like a fool. On the previous occasion you discovered that Purcell had been at the trouble of ungumming the envelope, which he had undoubtedly addressed with his own hand, for the express purpose of taking out the right contents, which were already in it, and putting in the wrong ones. Perhaps you made some other discoveries which you did not mention," Mr Penfield added, after a slight pause; and as Thorndyke only bowed slightly, which was not very explicit, he further added: "Would it be indiscreet or impertinent to inquire whether you did, in fact, make any further discoveries? Whether, for instance, you arrived at any opinion as to the nature of the enclosures, which were, I think, the objects of your investigations?"

Thorndyke hesitated. For a moment he was disposed to take the old solicitor into his confidence. But experience had taught him, as it teaches most of us, that when the making or withholding of confidences are alternatives, he chooses the better part who keeps his own counsel. Nevertheless, he gave Penfield a cautionary hint.

"Those enclosures," said he, "have ceased to interest me. Any opinions that I formed as to their nature had better be left unstated. I seek no verification of them. Opinions held but not disclosed commit the holder to nothing, whereas actual knowledge has its responsibilities. I do not know what those enclosures were and I do not want to know."

For some moments after Thorndyke finished speaking there was a slightly uncomfortable silence. Mr Penfield's dry facetiousness evaporated rather suddenly, and he found himself reading a somewhat alarming significance into Thorndyke's ambiguous and even cryptic reply. "He did not know and he did not want to know." Now, Mr Penfield did know, and would have given a good deal to be without that knowledge, for to possess the knowledge was to be an accessory. Was that what Thorndyke meant? Mr Penfield had a dark suspicion that it was.

"Probably you are right," he said presently. "You know what opinions you formed and I do not. But there is one point that I should like to have made clear. We are both acting in Mrs Purcell's interest, but her husband is also my client. Is there any conflict in our purposes with regard to him?"

"I think not," replied Thorndyke. "At any rate, I will say this much: that I should under no circumstances take any action that might be prejudicial to him without your concurrence, or at least without placing you in possession of all the facts. But I feel confident that no such necessity will arise. We are dealing with separate aspects of the case, but it would be foolish for us to get at cross-purposes."

"Exactly," said Mr Penfield. "That is my own feeling. And with regard to this letter: if it should yield any further suggestions and you should consider them as being of any interest to me, perhaps you would be so good as to inform me of them."

"I will, certainly," Thorndyke replied; "and, by the way, what are you going to do? Shall you issue any further advertisement?"

"I had not intended to," said Mr Penfield; "but perhaps it would be well to try to elicit a further reply. I might ask Purcell to send a receipt for the legacy, which I shall pay into his bank. He knows the amount, so that I need not state it."

"I think that would be advisable," said Thorndyke, "but my impression is that there will be no reply."

"Well, we shall see," said Penfield, rising and drawing on his gloves. "If an answer comes, you shall see it; and if there is no answer, I will advise you to that effect. You will agree with me that we keep our own counsel about the matters that we have discussed," and as Thorndyke assented, he added: "of course the actual receipt of the letter is no secret."

With this and a stiff handshake Mr Penfield took his departure, cogitating profoundly as he wended his way eastward, wondering how much Thorndyke really knew about those unfortunate enclosures and how he came by his knowledge.

Meanwhile Thorndyke, as soon as he was alone, resumed his examination of the letter, calling in now the aid of more exact methods. Placing on the table a microscope specially constructed for examining documents, he laid the envelope on the stage and inspected the post-mark at the point where the tail of the *l* touched it. The higher magnification at once resolved any possible uncertainty. The written line was on top of the postmark beyond all doubt. But it also brought another anomaly into view. It was now evident that the indentation of the post-mark did not coincide exactly with the whole width of the printed line. The indented line was somewhat narrower. It consisted of a furrow, deepest in the middle, which followed the printed line but did not completely occupy it, and in one or two places strayed slightly outside it. On turning the envelope over and testing the other post-mark, the same peculiarity was observable. The indentation was a thing separate from the printed mark, and had been produced by a separate operation, apparently with a bluntly pointed tool, which would account for its excessive depth.

It was an important discovery in two respects. First, it confirmed the other evidence that the letter had never been posted; and, secondly, it threw some light on the means by which the post-mark had been produced. What was the object of the indentation? Evidently to imitate the impression of metal types and disguise the method that had actually been used.

What was that method? It was not photography, for the marks were in printers' ink. It was not copperplate, for the engraved plate throws up a line in relief, whereas these lines were flat, like the lines of a lithograph. In fact, lithography appeared to be the only alternative; and with this view the appearances agreed completely, particularly the thick black ink, quite different from the rather fluid ink used by the post office.

From the post-marks Thorndyke now transferred his attention to the writing. He had been struck by the exact resemblance of the name "Penfield" on the envelope to the same name in the letter. Each was a perfect facsimile of the other. Placing them together, he could not see a single point of difference or variation between them. With a delicate caliper gauge he measured the two words, taking the total length, the height of each letter, and the distance between various points. In all cases the measurements were practically identical. Now such perfect repetition as this does not happen in natural writing. It is virtually diagnostic of forgery – of a forgery by means of a careful tracing from an original. And Thorndyke had no doubt that this was such a forgery.

Confirmation was soon forthcoming. An exploration with the microscope of the surfaces of the envelope and the letter showed in both a number of minute spindle-shaped fragments of rubber. Something had been rubbed out. Then, on examining the words by transmitted light powerful enough to turn the jet-black writing into a deep purple, there could be seen through the ink a broken grey line, the remains of a pencil line, which the ink had partly protected from the rubber. Similar remains of a pencil tracing were to be seen in other parts of the letter, especially in the signature. In short, there was no possible doubt that the whole production, letter and post-marks alike, was a forgery.

The next question was, Who was the forger? But the answer to that seemed to be contained in the further question, What was the purpose of the forgery? For the evident purpose of this letter was to furnish evidence that Purcell was still alive, and as such it had been accepted by Mr Penfield. That distinctly pointed to Varney, who had already made two false, or at least incorrect, statements, apparently with the same object. The skill with which the forgery had been executed also pointed to him, for an engraver must needs be a skilful copyist. There was only one doubtful point. Whoever had prepared this letter was a lithographer; not a mere draughtsman, but a printer as well. Now was Varney a lithographer? It was extremely probable. Many etchers and mezzo-tinters work also on the stone. But until it had been ascertained that he was, the authorship of the letter must be left in suspense. But assuming the letter to be Varney's work, it was evident that Mr Penfield's visit had added materially to the body of circumstantial evidence. It had established that Purcell had worn a moustache apparently identical in character with that of the elusive Bromeswell, which, taken in conjunction with all the other known facts, made it nearly a certainty that Bromeswell and Purcell were one and the same person. But that assumption had been seen to lead to the inference that Purcell was dead, and that Varney was responsible for, or implicated in, the circumstances of his death.

Then there was this letter. It was a forged letter, and its purpose was to prove that Purcell was alive. But the fact that it was necessary to forge a letter to prove that he was alive was in itself presumptive evidence that he was not alive. Subject to proof that Varney was a lithographer and therefore capable of producing this forgery, the evidence that Mr Penfield had brought furnished striking confirmation of the hypothesis that Thorndyke had formed as to what had become of Daniel Purcell.

CHAPTER TEN

In Which Thorndyke Sees
a New Light

"We shall only be three at dinner, after all," said Margaret. "Mr Rodney will be detained somewhere, but he is coming in for a chat later in the evening."

Varney received the news without emotion. He could do without Rodney. He would not have been desolated if the other guest had been a defaulter, too. At any rate, he hoped that he would not be needlessly punctual, and thus shorten unduly the *tête-à-tête* with Margaret which he, Varney, had secured by exercising the privilege of an old friend to arrive considerably before his time.

"You have only met Dr Thorndyke once before, I think?" said Margaret.

"Yes; at Sennen, you know, the day that queer letter came from Mr Penfield, and I didn't see much of him then. I remember that I was a little mystified about him; couldn't quite make out whether he was a lawyer, a doctor, or a man of science."

"As a matter of fact, he is all three. He is what is called a medical jurist – a sort of lawyer who deals with legal cases that involve medical questions. I understand that he is a great authority on medical evidence."

"What legal cases do involve medical questions?"

"I don't know much about it," replied Margaret, "but I believe they include questions of survivorship and cases of presumption of death."

"Presumption of death!" repeated Varney. "What on earth does that mean?"

"I am not very clear about it myself," she replied, "but from what I am told I gather that it is a sort of legal proceeding that takes place when a person disappears permanently and there is uncertainty as to whether he or she is dead or alive. An application is made to the court for permission to presume that the person is dead, and if the court gives the permission the person is then legally presumed to be dead, and his will can be administered and his affairs wound up. That is an instance of the kind of case that Dr Thorndyke undertakes. He must have had quite a lot of experience of persons who have disappeared, and for that reason Mr Rodney advised me to consult him about Dan."

"Do you mean with a view to presuming his death?" asked Varney, inwardly anathematizing Dan for thus making his inevitable appearance in the conversation, but keenly interested nevertheless.

"No," replied Margaret. "I consulted him quite soon after Dan went away. What I asked him to do was to find out, if possible, what had become of him, and if he could discover his whereabouts to get into touch with him."

"Well," said Varney, "he doesn't seem to have had much luck up to the present. He hasn't been able to trace Dan, has he?"

"No," she replied – "at least, I suppose not. But we know where the lost sheep is now. Had you heard about the letter?"

"The letter?"

"Yes. From Dan. He wrote to Mr Penfield a few days ago."

"Did he, though?" said Varney, with well-simulated surprise. "From somewhere abroad, I suppose?

"No. The post-mark was Woodbridge – there was no address," and here Margaret briefly explained the circumstances.

"It sounds rather as if he were afloat," said Varney. "That is an ideal coast for lurking about in a smallish yacht. There is endless cover in the rivers and the creeks off the Colne, the Roach, the Crouch, and the Blackwater. But it looks as if he had made more preparation for the flitting than we thought at the time. He hasn't written to you?"

Margaret shook her head. The affront was too gross for comment.

"It was beastly of him," said Varney. "He might have sent you just a line. However, Dr Thorndyke will have something to go on now. He will know whereabouts to look for him."

"As far as I am concerned," Margaret said coldly, "the affair is finished. This insult was the last straw. I have no further interest in him, and I hope I may never see him again. But," she added earnestly, after a brief pause, "I should like to be rid of him completely. I want my freedom."

As she spoke – with unusual emphasis and energy – she looked, for a moment, straight into Varney's eyes. Then suddenly she flushed scarlet and turned her head away.

Varney was literally overwhelmed. He felt the blood rush to his head and tingle in the tips of his fingers. After one swift glance he, too, turned away his head. He did not dare to look at her. Nor, for some seconds, did he dare to trust his voice. At last it had come! In the twinkling of an eye his dim hopes, more than half distrusted, had changed into realities. For there could be no doubt. That look into his eyes, that sudden blush, what could they be but an unpremeditated, unintended confession? She wanted her freedom. That unguarded glance told him why; and then her mantling cheeks, while they rebuked the glance, but served to interpret its significance.

With an effort he regained his normal manner. His natural delicacy told him that he must not be too discerning. He must take no cognizance of this confidence that was never intended. She must still think that her secret was locked up in her own breast, secure from every eye, even from his.

And yet what a pitiful game of cross-purposes they were playing! She wanted her freedom! And behold! she was free, and he knew it and could not tell her. What a tangle it was! And how was it ever going to be straightened out? In life, Purcell had stood between him and liberty; and now the ghost – nay, less than the ghost, the mere unsubstantial name – of Purcell stood between him and a lifelong happiness that Fortune was actually holding out to him.

It was clear that, sooner or later, the ghost of Purcell would have to be laid. But how? And here it began to dawn upon him that the, ingenious letter, on which he had been congratulating himself, had been a tactical mistake. He had not known about Dr Thorndyke, and he had never heard before of the possibility of presuming a person's death. He had been busying himself to produce convincing evidence that Purcell was alive, whereas it was possible that Thorndyke had been considering the chances of being able to presume his death. It was rather a pity, for Purcell had got to be disposed of before he could openly declare himself to Maggie; and this method of legal presumption of death appeared to be the very one that suited the conditions. He wished he had known about it before.

These reflections flashed through his mind in the silence that had followed Margaret's unguarded utterance. For the moment Varney had been too overcome to reply. And Margaret suddenly fell silent with an air of some confusion. Recovering himself, Varney now replied in a tone of conventional sympathy:

"Of course you do. The bargain is off on the one side, and it is not reasonable that it should hold on the other. You don't want to be shackled for ever to a man who has gone out of your life. But I don't quite see what is to be done."

"Neither do I," said Margaret. "Perhaps the lawyers will be able to make some suggestion – and I think I hear one of them arriving."

A moment or two later the door opened and the housemaid announced "Dr Thorndyke." Varney stood up, and as the guest was ushered in he looked with deep curiosity, not entirely unmingled with awe, at this tall, imposing man, who held in his mind so much recondite knowledge and doubtless so many strange secrets.

"I think you know Mr Varney," said Margaret, as she shook hands, "though you hadn't much opportunity to improve his acquaintance at Sennen."

"No," Thorndyke agreed. "Mr Penfield's bombshell rather distracted our attention from the social aspects of that gathering. However, we are free from his malign influence this evening."

"I am not sure that we are," said Varney. "Mrs Purcell tells me that he has just produced another mysterious letter."

"I shouldn't call it 'mysterious,'" said Thorndyke. "On the contrary, it resolves the mystery. We now know, approximately, where Mr Purcell is."

"Yes, it ought to be easy to get on his track now. That, I understand, is what you have been trying to do. Do you propose to locate him more exactly?"

"I see no reason for doing so," replied Thorndyke. "His letter answers Mr Penfield's purpose, which was to produce evidence that he is alive. But his letter does raise certain questions that will have to be considered. We shall hear what Mr Rodney has to say on the subject. He is coming tonight, isn't he?"

"He is not coming to dinner," said Margaret, "but he is going to drop in later. There goes the gong. Shall we go into the dining-room?"

Thorndyke held the door open, and they crossed the corridor to the pleasant little room beyond. As soon as they had taken their places at the table, Margaret led off the conversation with a rather definite change of subject.

"Have you brought any of your work to show us, Mr Varney?" she asked.

"Yes," he replied; "I have brought one or two etchings that I don't think you have seen and a couple of aquatints."

"Aquatints," said Margaret. "Isn't that a new departure?"

"No. It is only a revival. I used to do a good deal of aquatint work, but I have not done any for quite a long time until I attacked these two. I like a change of method now and again. But I always come back to etchings."

"Do you work much with the dry point?" asked Thorndyke.

"Not the pure dry point," was the reply. "Of course, I use it to do finishing work on my etchings, but that is a different thing. I have done very few dry points proper. I like the bitten line."

"I suppose," said Thorndyke, "an etcher rather looks down on lithography?"

"I don't think so," replied Varney. "I don't certainly. It is a fine process and an autograph process, like etching and mezzotint. The finished print is the artist's own work, every bit of it, as much as an oil painting."

"Doesn't the printer take some of the credit?" Thorndyke asked.

"I am assuming that the artist does his own printing. If he doesn't, I should not call him a lithographer. He is only a lithographic draughtsman. When I used to work at lithography I always did my own printing. It is more than half the fun. I have the little press still."

"Then perhaps you will revive that process, too, one day?"

"I don't think so," Varney replied. "The flat surface of a lithograph is rather unsatisfying after the rich raised lines of an etching. I shall never go back to lithography, except, perhaps, for some odd jobs;" and here a spirit of mischievous defiance impelled him to add: "I did a little lithograph only the other day, but I didn't keep it. It was a crude little thing."

Thorndyke noted the statement with a certain grim appreciation. In spite of himself, he could not but like Varney; and this playful, sporting attitude in respect of a capital crime appealed to him as a new experience. It established him and Varney as opposing players in a sort of grim and tragic game, and it confirmed him in certain opinions that he had formed as to the antecedents and motives of the crime. For as to the reality of the crime he now had no doubt. The statement that Varney had just made in all the insolence of his fancied security had set the keystone on the edifice that Thorndyke had built up. Circumstantial evidence has a cumulative quality. It advances by a sort of geometrical progression, in which each new fact multiplies the weight of all the others. The theory that Varney had made away with Purcell involved the assumption that Varney was a lithographer who was able to print. It was now established that Varney was a lithographer and that he owned a press. Thus the train of circumstantial evidence was complete.

It was a most singular situation. In the long pauses which tend to occur when good appetites coincide with a good dinner, the two men, confronting one another across the table, sat, each busy with his thoughts behind the closed shutters of his mind, each covertly observant of the other, and each the object of the other's meditations. To Varney had come once more that queer feeling of power that he had experienced at Sennen when Mr Penfield's letter had arrived; the sense of an almost godlike superiority and omniscience. Here were these simple mortals, full of wonder, perplexity, and speculation as to the vanished Purcell. And they were all wrong. But he knew everything. And he was the motive power behind all their ineffectual movements. It was he who, by the pressure of a finger, had set this puppet-show in motion, and he had but to tweak a string in his quiet studio and they were all set dancing again. Every one of them was obedient to his touch: Maggie, Penfield, Rodney, even this strong-faced, inscrutable man whose eye he had just met – all of them were the puppets whose movements, joint or separate, were directed by his guiding hand.

Thorndyke's reflections were more complex. From time to time he glanced at Varney – he was too good an observer to need to stare – profoundly interested in his appearance. No man could look less like a murderer than this typical artist with his refined face, dreamy yet vivacious, and his suave, gentle manners. Yet that, apparently, was what he was. Moreover, he was a forger of bank-notes – perhaps of other things, too, as suggested by the very expert production of this letter – and had almost certainly uttered the forged notes. That was, so to speak, the debit side of his moral account, and there was no denying that it was a pretty heavy one.

On the other hand, he was evidently making a serious effort to earn an honest living. His steady industry was clear proof of that. It was totally unlike a genuine criminal to work hard and with enthusiasm for a modest income. Yet that was what he was evidently doing. It was a very singular contradiction. His present mode of life, which was evidently adapted to his temperament, seemed totally irreconcilable with his lurid past. There seemed to be two Varneys: the criminal Varney, practising felonies and not stopping short of murder, and the industrious, artistic Varney, absorbed in his art and content with the modest returns that it yielded.

Which of them was the real Varney? As he debated this question, Thorndyke turned to the consideration of the other partner in the criminal firm. And this seemed to throw an appreciable light on the question. Purcell had clearly been the senior partner. The initiative must have been his. The starting-point of the banknote adventure must have been the theft of the note-moulds at Maidstone. That had been Purcell's exploit, probably a lucky chance of which he had taken instant advantage. But the moulds were of no use to him without an engraver, so he had enlisted Varney's help. Now, to what extent had that help been willingly given?

It was, of course, impossible to say. But it was possible to form a reasonable opinion by considering the characters of the two men. On the one hand, Varney, a gentle, amiable, probably pliable man. On the other, Purcell, a strong, masterful bully, brutal, selfish, unscrupulous, ready to trample ruthlessly on any rights or interests that conflicted with his own desires. That was, in effect, the picture of him that his wife had painted – the wife whom he had married, apparently against her inclination, by putting pressure on her father, who was his debtor. Purcell was a money-lender, a usurer; and even at that a hard case, as Mr Levy's observations seemed to hint. Now, a usurer has certain affinities with a blackmailer. Their methods are somewhat similar. Both tend to fasten on their victim and bleed him continuously. Both act by getting a hold on the victim and putting on the screw when necessary, and both are characterized by a remorseless egoism.

Now, Purcell was clearly of the stuff of which blackmailers are made. Was it possible that there was an element of blackmail in his relations with Varney? The appearances strongly suggested it. Here were two men jointly engaged in habitual crime. Suddenly one of them is eliminated by the act of the other, and forthwith the survivor rids himself of the means of repeating the crime and settles down to a life of lawful industry. That was what had happened. The instant Varney had got rid of Purcell he had proceeded to get rid of the paper blanks by sending them to Mr Penfield instead of printing them and turning them into money; and by thus denouncing the firm had made it impossible, in any case, to continue the frauds. Then he had settled down to regular work in his studio. That seemed to be the course of events.

It was extremely suggestive. Purcell's disappearance coincided with the end of the criminal adventure and the beginning of a reputable mode of life. That seemed to supply the motive for the murder – if it had been a murder. It suggested that no escape from the life of crime had been possible so long as Purcell was alive, that Purcell had obtained some kind of hold on Varney which enabled him to compel the latter to continue in the criminal partnership; and that Varney had taken the only means that were possible to rid himself of his parasite. That was what it looked like.

Of course, this was mere guesswork. No proof was possible. But it agreed with all the facts, and it made Varney's apparent dual personality understandable. The real and essential Varney appeared to be the artist, not the criminal. He appeared to be a normal man, who had committed a murder under exceptional circumstances. With the banknote business Thorndyke was not concerned, and he had no knowledge of its circumstances. But the murder was his concern, and he set himself to consider it.

The hypothesis was that Purcell had been, in effect, a blackmailer, and that Varney had been his victim. Now, it must be admitted that Thorndyke held somewhat unconventional views on the subject of blackmail. He considered that a blackmailer acts entirely at his own risk, and that the victim (since the law can afford him but a very imperfect protection) is entitled to take any available measures for his own defence, including the elimination of the blackmailer. But if the blackmailer acts at his own risk, so does the victim who elects to make away with him. Morally, the killing of a blackmailer may be justifiable homicide, but it has no such legal status. In law self-defence means defence against bodily injury; it does not include defence against moral injury. Whoever elects to rid himself of a blackmailer by killing him accepts the risk of a conviction on a charge of murder. But that appeared to be Varney's position. He had accepted the risk. It was for him to avoid the consequences if he could. As to Thorndyke himself, though he might, like the Clerk of Arraigns at the Old Bailey wish the offender "a good deliverance," his part was to lay bare the hidden facts. He and Varney were players on opposite sides. He would play impersonally, without malice and with a certain good will to his opponent. But he must play his own hand and leave his opponent to do the same.

These reflections passed swiftly through his mind in the intervals of a very desultory conversation. As he reached his conclusion, he once more looked up at Varney. And then he received something like a shock. At the moment no one was speaking, and Varney was sitting with his eyes somewhat furtively fixed on Margaret's downcast face. Now, to an experienced observer there is something perfectly unmistakable in the expression with which a man looks at a woman with whom he is deeply in love. And such was the expression that Thorndyke surprised on Varney's face. It was one of concentrated passion, of adoration.

Thorndyke was completely taken aback. This was an entirely new situation, calling for a considerable revision of his conclusions and also of his sympathies. An eliminated blackmailer is one thing; Uriah's wife is another and a very different one. Thorndyke was rather puzzled, for though the previous hypothesis hung fairly together, it was now weakened by the possibility that the murder had been committed merely to remove a superfluous husband. Not that it made any practical difference. He was concerned with the fact of Purcell's murder. The motives were no affair of his.

His reflections were interrupted by a question from Margaret.

"You haven't been down to Cornwall, I suppose, since you came to see us at Sennen in the summer?"

"No, I have not; but Professor D'Arcy has, and he is starting for another trip at the end of next month."

"Is he still in search of worms? It was worms that you were going to look for, wasn't it?"

"Yes, marine worms. But he is not fanatical on the subject. All marine animals are fish that come to his net."

"You are using the word 'net' in a metaphorical sense, I presume," said Varney. "Or does he actually use a net?"

"Sometimes," replied Thorndyke. "A good many specimens can be picked up by searching the shore at low tide, but the most productive work is done with the dredge. Many species are found only below low-water mark."

"Is there anything particularly interesting about marine worms?" Margaret asked. "There always seems something rather disgusting about a worm, but I suppose that is only vulgar prejudice."

"It is principally unacquaintance with worms," replied Thorndyke. "They are a highly interesting group of animals, both in regard to structure and habits. You ought to read Darwin's fascinating book on earthworms and learn what an important part they play in the fashioning of the earth's surface. But the marine worms are not only interesting, some of them are extraordinarily beautiful creatures."

"That was what Philip Rodney used to say," said Margaret, "but we didn't believe him, and he never showed us any specimens."

"I don't know that he ever got any," said Varney. "He made great preparations in the way of bottles and jars, and then he spent most of his time sailing his yacht or line-fishing from a lugger. The only tangible result of his preparations was that remarkable jury button that he fixed on Dan's oilskin coat. You remember that button, Mrs Purcell?"

"I remember something about a button, but I have forgotten the details. What was it?"

"Why, Dan lost the top button from his oiler and never got it replaced. One day he lent the coat to Philip to go home in the wet, and as Phil was going out line-fishing the next day and his own oilers were on the yacht, he thought he would take Dan's. So he proceeded to fix on a temporary button, and a most remarkable job he made of it. It seems that he hadn't got either a button or a needle and thread, so he extemporized. He took the cork out of one of his little collecting bottles – it was a flat cork, waterproofed with paraffin wax, and it had a round label inscribed 'Marine Worms.' Well, as he hadn't a needle or thread he bored two holes through the cork with the little marlinspike in his pocket-knife, passed through them the remains of a fiddle-string that he had in his pocket, made two holes in the oilskin, threaded the catgut through them, and tied a reef-knot on the inside."

"And did it answer?" asked Margaret. "It sounds rather clumsy."

"It answered perfectly. So well that it never got changed. It was on the coat when Dan went up the ladder at Penzance, and it is probably on it still. Dan seemed quite satisfied with it."

There was a brief silence, during which Thorndyke looked down thoughtfully at his plate. Presently he asked:

"Was the label over the wax or under it?"

Varney looked at him in surprise, as also did Margaret. What on earth could it matter whether the label were over or under the wax?

"The label was under the wax," the former replied. "I remember Philip mentioning the fact that the label was waterproofed as well as the cork. He made quite a point of it, though I didn't see why. Do you?"

"If he regarded the label as a decorative adjunct," replied Thorndyke, "he would naturally make a point of the impossibility of its getting washed off, which was the object of the waxing."

"I suppose he would," Varney agreed in an absent tone, and still looking curiously at Thorndyke. He had a feeling that the latter's mildly facetious reply was not quite "in key" with the very definite question. Why had that question been asked? Had Thorndyke anything in his mind? Probably not. What could he have? At any rate, it was of no consequence to him, Varney.

In which he was, perhaps, mistaken. Thorndyke had been deeply interested in the history of the button. Here was one of those queer, incalculable trivialities which so often crop up in the course of a criminal trial. By this time, no doubt, that quaint button was detached and drifting about in the sea, or lying unnoticed on some lonely beach among the high-water jetsam. The mere cork would be hardly recognizable, but if the label had been protected by the wax it would be identifiable with absolute certainty. And if ever it should be identified, its testimony would go to prove the improbability that Daniel Purcell ever went ashore at Penzance.

CHAPTER ELEVEN

In Which Varney Has an Inspiration

The adjournment to the drawing-room was the signal for Varney to fetch his portfolio and exhibit his little collection, which he did with a frank interest and pleasure in his works that was yet entirely free from any appearance of vanity. Thorndyke examined the proofs with a curiosity that was not wholly artistic. Varney interested him profoundly. There was about him a certain reminiscence of Benvenuto Cellini: a combination of the thoroughgoing rascal with the sincere and enthusiastic artist. But Thorndyke could not make up his mind how close the parallel was. From Cellini's grossness Varney appeared to be free; but how about the other vices? Had Varney been forced into wrongdoing by the pressure of circumstances on a weak will? Or was he a criminal by choice and temperament? That was what Thorndyke could not decide.

An artist's work may show only one side of his character, but it shows that truthfully and unmistakably. A glance through Varney's works made it clear that he was an artist of no mean talent. There was not only skill, which Thorndyke had looked for, but a vein of poetry, which he noted with appreciation and almost with regret.

"You don't seem to value your aquatints," he said, "but I find them very charming. This seascape with the fleet of luggers half hidden in the mist, and the lighthouse peeping over the top of the fogbank, is really wonderful. You couldn't have done that with the point."

"No," Varney agreed; "every process has its powers and its limitations."

"The lighthouse, I suppose, is no lighthouse in particular?"

"Well, no; but I had the Wolf in my mind when I planned this plate. As a matter of fact, I saw a scene very like this when I was sailing round with Purcell to Penzance the day he vanished. The lighthouse looked awfully ghostly with its head out of the fog and its body invisible."

"Wasn't that the time you had to climb up the mast?" asked Margaret.

"Yes; when the jib halyard parted and the jib went overboard. It was rather a thrilling experience, for the yacht was out of control for the moment and the Wolf rock was close under our lee. Dan angled for the sail while I went aloft."

Thorndyke looked thoughtfully at the little picture, and Varney watched him with outward unconcern but with secret amusement and a sort of elfish mischief.

And again he was conscious of a sense of power, of omniscience. Here was this learned, acute lawyer and scientist looking in all innocence at the very scene on which he, Varney, had looked as he was washing the stain of Purcell's blood from the sail. Little did he dream of the event which this aquatint commemorated! For all his learning and his acuteness, he, Varney, held him in the hollow of his hand.

To Thorndyke the state of mind revealed by this picture was as surprising as it was illuminating. This was, in effect, a souvenir of that mysterious and tragic voyage. Whatever had happened on that voyage was clearly the occasion of no remorse. There was no shrinking from the memory of that day, but rather evidence that it was recalled with a certain satisfaction. In that there seemed a most singular callousness. But what did that callous indifference, or even satisfaction, suggest? A man who had made away with a friend with the express purpose of getting possession of that friend's wife would surely look back on the transaction with some discomfort; indeed, would avoid looking back on it at all. Whereas one who had secured his liberty by eliminating his oppressor could hardly be expected to feel either remorse or regrets. It looked as if the blackmail theory were the true one, after all.

"That will be Mr Rodney," Margaret said, looking expectantly at the door.

"I didn't hear the bell," said Varney. Neither had Thorndyke heard it; but he had not been listening, whereas Margaret apparently had, which perhaps accounted for the slightly preoccupied yet attentive air that he had noticed once or twice when he had looked at her.

A few moments later John Rodney entered the room unannounced, and Margaret went forward quickly to welcome him. And for the second time that evening Thorndyke found himself looking, all unsuspected, into the secret chamber of a human heart.

As Margaret had advanced towards the door, he and Varney stood up. They were thus both behind her when Rodney entered the room. But on the wall by the door was a small mirror, and in this Thorndyke had caught an instantaneous glimpse of her face as she met Rodney. That glimpse had told him what, perhaps, she had hardly guessed herself; but the face which appeared for a moment in the mirror and was gone was a face transfigured. Not, indeed, with the expression of passionate adoration that he had seen on Varney's face. That meant passion consciously recognized and accepted. What Thorndyke saw on Margaret's face was a softening, a tender, joyful welcome such as a mother might bestow on a beloved child. It spoke of affection rather than passion. But it was unmistakable. Margaret Purcell loved John Rodney. Nor, so far as Thorndyke could judge, was the affection only on one side. Rodney, facing the room, naturally made no demonstration; but still, his greeting had in it something beyond mere cordiality.

It was an extraordinarily complex situation, and there was in it a bitter irony such as De Maupassant would have loved. Thorndyke glanced at Varney, from whom Margaret's face had been hidden, with a new interest. Here was a man who had made away with an unwanted husband, perhaps with the sole purpose of securing the reversion of the wife; and behold! he had only created a vacancy for another man.

"This is a great pleasure, Thorndyke," said Rodney, shaking hands heartily. "Quite an interesting experience, too, to see you in evening clothes, looking almost human. I am sorry I couldn't get here to dinner. I should like to have seen you taking food like an ordinary mortal."

"You shall see him take some coffee presently," said Margaret. "But doesn't Dr Thorndyke usually look human?"

"Well," replied Rodney, "I won't say that there isn't a certain specious resemblance to a human being. But it is illusory. He is really a sort of legal abstraction like John Doe or Richard Roe. Apart from the practice of the law there is no such person."

"That sounds to me like a libel," said Margaret.

"Yes," agreed Varney. "You've done it now, Rodney. It must be actionable to brand a man as a mere hallucination. There will be wigs on the green – barrister's wigs – when Dr Thorndyke begins to deal out writs."

"Then I shall plead justification," said Rodney, "and I shall cite the present instance. For what do these pretences of customary raiment and food consumption amount to? They are mere camouflage, designed to cover a legal inquiry into the disappearances from his usual places of resort of one Daniel Purcell."

"Now you are only making it worse," said Margaret, "for you are implicating me. You are implying that my little dinner party is nothing more than a camouflaged legal inquisition."

"And you are implicating me, too," interposed Varney, "as an accessory before, during, and after the fact. You had better be careful, Rodney. It will be a joint action, and Dr Thorndyke will produce scientific witnesses who will prove anything he tells them to."

"I call this intimidation," said Rodney. "The circumstances seem to call for the aid of tobacco – I see that permission has been given to smoke."

"And perhaps a cup of coffee might help," said Margaret, as the maid entered with the tray.

"Yes, that will clear my brain for the consideration of my defence. But still, I must maintain that this is essentially a legal inquisition. We have assembled primarily to consider the position which is created by this letter that Penfield has received."

"Nothing of the kind," said Margaret. "I asked you primarily that I might enjoy the pleasure of your society, and, secondly, that you might enjoy the pleasure of one another's – "

"And yours."

"Thank you. But as to the letter, I don't see that there is anything to discuss. We now know where Dan is, but that doesn't seem to alter the situation."

"I don't agree with you in either respect," said Rodney. "There seems to me a good deal to discuss; and our knowledge as to Dan's whereabouts alters the situation to this extent: that we can get into touch with him if we want to – or at least Dr Thorndyke can, I presume."

"I am not so sure of that," said Thorndyke. "But we could consider the possibility if the necessity should arise. Had you anything in your mind that would suggest such a necessity?"

"What I have in my mind," replied Rodney, "is this. Purcell has left his wife for reasons known only to himself. He has never sent a word of excuse, apology, or regret. Until this letter arrived it was possible to suppose that he might be dead, or have lost his memory, or in some other way be incapable of communicating with his friends. Now we know that he is alive, that he has all his faculties – except the faculty of behaving like a decent and responsible man – and that he has gone away and is staying away of his own free will and choice. If there was ever any question as to his coming back, there is none now; and if there could ever have been any excuse or extenuation of his conduct, there is now none. We see that although he has never sent a message of any kind to his wife, yet, when the question of a sum of money arises, he writes to his solicitor with the greatest promptitude. That letter is a gross and callous insult to his wife."

Thorndyke nodded. "That seems to be a fair statement of the position," said he. "And I gather that you consider it possible to take some action?"

"My position is this," said Rodney. "Purcell has deserted his wife. He has shaken off all his responsibilities as a husband. But he has left her with all the responsibilities and disabilities of a wife. He has taken to himself the privileges of a bachelor, but she remains a married woman. That is an intolerable position. My contention is that, since he has gone for good, the tow-rope ought to be cut. He should be set adrift finally and completely and she should be liberated."

"I agree with you entirely and emphatically," said Thorndyke. "A woman whose husband has left her should, if she wishes it, revert to the status of a spinster."

"And she does wish it," interposed Margaret.

"Naturally," said Thorndyke. "The difficulty is in respect of ways and means. Have you considered the question of procedure, Rodney?"

"It seems to me," was the reply, "that the ways and means are provided by the letter itself. I suggest that the terms of that letter and the circumstances in which it was written afford evidence of desertion, or at least good grounds of action."

"You may be right," said Thorndyke, "but I doubt if it would be accepted as evidence of an intention not to return. It seems to me that a court would require something more definite. I suppose an action for restitution, as a preliminary, would not be practicable?"

Rodney shook his head emphatically, and Margaret pronounced a most decided refusal.

"I don't want restitution," she exclaimed, "and I would not agree to it. I would not receive him back on any terms."

"He wouldn't be likely to come back," said Thorndyke, "and if he did not, his failure to comply with the order of the court would furnish definite grounds for further action."

"But he might come back, at least temporarily," objected Margaret, "if only by way of retaliation."

"Yes," agreed Rodney, "it is perfectly possible; in fact, it is rather the sort of thing that Purcell would do – come back, make himself unpleasant, and then go off again. No; I am afraid that cat won't jump."

"Then," said Thorndyke, "we are in difficulties. We want the marriage dissolved, but we haven't as much evidence as the court would require."

"Probably more evidence could be obtained," suggested Rodney, "and of a different kind. Didn't Penfield say something about an associate or companion? Well, that is where our knowledge of Purcell's whereabouts should help us. If it were possible to locate him exactly and keep him under observation, evidence of the existence of that companion might be forthcoming, and then the case would be all plain sailing."

Thorndyke had been expecting this suggestion and considering how he should deal with it. He could not undertake to search the Eastern Counties for a man who was not there, nor could he give his reasons for not undertaking that search. Until his case against Varney was complete he would make no confidences to anybody. And as he reflected he watched Varney (who had been a keenly interested listener to the discussion), wondering what he was thinking about it all, and noting idly how neatly and quickly he rolled his cigarettes and how little he was inconvenienced by his contracted finger, the third finger of his left hand.

"I think, Rodney," he said, "that you overestimate the ease with which we could locate Purcell. The Eastern Counties offer a large area in which to search for a man – who may not be there, after all. The post-mark on the letter tells us nothing of his permanent abiding-place, if he has one. Varney suggests that he may be afloat, and if he is, he will be very mobile and difficult to trace. And it would be possible for him to change his appearance – by growing a beard, for instance – sufficiently to make a circulated description useless."

Rodney listened to these objections with hardly veiled impatience. He had supposed that Thorndyke's special practice involved the capacity to trace missing persons, yet as soon as a case calling for this special knowledge arose, he raised difficulties. That was always the way with these confounded experts. Now, to him – though, to be sure, it was out of his line – the thing presented no difficulties at all. To no man does a difficult thing look so easy as to one who is totally unable to do it.

Meanwhile Thorndyke continued to observe Varney, who was evidently reflecting profoundly on the impasse that had arisen. He, of course, could see the futility of Rodney's scheme. He, moreover, since he was in love with Margaret, would be at least as keen on the dissolution of this marriage as Rodney. Thorndyke, watching his eager face, began to hope that he might make some useful suggestion. Nor was he disappointed. Suddenly Varney looked up, and, addressing himself to Rodney, said:

"I've got an idea. You may think it bosh, but it is really worth considering. It is this. There is no doubt that Dan has cleared out for good, and it is rather probable that he has made some domestic arrangements of a temporary kind. You know what I mean. And he might be willing to have the chance of making them permanent, because he is not free in that respect any more than his wife is. Now what I propose is that we put in an advertisement asking him to write to his wife, or to Penfield, stating what his intentions are. It is quite possible that he might, in his own interests, send a letter that would enable you to get a divorce without any other evidence. It is really worth trying."

Rodney laughed scornfully. "You've missed your vocation, Varney," said he. "You oughtn't to be tinkering about with etchings. You ought to be in the Law. But I'm afraid the mackerel wouldn't rise to your sprat."

Thorndyke could have laughed aloud. But he did not. On the contrary, he made a show of giving earnest consideration to Varney's suggestion, and finally said:

"I am not sure that I agree with you, Rodney. It doesn't seem such a bad plan."

In this he spoke quite sincerely. But then he knew, which Rodney did not, that if the advertisement were issued there would certainly be a reply from Purcell; and, moreover, that the reply would be of precisely the kind that would be most suitable for their purpose.

"Well," said Rodney, "it seems to me rather a wild-cat scheme. You are proposing to ask Purcell to give himself away completely. If you knew him as well as I do you would know that no man could be less likely to comply. Purcell is one of the most secretive men I have ever known, and you can see for yourself that he has been pretty secret over this business."

"Still," Thorndyke persisted, "it is possible, as Varney suggests, that it might suit him to have the tow-rope cut, as you express it. What do you think, Mrs Purcell?"

"I am afraid I agree with Mr Rodney. Dan is as secret as an oyster, and he hasn't shown himself at all well disposed. He wouldn't make a statement for my benefit. As to the question of another woman, I have no doubt that there is one, but my feeling is that Dan would prefer to have a pretext for not marrying her."

"That is exactly my view," said Rodney. "Purcell is the sort of man who will get as much as he can and give as little in exchange."

"I don't deny that," said Varney, "but I still think that it would be worth trying. If nothing came of it we should be no worse off."

"Exactly," agreed Thorndyke. "It is quite a simple proceeding. It commits us to nothing and it is very little trouble, and if by any chance it succeeded, see how it would simplify matters. In place of a crowd of witnesses collected at immense trouble and cost you would have a letter which could be put in evidence, and which would settle the whole case in a few minutes."

Rodney shrugged his shoulders and secretly marvelled how Thorndyke had got his great reputation.

"There is no answering a determined optimist," said he. "Of course, Purcell may rise to your bait. He may even volunteer to go into the witness-box and make a full confession and offer to pay our costs. But I don't think he will."

"Neither do I," said Thorndyke. "But it is bad practice to reject a plan because you think it probably will not succeed when it is possible and easy to give it a trial. Have you any objection to our carrying out Mr Varney's suggestion?"

"I have no objection to *your* carrying it out," replied Rodney, "and I don't suppose Mrs Purcell has, but I don't feel inclined to act on it myself."

Thorndyke looked interrogatively at Margaret. "What do you say, Mrs Purcell?" he asked.

"I am entirely in your hands," she replied. "It is very good of you to take so much trouble, but I fear you will have your trouble for nothing."

"We shan't lose much on the transaction even then," Thorndyke rejoined, "so we will leave it that I insert the advertisement in the most alluring terms that I can devise. If anything comes of it you will hear before I shall."

This brought the discussion to an end. If Rodney had any further ideas on the subject he reserved them for the benefit of Margaret or Mr Penfield, having reached the conclusion that Thorndyke was a pure specialist – and probably overrated at that – whose opinions and judgment on general law were not worth having. The conversation thus drifted into other channels, but with no great vivacity, for each of the four persons was occupied inwardly with the subject that had been outwardly dismissed.

Presently Varney, who had been showing signs of restlessness, began to collect his etchings in preparation for departure. Thereupon Thorndyke also rose to make his farewell.

"I have had a most enjoyable evening, Mrs Purcell," he said, as he shook his hostess' hand. And he spoke quite sincerely. He had

had an extremely enjoyable evening, and he hoped that the entertainment was even now not quite at an end. "May we hope that our plottings and schemings will not be entirely unfruitful?"

"You can hope as much as you like," said Rodney, "if hopefulness is your speciality, but if anything comes of this plan of Varney's, I shall be the most surprised man in London."

"And I hope you will give the author of the plan all the credit he deserves," said Thorndyke.

"He has got that now," Rodney replied with a grin.

"I doubt if he has," retorted Thorndyke. "But we shall see. Are we walking the same way, Varney?"

"I think so," replied Varney, who had already decided, for his own special reasons, that they were; in which he was in complete, though unconscious, agreement with Thorndyke.

"Rodney seems a bit cocksure," the former remarked, as they made their way towards the Brompton Road, "but it is no use taking things for granted. I think it quite possible that Purcell may be willing to cut his cable. At any rate, it is reasonable to give him the chance."

"Undoubtedly," agreed Thorndyke. "There is no greater folly than to take failure for granted and reject an opportunity. Now, if this plan of yours should by any chance succeed, Mrs Purcell's emancipation is as good as accomplished."

"Is it really?" Varney exclaimed eagerly.

"Certainly," replied Thorndyke. "That is, if Purcell should send a letter the contents of which should disclose a state of affairs which would entitle his wife to a divorce. But that is too much to hope for unless Purcell also would like to have the marriage dissolved."

"I think it quite possible that he would, you know," said Varney. "He must have had strong reasons for going off in this way, and we know what those strong reasons usually amount to. But would a simple letter, without any witnesses, be sufficient to satisfy the court?"

"Undoubtedly," replied Thorndyke. "A properly attested letter is good evidence enough. It is just a question of what it contains. Let us suppose that we have a suitable letter. Then our procedure is perfectly simple. We produce it in court, and it is read and put in evidence. We say to the judge: 'Here is a letter from the respondent to the petitioner, or her solicitor, as the case may be. It is in answer to an advertisement, also read and put in evidence; the handwriting has been examined by the petitioner, by her solicitor, and by the respondent's banker, and each of them swears that the writing and the signature are those of the respondent. In that letter the respondent clearly and definitely states that he has left his wife for good; that under no circumstances will he ever return to her; that he refuses hereafter to contribute to her support; and that he has transferred his affections to another woman, who is now living with him as his wife.' On that evidence I think we should have no difficulty in obtaining a decree."

Varney listened eagerly. He would have liked to make a few notes, but that would hardly do, though Thorndyke seemed to be a singularly simple-minded and confiding man. And he was amazingly easy to pump.

"I don't suppose Purcell would give himself away to that extent," he remarked, "unless he was really keen on a divorce."

"It is extremely unlikely in any case," Thorndyke agreed. "But we have to bear in mind that if he writes at all it will be with the object of stating his intentions as to the future and making his position clear. I shall draft the advertisement in such a way as to elicit this information, if possible. If he is not prepared to furnish the information he will not reply. If he replies it will be because, for his own purposes, he is willing to furnish the information."

"Yes, that is true. So that he may really give more information than one might expect. I wonder if he will write. What do you think?"

"It is mere speculation," replied Thorndyke. "But if I hadn't some hopes of his writing I shouldn't be at the trouble of putting in the advertisement. But perhaps Rodney is right: I may be unreasonably optimistic."

At Piccadilly Circus they parted and went their respective ways, each greatly pleased with the other and both highly amused. As soon as Thorndyke was out of sight, Varney whipped out his notebook, and by the light of a street lamp made a careful précis of the necessary points of the required letter. That letter also occupied Thorndyke's mind, and he only hoped that the corresponding agent of Daniel Purcell, deceased, would not allow his enthusiasm to carry him to the extent of producing a letter the contents of which would stamp the case as one of rank collusion. For in this letter Thorndyke saw a way, and the only way, out for Margaret Purcell. He knew, or at least was fully convinced, that her husband was dead. But he had no evidence that he could take into court, nor did he expect that he ever would have. It would be years before it would be possible to apply to presume Purcell's death, and throughout those years Margaret's life would be spoiled. This letter was a fiction. The erring husband was a fiction. But it would be better that Margaret should be liberated by a fiction than that she should drag out a ruined life shackled to a husband who was himself a fiction.

CHAPTER TWELVE

In Which Varney Once More Pulls the Strings

For the second time, in connection with the death of Daniel Purcell, Mr Varney found it necessary to give an attentive eye to the movements of the postman. He had ascertained from the post office the times at which letters were delivered in the neighbourhood of Margaret's flat; and now, in the gloom of a December evening, he lurked in the vicinity until he saw the postman approaching down the street and delivering letters at the other flats on his way. Then he entered the now familiar portals, and made his way quietly up the stairs until he reached Margaret's outer door. Here he paused for a few moments, standing quite still and listening intently. If he had been discovered he would have simply come to pay a call. But he was not, and the silence from within suggested that there was nobody in the hall. With a furtive look round, he drew a letter from his pocket and silently slipped it into the letter-box, catching the flap on his finger as it fell to prevent it from making any sound. Then he turned and softly stole down the stairs; and as he reached the ground floor the postman walked into the entry.

It was not without reluctance that he came away. For she was behind that door, almost certainly – she, his darling, for whose freedom from the imaginary shackles that she wore he was carrying out this particular deception. But his own guilty conscience made it seem to him that he had better not be present when the fabricated letter arrived. So he tore himself from the beloved pre-cincts and went his way, thinking his thoughts and dreaming his dreams.

Varney's surmise was correct. Margaret was within. But it was perhaps as well that he had refrained from paying a call, for she was not alone, and his visit would not have been entirely welcome. About half an hour before his arrival Jack Rodney had ascended those stairs, and had been admitted in time to join Margaret at a somewhat belated tea.

"My excuse for coming to see you," said Rodney, "is in my pocket – the front page of *The Times*."

"I don't know what you mean by an excuse," Margaret replied. "You know perfectly well that I am always delighted to see you. But perhaps you mean an excuse to yourself for wasting your time in gossiping with me."

"Indeed, I don't," said he. "I count no time so profitably employed as that which I spend here."

"I don't quite see what profit you get," she rejoined, "unless it is the moral benefit of doing a kindness to a lonely woman."

"I should like to take that view if I honestly could. But the fact is that I come here for the very great pleasure of seeing you and talking to you, and the profit that I get is that very great pleasure. I only wish the proprieties allowed me to come oftener."

"So do I," she said frankly. "But you know that, too. And now tell me what there is in the front page of *The Times* that gave you this sorely needed excuse."

Rodney laughed in a boisterous, schoolboy fashion as he drew from his pocket a folded leaf of the newspaper. "It's the great advertisement," said he. "The Thorndyke-Varney or Varney-Thorndyke advertisement. It came out yesterday morning. Compose yourself to listen, and I'll read it out to you."

He opened the paper out, refolded it into a convenient size, and with a portentous preliminary "Ahem!" read aloud in a solemn sing-song:

" 'Purcell, D, is earnestly requested to communicate to M or her solicitor his intentions with regard to the future. If his present arrangements are permanent, she would be grateful if he would notify her to that effect, in order that she may make the necessary modifications in her own.' "

As he finished, he looked up at her and laughed contemptuously.

"Well, Maggie," said he, "what do you think of it?"

She laughed merrily, and looked at him with hardly disguised fondness and admiration. "What a schoolboy you are, John!" she exclaimed. "How annoyed Dr Thorndyke would be if he could hear you! But it is rather funny. I can imagine Dan's face when he reads it – if he ever does read it."

"So can I," chuckled Rodney. "I can see him pulling down his lower lip and saying, 'Gur!' in that pleasant way that he has. But isn't it a perfectly preposterous exhibition? Just imagine a man of Thorndyke's position doing a thing like this! Why, it is beneath the dignity of a country attorney's office-boy. I can't conceive how he got his reputation. He seems to be an absolute greenhorn."

"Probably he is quite good at his own speciality," suggested Margaret.

"But this *is* his own speciality. The truth is that the ordinary lawyer's prejudice against experts is to a great extent justified. They are really humbugs and pretenders. You saw what his attitude was when I suggested that he should get Dan under observation. Of course, it was the obvious thing to do, and one would suppose that it would be quite in his line. Yet as soon as I made the suggestion he raised all sorts of difficulties; whereas a common private inquiry agent would have made no difficulty about it at all."

"Do you think not?" Margaret asked, a little eagerly. "Perhaps it might be worth while to employ one. It would be such a blessed thing to get rid of Dan for good."

"It would, indeed," Rodney agreed heartily. "But perhaps we had better see if Thorndyke gets a bite. If he fails we can try the other plan."

Margaret was slightly disappointed. She wanted to see some progress made, and was a little impatient of the law's delays. But the truth is that Rodney had been speaking rather at random. When he came to consider what information he had to give to a private detective, the affair did not look quite such plain sailing.

"Perhaps," said Margaret, "Dr Thorndyke was right in giving Mr Varney's plan a trial. We are no worse off if it fails; and if it were by any chance to succeed, oh, what a relief it would be! Not that there is the slightest chance that it will."

"Not a dog's chance," agreed Rodney, "and Thorndyke was an ass to have anything to do with the advertisement. He should have let Varney put it in. No one expects an artist to show any particular legal acumen."

"Poor Mr Varney!" murmured Margaret with a faint smile; and at this moment the housemaid entered the room with a couple of letters on a salver. Margaret took the letters, and, having thanked the maid, laid them on the table by her side.

"Won't you read your letters?" said Rodney. "You are not going to make a stranger of me, I hope."

"Thank you," she replied. "If you will excuse me I will just see whom they are from."

She took up the top letter, opened it, glanced through it, and laid it down. Then she picked up the second letter, and as her glance fell on the address she uttered a little cry of amazement.

"What is it?" asked Rodney.

She held the envelope out for him to see. "It's from Dan!" she exclaimed; and forthwith she tore it open and eagerly took out the letter.

As she read it, Rodney watched her with mingled amusement, vexation, and astonishment. The utterly inconceivable thing had happened. Thorndyke had taken odds of a million to one against and it had come off. That was just a piece of pure luck. It reflected no particular credit on Thorndyke's judgment; but still, Rodney rather wished he had been less dogmatic.

When she had quickly read through the letter, Margaret handed it to him without comment. He took it from her and rapidly ran through the contents.

"Dear Maggie" (it ran),

"I have just seen your quaint advertisement, and send you a few lines, as requested. I don't know what you mean by 'modifying your arrangements,' but I can guess. However, that is no concern of mine, and whatever your plans may be, I don't want to stand in your way. So I will give you a plain statement, and you can do what you like.

"My present arrangements are quite permanent. You have seen the last of yours truly. I have no intention of ever coming back – and I don't suppose you particularly want me. It may interest you to know that I have made fresh domestic arrangements – necessarily a little unorthodox, but also quite permanent.

"With regard to financial questions, I am afraid I can't contribute to your 'arrangements,' whatever they may be. You have enough to live on, and I have new responsibilities; but if you can get anything out of Levy you are welcome to it. You will be the first person who ever has. You can also try Penfield, and I wish you the best of luck. And that is all I have got to say on the subject.

With best wishes,

Yours sincerely

Daniel Purcell."

Rodney returned the letter with an expression of disgust. "It is a brutal, hoggish letter," said he, "typical of the writer. Where does he write from?"

"The post-mark is Wivenhoe. It was posted last night at seven-thirty."

"That looks as if Varney were right and he were afloat; but it is a queer time of year for yachting on the East Coast. Well, I suppose you are not much afflicted by the tone of that letter?"

"Not at all. The more brutal the better. I shall have no qualms now. But the question is, will the letter do? What do you think?"

"It ought to do well enough – if it isn't a little too good to be true."

"I don't quite understand. You don't doubt the truth of what he says, do you?"

"Not at all. What I mean is this: Divorce judges are pretty wary customers. They have to be. The law doesn't allow married people, who are tired of one another and would like to try a fresh throw of the dice, to make nice little mutual arrangements to get their marriage dissolved. That is called collusion. And then there is a mischievous devil called the King's Proctor, whose function is to 'prevent us, O Lord, in all our doings' and to trip up poor wretches who have got a decree and think they have escaped, and to send them back to cat-and-dog matrimony until death do them part. Now, the only pitfall about this letter of Dan's is that it is so very complete. He makes things so remarkably easy for us. He leaves us nothing to prove. He admits everything in advance, and covers the whole of our case in our favour. That letter might have been dictated by a lawyer in our interest."

Margaret looked deeply disappointed. "You don't mean to say that we shan't be able to act on it!" she exclaimed in dismay.

"I don't say that," he replied, "and I certainly think it will be worth trying. But I do wish that we could produce evidence that he is living with some woman, as he appears to state. That would be so much more convincing. However, I will get an opinion from a counsel who has had extensive experience of divorce practice – a man like Barnby, for instance. I could show him a copy of the letter and hear what he thinks."

"Why not Dr Thorndyke?" said Margaret. "He was really right, after all, and we shall have to show him the letter."

"Yes, and he must see the original. But as to taking his opinion – well, we shall have to do that as a matter of courtesy, but I don't set much value on his judgment. You see, he chose to go double Nap on this letter, and he happened to win. Events prove that he was right to take the chance, but it was primitive strategy. It doesn't impress me.

Margaret made no immediate rejoinder. She was not a lawyer, and to her the fact that the plan had succeeded was evidence that it was a good plan. Accordingly, her waning faith in Thorndyke was strongly revived.

"I can't help hoping," she said presently, "that this letter will secure a decision in our favour. It really ought to. You see, there is no question of arrangement or collusion on my side. Our relations were perfectly normal and pleasant up to the moment of Dan's disappearance. There were no quarrels, no differences, nothing to hint at any desire for a change in our relations; and I have waited six months for him to come back, and have taken no action until he made it clear that he had gone for good. Don't you think that I have a fair chance of getting my freedom?"

"Perhaps you are right, Maggie," he replied. "I may be looking out for snags that aren't there. Of course, you could call me and Philip and Varney to prove that all was normal up to the last, and Penfield and Thorndyke to give evidence of your efforts to trace Dan. Yes, perhaps it is a better case than I thought. But all the same, I will show the letter to Barnby when Thorndyke has seen it and get his opinion without prejudice."

He paused and reflected profoundly for a while. Suddenly he looked up at Margaret, and in his eyes there was a new light.

"Supposing, Maggie," he said in a low, earnest voice, "you were to get this marriage dissolved. Then you would be free – free to marry. You know that years ago, when you were free, I loved you. You know that, because I told you; and I thought, and I still think, that you cared for me then. The fates were against us at that time, but in the years that have passed there has been no change in me. You are the only woman I have ever wanted. Of course, I have kept my feelings to myself. That had to be. But if we can win back your freedom, I shall ask you to be my wife, unless you forbid me. What shall you say to me, Maggie?"

Margaret sat with downcast eyes as Rodney was speaking. For a few moments she had appeared pale and agitated, but she was now quite composed, and nothing but a heightened colour hinted at any confusion. At the final question she raised her head and looked Rodney frankly in the face.

"At present, John," she said quietly, "I am the wife of Daniel Purcell, and as such have no right to contemplate any other marriage. But I will be honest with you. There is no reason why I should not be. You are quite right, John. I loved you in those days that you speak of, and if I never told you, you know why. You know how I came to marry Dan. It seemed to me then that I had no choice. Perhaps I was wrong, but I did what I thought was my duty to my father.

"In the years that have passed since then – the long, grey years – I have kept my covenant with Dan loyally in every respect. If I have ever looked back with regret, it has been in secret. But through those years you have been a faithful friend to me, and of all my friends the best beloved. And so you are now. That is all I can say, John."

"It is enough, Maggie," he said, "and I thank you from my heart for saying so much. Whatever your answer might have been, I would have done everything in my power to set you free. But now I shall venture to have a hope that I hold a stake in your freedom."

She made no answer to this, and for some time both sat silently engrossed with their own thoughts, and each thinking much the same thoughts as the other. The silence was at length broken by Rodney.

"It was an awful blow to me when I came home from my travels and found you married. Of course, I guessed what had happened, though I never actually knew. I assumed that Dan had put the screw on your father in some way."

"Yes. He had lent my father money, and the bills could not be met."

"What a Juggernaut the fellow is!" exclaimed Rodney. "An absolutely ruthless egoist. By the way, was he in the habit of lending money? I notice that he refers in this letter to a person named Levy. Who is Levy? And what does Dan do for a livelihood? He is out of the paper trade, isn't he?"

"I think so. The truth is, I have never known what his occupation is. I have suspected that he is principally a money-lender. As to Mr Levy, I have always thought he was a clerk or manager, but it rather looks as if he were a partner."

"We must find out," said Rodney. "And there is another thing that we must look into – that mysterious letter that Penfield received from Dan. Did you ever learn what was in it?"

"Never. Mr Penfield refused to divulge the slightest hint of its contents. But I feel convinced that it was in some way connected with Dan's disappearance. You remember it arrived on the very day that Dan went away. I think Dr Thorndyke called on Mr Penfield to see if he could glean any information, but I assume that he didn't succeed."

"We can take that for granted," said Rodney. "I don't think Thorndyke would get much out of a wary old bird like Penfield. But we must find out what was in that letter. Penfield will have to produce it if we put him in the witness-box, though he will be a mighty slippery witness. However, I will see Thorndyke and ask him about it when I have consulted Barnby. Perhaps I had better take charge of the letter."

Margaret handed him the letter, which he put securely in his wallet, and the plan of action being now settled, he stayed only for a little further gossip, and then took his leave.

On the following afternoon he called by appointment on Thorndyke, who, having admitted him, closed the "oak" and connected the bell with the laboratory upstairs, where his assistant, Polton, was at work.

"So," he said, "our fish has risen to the tin minnow, as I gather from your note."

"Yes. You have had better luck than I expected."

"Or than I deserved, you might have added if you had been less polite. Well, I don't know that I should agree. I consider it bad practice to treat an improbability as an impossibility. But what does he say?"

"All that we could wish – and perhaps a little more. That is the only difficulty. He makes things a little too easy for us – at least, that is my feeling. But you had better see the letter."

He took it from his wallet and passed it to Thorndyke, who glanced at the post-mark, and when he had taken out the letter looked quickly into the interior of the envelope.

"Wivenhoe," he remarked. "Some distance from Woodbridge, but in the same district."

He read carefully through the text, noting at the same time the peculiarities that he had observed in the former letter. In this case, too, the post-marks had been made when the envelope was empty – a curious oversight on the part of Varney in view of the care and ingenuity otherwise displayed. Indeed, as he read through the letter, Thorndyke's opinion of that cunning artificer rose considerably. It was a most skilful and tactful production. It did certainly make things almost suspiciously easy, but then that was its function. The whole case for the petition rested on it. But the brutal attitude of the imaginary truant was admirably rendered, and, so far as he could judge, the personality of the missing man convincingly represented.

"It is not a courteous epistle," he remarked tentatively.

"No," agreed Rodney, "but it is exactly the sort of letter that one would expect from Purcell. It gives you his character in a nutshell."

This was highly satisfactory and very creditable to Varney.

"You mentioned in your note that you were going to take Barnby's opinion on it. Have you seen him?"

"Yes, and he thinks the same as I do: that it would be a little risky to base a petition on this letter alone. The judge might smell a rat. He considers that if we could produce evidence that Purcell is actually living with another woman, this letter would be good evidence of desertion. He suggested putting a private inquiry agent on Purcell's tracks. What do you say to that?"

"In the abstract it is an excellent suggestion. But how are you going to carry it out? You speak of putting the agent on Purcell's tracks. But there are no tracks. There is no place in which he is known to have been staying; there is no person known to us who has seen him since he landed at Penzance. You would start your sleuth without a scent to wander about Essex and Suffolk looking for a man whom he had never seen and would probably not recognize if he met him, and who is possibly not in either of those counties at all. It really is not a practicable scheme."

Rodney emitted a discontented grunt. "Doesn't sound very encouraging certainly," he admitted. "But how do the police manage in a case of the kind?"

"By having, not one agent but a thousand, and all in communication through a central office. And even the police fail if they haven't enough data. But with regard to Barnby, of course his opinion has great weight. He knows the difficulties of these cases, and his outlook will probably be the judge's outlook. But did you make clear to him the peculiarities of this case? – the character of the petitioner, her excellent relations with her husband, the sudden, unforeseen manner of the disappearance, and the total absence of any grounds for a suspicion of collusion? Did you present these points to him?"

"No, I didn't. We merely discussed the letter."

"Well, see him again and put the whole case to him. My feeling is that a petition would probably succeed."

"I hope you are right," said Rodney, more encouraged than he would have liked to admit. "I'll see Barnby again. Oh, and there is another point. That letter that Purcell sent to Penfield by mistake in June. It probably throws some light on the disappearance, and might be important as evidence on our side. I suppose Penfield did not tell you what was in it or show it to you?"

"No, he would say nothing about it; but he allowed me, at my request, to examine the envelope."

Rodney grinned. "He might also have shown you the postman who delivered the letter. But if he won't tell us anything, we might put him in the witness-box and make him disgorge his secret."

"Yes, and you may have to if the court demands to have the letter produced. But I strongly advise you to avoid doing so if you can. I have the impression that the production of that letter would be very much the reverse of helpful – might, in fact, be fatal to the success of the case and would in addition be very disagreeable to Mrs Purcell."

Rodney looked at him in astonishment. "Then you know what was in the letter?" said he.

"No; but I have formed certain opinions which I have no doubt are correct, but which I do not feel at liberty to communicate. I advise you to leave Mr Penfield alone. Remember that he is a lawyer, that he is Mrs Purcell's friend, that he does know what is in the letter, and that he thinks it best to keep his knowledge to himself. But he will have to be approached on the question as to whether he is willing to act for Mrs Purcell against her husband. If you undertake that office you can raise the question of the letter with him, but I would urge you most strongly not to force his hand."

Rodney listened to this advice with a slightly puzzled expression. Like Mr Penfield, he viewed Thorndyke with mixed feelings, now thinking of him as an amateur, a doctor who dabbled ineffectively in law, and now considering the possibility that he might command some means of acquiring knowledge that were not available to the orthodox legal practitioner. Here was a case in point. He had examined the envelope of that mysterious letter "at his own request" and evidently for a specific purpose, and from that inspection he had in some unaccountable way formed a very definite opinion as to what the envelope had contained. That was very curious. Of course, he might be wrong; but he seemed to be pretty confident. Then there was the present transaction. Rodney himself had rejected Varney's suggestion with scorn. But Thorndyke had adopted it quite hopefully, and the plan had succeeded in the face of all probabilities. Could it be that Thorndyke had some unknown means of gauging those probabilities? It looked rather like it.

"You are only guessing at the nature of that letter," he said tentatively, "and you may have guessed wrong."

"That is quite possible," Thorndyke agreed. "But Penfield isn't guessing. Put the case to him, hear what he says, and follow his advice. And if you see Barnby again it would be better to say nothing about that letter. Penfield will advise you to keep it out of the case if you can, and that is my advice, too."

When Rodney took his departure, which he did a few minutes later, he carried with him a growing suspicion that he had underestimated Thorndyke; that the latter, perhaps, played a deeper game than at first sight appeared; and that he played with pieces unknown to traditional legal practice.

For some time after his visitor had left Thorndyke remained wrapped in profound thought. In his heart he was sensible of a deep distaste for this case that he was promoting. If it were to succeed, it could only be by misleading the court. It is true that the parties were acting in good faith, that the falsities which they would present were falsities that they believed to be true. But the whole case was based on a fiction, and Thorndyke detested fictions. Nor was he satisfied with his own position in an ethical sense. He knew that the case was fictitious, that the respondent was a dead man, and that the documents to be produced in evidence were forgeries. He was, in fact, an accessory to those forgeries. He did not like it at all. And he was not so optimistic as to the success of the petition as he had led Rodney to believe, though he was not very uneasy on that score. What troubled him was that this was, in effect, a bogus case, and that he was lending it his support.

But what was the alternative? His thoughts turned to Margaret, sweet-faced, sweet-natured, gracious-mannered, the perfect type of an English gentlewoman; and he thought of the fine, handsome, high-minded gentleman who had just gone away. These two loved one another – loved as only persons of character can love. Their marriage, if it could be achieved, would secure to them a lifelong happiness, in so far as such happiness is attainable by mortals. But between them and their happiness stood the fiction of Daniel Purcell. In order that they might marry, Purcell must either be proved to be dead or assumed to be alive.

Could he be proved to be dead? If he could, that were the better way, because it would demonstrate the truth. But was it possible? In a scientific sense it probably was. Science can accept a conclusion with reservations. But the law has to say "yes" or "no" without any reservations at all. This was not a case of death merely presumed. It was a death alleged to have occurred at a specific time and place and in a specific manner; and inseparably bound up with it was a charge of murder. If Purcell was dead, Varney had murdered him, and the murder was the issue that would be tried. But no jury would entertain for a moment the guilt of the accused on such evidence as Thorndyke could offer. And an acquittal would amount to a legal decision that Purcell was not dead. On that decision Margaret's marriage to Rodney would be impossible.

Thus Thorndyke's reflections led him back, as they always did, to the conclusion that Purcell's death was incapable of legal proof, and must ever remain so, unless by some miracle new and con-clusive evidence should come to light. But to wait for a miracle to happen was an unsatisfactory policy. If Purcell could not be proved to be dead, and if such failure of proof must wreck the happiness of two estimable persons, then it would appear that it might be allowable to accept what was the actual legal position and assume that he was alive.

So, once again, Thorndyke decided that he had no choice but to continue to share with Varney the secret of Purcell's death and to hold his peace. And if this must be, the petition must take its course, aided and abetted, if necessary, by him. After all, nobody would be injured and nothing done which was contrary either to public policy or private morals. There were only two alternatives, as matters stood. The fiction of Purcell as a living man would either keep Margaret and Rodney apart, as it was doing now, or it would be employed (with other fictions) to enable them to be united. And it was better that they should be united.

CHAPTER THIRTEEN

In Which the Medico-Legal Worm Arrives

Romance lurks in unsuspected places. As we go our daily round, we are apt to look distastefully upon the scenes made dull by familiarity, and to seek distraction by letting our thoughts ramble far away into time and space, to ages and regions in which life seems more full of colour. In fancy, perchance, we thread the ghostly aisles of some tropical forest, or linger on the white beach of some lonely coral island, where the coconut palms, shivering in the sea breeze, patter a refrain to the song of the surf; or we wander by moonlight through the narrow streets of some Southern city and hear the thrum of the guitar rise to the shrouded balcony; and behold! all the time Romance is at our very doors.

It was on a bright afternoon early in March that Thorndyke sat, with Philip Rodney by his side, on one of the lower benches of the lecture theatre of the Royal College of Surgeons. Not a likely place, this, to encounter Romance. Yet there it was – and Tragedy, too – lying unnoticed at present on the green baize cover of the lecturer's table, its very existence unsuspected.

Meanwhile Thorndyke and Philip conversed in quiet undertones, for it still wanted some minutes to the hour at which the lecture would commence.

"I suppose," said Philip, "you have had no report from that private detective fellow – I forget his name?"

"Bagwell. No, excepting the usual weekly note stating that he is still unable to pick up any trace of Purcell."

"Ah," commented Philip, "that doesn't sound encouraging. Must be costing a lot of money, too. I fancy my brother and Maggie Purcell are both beginning to wish they had taken your advice and relied on the letter by itself. But Jack was overborne by Barnby's insistence on corroborative evidence, and Maggie let him decide. And now they are sorry they listened to Barnby. They hadn't bargained for all this delay."

"Barnby was quite right as to the value of the additional evidence," said Thorndyke. "What he didn't grasp was the very great difficulty of getting it. But I think I hear the big-wigs approaching."

As he spoke, the usher threw open the lecturer's door. The audience stood up, the president entered, preceded by the mace-bearer and followed by the officers and the lecturer, and took his seat; the audience sat down, and the lecture began without further formalities.

The theatre was nearly full. It usually was when Professor D'Arcy lectured; for that genial savant had the magnetic gift of infusing his own enthusiasm into the lecture and so into his audience, even when, as on this occasion, his subject lay on the outside edge of medical science. Today he was lecturing on the epidermic appendages of the marine worms, and from the opening sentence he held his audience as by a spell, standing before the great blackboard with a bunch of coloured chalks in either hand, talking with easy eloquence – mostly over his shoulder – while he covered the black surface with those delightful drawings that added so much to the charm of his lectures. Philip watched his flying fingers with fascination, and struggled frantically to copy the diagrams into a large notebook with the aid of a handful of coloured pencils; while Thorndyke, not much addicted to note-taking, listened and watched with concentrated attention, mentally docketing and pigeon-holing any new or significant facts in what was to him a fairly familiar subject.

The latter part of the lecture dealt with those beautiful sea worms that build themselves tubes to live in – worms like the Serpula, that make their shelly or stony tubes by secretion from their own bodies, or, like the Sabella or Terebella, build them up with sand-grains, little stones or fragments of shell. Each, in turn, appeared in lively portraiture on the blackboard, and the trays on the table were full of specimens which were exhibited by the lecturer, and which the audience were invited to inspect more closely after the lecture.

Accordingly, when the last words of the peroration had been pronounced, the occupants of the benches trooped down into the arena to look at the exhibits and seek further details from the genial Professor. Thorndyke and Philip held back for a while on the outskirts of the crowd; but the Professor had seen them on their bench, and now approached, greeting them with a hearty handshake and a facetious question.

"What are you doing here, Thorndyke? Is it possible that there are medico-legal possibilities even in a marine worm?"

"Oh, come, D'Arcy!" protested Thorndyke, "don't make me such a hidebound specialist. May I have no rational interests in life? Must I live for ever in the witness-box like a marine worm in its tube?"

"I suspect you don't get very far out of your tube," said the Professor, with a chuckle and a sly glance at Philip.

"I got far enough out last summer," retorted Thorndyke, "to come and aid and abet you in your worm-hunting. Have you forgotten Cornwall?"

"No, to be sure," was the reply. "But that was only a momentary lapse, and I expect you had ulterior motives. However, the association of Cornwall, worm-hunting, and medical juris-prudence reminds me that I have something in your line. A friend of mine, who was wintering in Cornwall, picked it up on the beach at Morte Hoe and sent it to me. Now, where is it? It is on this table somewhere. It is a ridiculous thing – a small, flat cork, evidently from a zoologist's collecting-bottle, for it has a label stuck on it with the inscription 'Marine Worms.' It seems that our zoologist was a sort of Robinson Crusoe, for he had bored a couple of holes through it and evidently used it as a button. But the most ludicrous thing about it is that a Terebella has built its tube on it, as if the worm had been prowling about, looking for lodgings, and had read the label and forthwith had engaged the apartments. Ah! here it is."

He pounced on a little cardboard box, and, opening it, took out the cork button and laid it in Thorndyke's palm.

As the Professor was describing the object, Philip looked at him with a distinctly startled expression, and uttered a smothered exclamation. He was about to speak, but suddenly checked himself and looked at Thorndyke, who flashed at him a quick glance of understanding.

"Isn't that a quaint coincidence?" chuckled the Professor – "I mean that the worm should have taken up its abode and actually built his tube on the label?"

"Very quaint," replied Thorndyke, still looking with deep interest at the object that lay in his hand.

"You realize," Philip said in a low voice, as the Professor turned away to answer a question, "that this button came from Purcell's oilskin coat?"

"Yes, I remember the incident. I realized what it was as soon as D'Arcy described the button."

He glanced curiously at Philip, wondering whether he, too, realized exactly what this queer piece of jetsam was. For to Thorndyke its message had been conveyed even before the Professor had finished speaking. In that moment it had been borne to him that the unlooked-for miracle had happened, and that Margaret Purcell's petition need never be filed.

"Well, Thorndyke," said the Professor, "my friend's treasure trove seems to interest you. I thought it would as an instance of the possibilities of coincidence. Quite a useful lesson to a lawyer, by the way."

"Exactly," said Thorndyke. "In fact, I was going to ask you to allow me to borrow it to examine at my leisure."

The Professor was delighted. "There, now," he chuckled, with a mischievous twinkle at Philip, "what did I tell you? He hasn't come here for the comparative anatomy at all. He has just come to grub for legal data. And now, you see, the medico-legal worm has arrived, and is instantly collared by the medical jurist. Take him, by all means, Thorndyke. You needn't borrow him. I present him as a gift to your black museum. You needn't return him."

Thorndyke thanked the Professor, and, having packed the specimen with infinite tenderness in its cotton wool, bestowed the box in his waistcoat pocket. A few minutes later he and Philip took their leave of the Professor and departed, making their way through Lincoln's Inn to Chancery Lane.

"That button gave me quite a shock for a moment," said Philip, "appearing out of the sea on the Cornish coast; for, of course, it was on Purcell's coat when he went ashore – at least, I suppose it was. I understood Varney to say so."

"He did," said Thorndyke. "He mentioned the incident at dinner one evening, and he then said definitely that the cork button was on the coat when Purcell went up the ladder."

"Yes, and it seemed rather mysterious at first, as Purcell went right away from Cornwall. But there is probably quite a simple explanation. Purcell went to the East Coast by sea, and it is most likely that, when he got on board the steamer, he obtained a proper button from the steward, cut off the jury button, and chucked it overboard. But it is a queer chance that it should have come back to us in this way."

Thorndyke nodded. "A very queer chance," he agreed.

As he spoke, he looked at Philip with a somewhat puzzled expression. He was, in fact, rather surprised. Philip Rodney was a doctor, a man of science, and an unquestionably intelligent person. He knew all the circumstances that were known, and he had seen and examined the button; and yet he had failed to observe the one vitally important fact that stared him in the face.

"What made you want to borrow the button?" Philip asked presently. "Was it that you wanted to keep it as a relic of the Purcell case?"

"I want to examine the worm-tube," replied Thorndyke. "It is a rather unusual one; very uniform in composition. Mostly, Terebella tubes are very miscellaneous as to their materials – sand, shell, little pebbles, and so forth. The material of this one seems to be all alike."

"Probably the stuff that the worm was able to pick up in the neighbourhood of Morte Hoe."

"That is possible," said Thorndyke; and the conversation dropped for a moment, each man occupying himself with reflections on the other.

To Philip it seemed rather surprising that a man like Thorndyke, full of important business, should find time, or even inclination, to occupy himself with trivialities like this. For, after all, what did it matter whether this worm-tube was composed of miscellaneous gatherings or of a number of similar particles? No scientific interest attached to the question. It seemed rather a silly quest. And yet Thorndyke had thought it worth while to borrow the specimen for this very purpose.

Thorndyke, for his part, was more than ever astonished at the mental obtuseness of this usually acute and intelligent man. Not only had he failed in the first place to observe a most striking and significant fact: he could not see that fact even when his nose was rubbed hard on it.

As they passed through Old Buildings and approached the main gateway, Philip slowed down.

"I am going into my brother's chambers here to have tea with him. Do you care to join us? He will be glad to see you."

Thorndyke, however, was in no mood for tea and gossip. He had got a first-class clue – a piece of really conclusive evidence. How conclusive it was and how far its conclusiveness went he could not tell at present; and he was eager to get to work on the assay of this specimen in an evidential sense – to see exactly what was the amount and kind of evidence that the sea had cast up on the shore of Morte Hoe. He therefore excused himself, and having bidden Philip adieu, he strode out into Chancery Lane and bore south towards the Temple.

On entering his chambers, he discovered his assistant, Polton, in the act of transferring boiling water from a copper kettle to a small silver teapot; whereby he was able to infer that his approach had been observed by the said Polton from his lookout in the laboratory above. The two men, master and man, exchanged friendly greetings, and Thorndyke then observed:

"I have got a job to do later on, Polton, when I have finished up the evening's work. I shall want to grind some small sections of a mineral that I wish to identify. Would you put out one or two small hones and the other things that I shall need?"

"Yes, sir," replied Polton. "I will put the mineral section outfit on a tray and bring it down after tea. But can't I grind the sections? It seems a pity for you to be wasting your time on a mechanical job like that."

"Thank you, Polton," replied Thorndyke. "Of course you could cut the sections as well as, or better than, I can. But it is possible that I may have to produce the sections in evidence, and in that case it will be better if I can say that I cut them myself and that they were never out of my own hands. The courts don't know you as I do, you see, Polton."

Polton acknowledged the compliment with a gratified smile, and departed to the laboratory. As soon as he was gone, Thorndyke brought forth the little cardboard box, and, having taken out the button, carried it over to the window, where, with the aid of his pocket lens, he made a long and careful examination of the worm-tube, the result of which was to confirm his original observation. The mineral particles of which the tube was built up were of various shapes and sizes, from mere sand-grains up to quite respectable little pebbles. But, so far as he could see, they were all of a similar material. What that material was an expert mineralogist would have been able, no doubt, to say offhand, and an expert opinion would probably have to be obtained. But in the meantime his own knowledge was enough to enable him to form a fairly reliable opinion when he had made the necessary investigations.

As he drank his tea, he reflected on this extraordinary windfall. Circumstances had conspired in the most singular manner against Varney. How much they had conspired remained to be seen. That depended on how much the worm-tube had to tell. But even if no further light were thrown on the matter by the nature of the mineral, there was evidence enough that Purcell had never landed at Penzance. The Terebella had already given that much testimony. And the cross-examination was yet to come.

Having finished tea, he fell to work on the reports and written opinions which had to be completed and sent off by the last post; and it was characteristic of the man that, though the button and its as yet half-read message lurked in the subconscious part of his mind as the engrossing object of interest, he was yet able to concentrate the whole of his conscious attention on the matters with which he was outwardly occupied. Twice during the evening Polton stole silently into the room, once to deposit on a side-table the little tray containing the mineral section appliances, and the second time to place on a small table near the fire a large tray bearing the kind of frugal, informal supper that Thorndyke usually consumed when alone and at work.

"If you wait a few moments, Polton, I shall have these letters ready for the post. Then we shall both be free. I don't want to see anybody tonight unless it is something urgent."

"Very well, sir," replied Polton. "I will switch the bell on to the laboratory, and I'll see that you are not disturbed unnecessarily."

With this he took up the letters which Thorndyke had sealed and stamped and reluctantly withdrew, not without a last wistful glance at the apparatus on the tray.

As the door closed behind him, Thorndyke rose, and, bringing forth the button from the drawer in which he had bestowed it, began operations at once. First, with a pair of fine forceps he carefully picked off the worm-tube half a dozen of the largest fragments and laid them on a glass slide. This he placed on the stage of the microscope, and, having fitted on a two inch objective, made a preliminary inspection under various conditions of light, both transmitted and reflected. When he had got clearly into his mind the general character of the unknown rock, he fetched from a store cabinet in the office a number of shallow drawers filled with labelled specimens of rocks and minerals, and he also placed on the table in readiness for reference one or two standard works on geology and petrology. But before examining either the books or the specimens in the drawers, he opened out a geological chart of the British Isles and closely scrutinized the comparatively small area with which the button was concerned – the Land's End and the north and south coast of Cornwall. A very brief scrutiny of the map showed him that the inquiry could now be narrowed down to a quite small group of rocks, the majority of which he could exclude at once by his own knowledge of the more familiar types; which was highly satisfactory. But there was evidently something more than this. Anyone who should have been observing him as he pored over the chart would have seen, by a suddenly increased attention, with a certain repressed eagerness, that some really illuminating fact had come into view; and his next proceedings would make clear to such an observer that the problem had already changed from one of search to a definite and particular identification.

From the chart he turned to the drawers of specimens, running his eye quickly over their contents, as if looking for some specific object; and this object he presently found in a little cardboard tray – a single fragment of a grey, compact rock, which he pounced upon at once, and, picking it out of its tray, laid it on the slide with the fragment from the worm-tube. Careful comparison gave the impression that they were identical in character, but the great difference in the size of the fragments compared was a source of possible error. Accordingly, he wrapped the specimen lightly in paper, and with a hammer from the tool drawer struck it a sharp blow, which broke it into a number of smaller fragments, some of them quite minute. Picking out one or two of the smallest from the paper and carefully noting the "conchoidal" character of the fracture, he placed them on a separate slide, which he at once labelled "stock specimen," labelling the other slide "worm-tube." Having taken this precaution against possible confusion, he laid the two slides on the stage of the microscope and once more made a minute comparison. And again the conclusion emerged that the fragments from the worm-tube were identical in all their characters with the fragment of the stock specimen.

It now remained to test this conclusion by more exact methods. Two more labelled slides having been prepared, Thorndyke laid them, label downwards, on the table and dropped on each a large drop of melted Canada balsam. In one drop, while it was still soft, he immersed two or three fragments from the worm-tube; in the other a like number of fragments of the stock specimen. Then he heated both slides over a spirit-lamp to liquefy the balsam and completely immerse the fragments, and laid them aside to cool while he prepared the appliances for grinding the sections.

This process was, as Polton had hinted, a rather tedious one. It consisted in rubbing the two slides backwards and forwards upon a wetted Turkey stone until the fragments of rock were ground to a flat surface. The flattened surfaces had then to be polished upon a smoother stone, and when this had been done the slides were once more heated over a spirit-lamp, the balsam liquefied, and each of the fragments neatly turned over with a needle on to its flat side. When the balsam was cool and set hard, the grinding process was repeated until each of the fragments was worn down to a thin plate or film with parallel sides. Then the slides were again heated, a fresh drop of balsam applied, and a cover-glass laid on top. The specimens were now finished and ready for examination.

On this, the final stage of the investigation, he bestowed the utmost care and attention. The two specimens were examined exhaustively and compared again and again by every possible method, including the use of the polariscope and the spectroscope, and the results of each observation were at once written down.

Finally, Thorndyke turned to the books of reference, and, selecting a highly technical work on petrology, checked his written notes by the very detailed descriptions that it furnished of rocks of volcanic origin. And once again the results were entirely confirmatory of the opinion that he had at first formed. No doubt whatever was left in his mind as to the nature of the particles of rock of which the worm had built its tube. But if his opinion was correct, he held evidence producible in a court of law that Daniel Purcell had never landed at Penzance; that, in fact, his dead body was even now lying at the bottom of the sea.

As he consumed his frugal supper, Thorndyke turned over the situation in his mind. He had no doubts at all. But it would be necessary to get his identification of the rock confirmed by a recognized authority who could be called as a witness, and whose statement would be accepted by the court as establishing the facts. There was no difficulty about that. He had a friend who was connected with the Geological Museum, and who was recognized throughout the world as a first-class authority on everything relating to the physical and chemical properties of rocks and minerals. He would take the specimens tomorrow to this expert, and ask him to examine them; and when the authoritative opinion had been pronounced, he would consider what procedure he should adopt. Already there was growing up in his mind a doubt as to the expediency of taking action on purely scientific evidence, and in answer to that doubt a new scheme began to suggest itself.

But for the moment he put it aside. The important thing was to get the expert identification of the rock, and so put his evidence on the basis of established fact. The conversion of scientific into legal evidence was a separate matter that could be dealt with later. And having reached this conclusion, he took a sheet of notepaper from the rack and wrote a short letter to his friend at the Museum, making an appointment for the following afternoon. A few minutes later he dropped it into the box of the Fleet Street post office, and for the time being dismissed the case from his mind.

CHAPTER FOURTEEN

In Which Mr Varney is Disillusioned

Thorndyke's visit to the Geological Museum was not a protracted affair, for his friend, Mr Burston, made short work of the investigation.

"You say you have examined the specimens yourself," said he. "Well, I expect you know what they are; just come to me for an official confirmation, h'm? However, don't tell me what your conclusion was. I may as well start with an open mind. Write it down on this slip of paper and lay it on the table face downwards. And now let us have the specimens."

Thorndyke produced from his pocket a cigar-case, from which he extracted a pill-box and the labelled microscope-slide.

"There are two little water-worn fragments in the pill-box," he explained, "and three similar ones which I have ground into sections. I am sorry the specimens are so small, but they are the largest I had."

Mr Burston took the pill-box, and, tipping the two tiny pebbles into the palm of his hand, inspected them through a Coddington lens.

"M'yes," said he; "I don't think it will be very difficult to decide what this is. I think I could tell you offhand. But I won't. I'll put it through the regular tests and make quite sure of it; and meanwhile you had better have a browse round the Museum."

He bustled off to some inner sanctum of the curator's domain, and Thorndyke adopted his advice by straying out into the galleries. But he had little opportunity to study the contents of the cases, for in a few minutes Mr Burston returned with a slip of paper in his hand.

"Now," he said facetiously, as they re-entered the room, "you see there's no deception."

He laid his slip of paper on the table beside Thorndyke's, and invited the latter to "turn up the cards." Thorndyke accordingly turned over the two slips of paper. Each bore the single word "phonolite."

"I knew you had spotted it," said Burston. "However, you have now got corroborative evidence, and I suppose you are happy. I only hope I haven't helped to send some poor devil to chokee or worse. Goodbye. Glad you brought the things to me."

He restored the pill-box and slide, and having shaken hands heartily returned to his lair, while Thorndyke went forth into Jermyn Street and took his way thoughtfully eastward.

In a scientific sense the Purcell case was now complete. But the more he thought about it the more did he feel the necessity for bringing the scheme of evidence into closer conformity with traditional legal practice. Even to a judge a purely theoretical train of evidence might seem inconclusive; to a jury, who had been well pounded by a persuasive counsel, it would probably appear quite unconvincing. It would be necessary to obtain corroboration along different lines and in a new direction; and the direction in which it would be well to explore in the first place was the ancient precinct of Lincoln's Inn, where, at 62, Old Buildings, Mr John Rodney had his professional chambers.

Now, at the very moment when Thorndyke was proceeding with swift strides from the neighbourhood of Jermyn Street towards Lincoln's Inn on business of the most critical importance to Mr Varney, it was decreed by the irony of Fate that the latter gentleman should be engaged in bringing his affairs to a crisis of another kind. For some time past he had been watching with growing impatience the dilatory proceedings of the lawyers in regard to Margaret's petition. Especially had he chafed at the farce of the private detective, searching, as he knew, for a man whose body was lying on the bed of the sea hundreds of miles away from the area of the search. He was deeply disappointed, too. For when his advertisement scheme had been adopted by Thorndyke, he had supposed that all was plain sailing; he had but to send the necessary letter, and the dissolution of the marriage could be proceeded with at once. That was how it had appeared to him. And as soon as the marriage was dissolved he would make his declaration, and in due course his heart's desire would be accomplished.

Very differently had things turned out. Months had passed, and not a sign of progress had been made. The ridiculous search for the missing man − ridiculous to him only, however − dragged on interminably, and made him gnash his teeth in secret. His omniscience was now a sheer aggravation; for it condemned him to look on at the futile activities that Barnby had suggested and Rodney initiated, recognizing all their futility, but unable to utter a protest. To a man of his temperament it was maddening.

But there was another source of trouble. His confidence in Margaret's feelings towards him had been somewhat shaken of late. It had seemed to him there had been a change in her bearing towards him − a slight change, subtle and indefinable, but a change. She seemed as friendly, as cordial as ever; she welcomed his visits and appeared always glad to see him, and yet there was a something guarded, so he felt, as if she were consciously restraining any further increase of intimacy.

The thought of it troubled him profoundly. Of course, it might be nothing more than a little extra carefulness, due to her equivocal position. She had need to keep clear of anything in the slightest degree compromising; that he realized clearly. But still, the feeling lurked in his mind that she had changed, at least in manner, and sometimes he was aware of a horrible suspicion that he might have been over-confident. More than once he had been on the point of saying something indiscreet, and as time went on he felt ever growing a yearning to have his doubts set at rest.

On this present occasion he was taking tea with Margaret by invitation, with the ostensible object of showing her a set of etchings of some of the picturesque corners of Maidstone. He always enjoyed showing her his works, because he could see that she enjoyed looking at them; and these etchings of her native town would, he knew, have a double appeal.

"What a lovely old place it is!" she exclaimed as she sipped her tea with her eyes fixed on the etchings that Varney had placed before her on a music-stand. "Why is it, Mr Varney, that an etching or a drawing of any kind is so much more like the place than a photograph? It can't be a question of accuracy, for the photograph is at least as accurate as a drawing, and contains a great deal more detail."

"Yes," agreed Varney, "and that is probably, the explanation. An artist puts down what he sees and what anyone else would see and recognize. A photograph puts down what is there, regardless of how the scene would look to a spectator. Consequently, it is full of irrelevant detail, which gets in the way of the real effect as the eye would see it; and it may show appearances that the eye never sees at all, as in the case of Muybridge's instantaneous photographs of galloping horses. A photograph of a Dutch clock might catch the pendulum in the middle of its swing, and then the clock would appear to have stopped. But an artist would always draw it at the end of its swing, where it pauses for an instant, and that is where the eye sees it when the clock is going."

"Yes, of course," said Margaret; "and now I understand why your etchings of the old streets and lanes show just the streets and lanes that I remember, whereas the photographs that I have all look more or less strange and unfamiliar. I suppose they are full of details that I never noticed; but your etchings pick out and emphasize the things that I used to look at with pleasure and which live in my memory. It is a long time since I have been to Maidstone. I should like to see it again; indeed, I am not sure that, if I were free to choose, I shouldn't like to live there again. It is a dear old town."

"Yes; isn't it? But you say 'if you were free to choose.' Aren't you free to choose where you will live?"

"In a sense I am, I suppose," she replied; "but I don't feel that I can make any definite arrangements for the future until – well, until I know what my own future is to be."

"But surely you know that now. You have got that letter of Dan's. That practically releases you. The rest is only a matter of time and legal formalities. If Jack Rodney had only got Penfield or some other solicitor to get the case started as soon as you had that letter, you would have had your decree by now and have been your own mistress. At least, that is my feeling on the subject. Of course, I am not a lawyer, and I may be wrong."

"I don't think you are," said Margaret. "I have thought the same all along, and I fancy Mr Rodney is beginning to regret that he did not follow Dr Thorndyke's advice and rely on the letter only. But he felt that he could hardly go against Mr Barnby, who has had so much experience in this kind of practice. And Mr Barnby was very positive that the letter was not enough."

"Yes, Barnby has crabbed the whole business; and now after all these months you are just where you were, excepting that you have dropped a lot of money on this ridiculous private detective. Can't you get Rodney to send the fellow packing and get the case started in earnest?"

"I am inclined to think that he is seriously considering that line of action, and I hope he is. Of course, I have not tried to influence him in the matter. It is silly for a lay person to embarrass a lawyer by urging him to do this or that against his judgment. But I must say that I have grown rather despondent as the time has dragged on and nothing has been done, and I shall be very relieved when a definite move is made. I have an impression that it will be quite soon."

"That is good hearing," exclaimed Varney, "because when a move is made it can't fail to be successful. How can it? On that letter Dan could offer no defence, and it is pretty obvious that he has no intention of offering any. And if there is no defence the case must go in your favour."

"Unless the judge suspects collusion, as Mr Barnby seems to think he may."

"But," protested Varney, "judges don't give their decisions on what they suspect, do they? I thought they decided on the evidence. Surely collusion would have to be proved like anything else; and it couldn't be, because there has been no collusion. And I don't see why anyone should suspect that there has been."

"I agree with you entirely, Mr Varney," said Margaret, "and I do hope you are right. You are making me feel quite encouraged."

"I am glad of that," said he, "and I am encouraging myself at the same time. This delay has been frightfully disappointing. I had hoped that by this time the affair would have been over and you would have been free. However, we may hope that it won't be so very long now."

"It will take some months, in any case," said Margaret.

"Yes, of course," he admitted; "but that is a mere matter of waiting. We can wait patiently when we see the end definitely in view. And what a relief it will be when it is over! Just think of it! When the words are spoken and the shackles are struck off! Won't that be a joyful day?"

As Varney was speaking, Margaret watched him furtively and a little uneasily. For there had come into his face an expression that she had seen more than once of late – an expression that filled her gentle soul with forebodings of trouble for this impulsive, warm-hearted friend. And now the note of danger was heightened by something significant in the words that he had used – something that expressed more than mere friendly solicitude.

"It will certainly be a relief when the whole business is over," she said quietly; "and it is most kind and sympathetic of you to take such a warm interest in my future."

"It isn't kind at all," he replied, "nor particularly sympathetic. I feel that I am an interested party. In a sense, your future is my future."

He paused for a few moments, and she looked at him in something like dismay. Vainly she cast about for some means of changing the current of the conversation, of escaping to some less perilous topic. Before she had time to recover from her confusion, he looked up at her and burst out passionately:

"Maggie, I want to ask you a question. I know I oughtn't to ask it, but you must try to forgive me. I can't bear the suspense any longer. I think about it day and night, and it is eating my heart out. What I want to ask you is this: When it is all over – when that blessed day comes and you are free, will you – can I hope that you may be willing to listen to me if I ask you to let me be your devoted servant, your humble worshipper, and to try to make up to you by love and faithful service all that has been missing from your life in the past? For years – for many years, Maggie – I have been your friend – a friend far more loving and devoted than you have ever guessed, for in those days I hardly dared to dream even of intimate friendship. But now the barrier between us is no longer immovable. Soon it will be cast down for ever. And then – can it be, Maggie, that my dream will come true? That you will grant me a lifelong joy by letting me be the guardian of your happiness and peace?"

For a moment there had risen to Margaret's face a flush of resentment, but it faded almost instantly and was gone, extinguished by a deep sense of the tragedy of this unfortunate but real and great passion. She had always liked Varney, and she had recognized and valued his quiet, unobtrusive friendship and the chivalrous deference with which he had been used to treat her. And now she was going to make him miserable, to destroy his cherished hopes of a future made happy in the realization of his great love for her. The sadness of it left no room for resentment, and her eyes filled as she answered unsteadily:

"You know, Mr Varney, that, as a married woman, I have no right to speak or think of the making of a new marriage. But I feel that your question must be answered; and I wish, dear Mr Varney, I wish from my heart that it could be answered differently. I have always valued your friendship – with very good reason; and I value your love, and am proud to have been thought worthy of it. But I cannot accept it. I can never accept it. It is dreadful to me, dear friend, to make you unhappy – you whom I like and admire so much. But it must be so. I have nothing but friendship to offer you, and I shall never have."

"Why do you say you will never have, Maggie?" he urged. "May it not be that you will change? That the other will come if I wait long enough? And I will wait patiently – wait until I am an old man if need be, so that only the door is not shut. I will never weary you with importunities, but just wait your pleasure. Will you not let me wait and hope, Maggie?"

She shook her head sadly. "No, Mr Varney" she answered. "Believe me, it can never be. There is nothing to wait for. There will be no change. The future is certain so far as that. I am so sorry, dear generous friend. It grieves me to the heart to make you unhappy. But what I have said is final. I can never say anything different."

Varney looked at her in incredulous despair. He could not believe in this sudden collapse of all his hopes; for his doubts of her had been but vague misgivings, born of impatience and unrest. But suddenly a new thought flashed into his mind.

"How do you know that?" he asked. "Why are you so certain? Is there anything now that you know of that – that must keep us apart for ever? You know what I mean, Maggie. Is there anything?"

She was silent for a few moments. Naturally, she was reluctant to disclose to another the secret that she had held so long locked in her own heart, and that even now she dared but to whisper to herself. But she felt that to this man, whose love she must reject and whose happiness she must shatter, she owed a sacred duty. He must not be allowed to wreck his life if a knowledge of the truth would save him.

"I will tell you, Mr Varney," she said. "You know how I came to marry Dan?"

"I think so," he replied. "He never told me, but I guessed."

"Well, if I had not married Dan I should have married John Rodney. There was no engagement and nothing was said; but we were deeply attached to one another, and we both understood. Then circumstances compelled me to marry Dan. Mr Rodney knew what those circumstances were. He cherished no resentment against me. He did not even blame me. He has remained my friend ever since, and he has formed no other attachment. I know that he has never forgotten what might have been, and neither have I. Need I say any more?"

Varney shook his head. "No," he replied gruffly. "I understand."

For some moments there was a deep silence in the room. Margaret glanced timidly at her companion, shocked at the sudden change in his appearance. In a moment all the enthusiasm, the eager vivacity, had died out of his face, leaving it aged, drawn, and haggard. He had understood, and his heart was filled with black despair. At a word all his glorious dream-castles had come crashing down, leaving the world that had been so sunny a waste of dust and ashes. So he sat for a while silent, motionless, stunned by the suddenness of the calamity. At length he rose and began, in a dull, automatic way, to collect his etchings and bestow them in his portfolio. When he had secured them and tied the ribbons of the portfolio, he turned to Margaret and, standing before her, looked earnestly in her face.

"Good-bye, Maggie," he said in a strange, muffled voice; "I expect I shan't see you again for some time."

She stood up, and with a little smothered sob held out her hand. He took it in both of his and, stooping, kissed it reverently.

"Good-bye again," he said, still holding her hand. "Don't be unhappy about me. It couldn't be helped. I shall often think of you and of how sweet you have been to me today; and I shall hope to hear soon that you have got your freedom. And I do hope to God that Rodney will make you happy. I think he will. He is a good fellow, an honest man, and a gentleman. He is worthy of you, and I wish you both long years of happiness."

He kissed her hand once more, and then, releasing it, made his way gropingly out into the hall and to the door. She followed him with the tears streaming down her face, and watched him, as she had watched him once before, descending the stairs. At the landing he turned and waved his hand, and even as she returned his greeting he was gone. She went back to the drawing-room still weeping silently, very sad at heart at this half-foreseen tragedy. For the time being, she could see, Varney was a broken man. He had come full of hope and he had gone away in despair; and something seemed to hint – it may have been the valedictory tone of his last words – that she had looked on him for the last time, that the final wave of his hand was a last farewell.

Meanwhile Varney, possessed by a wild unrest, hurried through the streets, yearning, like a wounded animal, for the solitude of his lair. He wanted to shut himself in his studio and be alone with his misery. Presently he hailed a taxicab, and from its window gazed out impatiently to measure its progress. Soon it drew up at the familiar entry, and when he had paid the driver he darted in and shut the door; but hardly had he attained the sanctuary that he had longed for than the same unrest began to engender a longing to escape. Up and down the studio he paced, letting the unbidden thoughts surge chaotically through his mind, mingling the troubled past with the future of his dreams – the sunny future that might have been – and this with the empty reality that lay before him.

On the wall he had pinned an early proof of the aquatint that Thorndyke had liked and that he himself rather liked. He had done it partly from bravado and partly as a memorial of the event that had set both him and Maggie free. Presently he halted before it and let it set the tune to his meditations. There was the lighthouse looking over the fog-bank just as it had looked on him when he was washing the bloodstain from the deck. By that time Purcell was overboard, at the bottom of the sea. His oppressor was gone. His life was now his own, and her life was her own.

He looked at the memorial picture, and in a moment it seemed to him to have become futile. The murder itself was futile, so far as he was concerned, though it had set Maggie free. To what purpose had he killed Purcell? It had been to ensure a future for himself; and behold! there was to be no future for him after all. Thus in the bitterness of his disappointment he saw everything out of proportion and in false perspective. He forgot that it was not to win Margaret but to escape from the clutches of his parasite that he had pulled the trigger on that sunny day in June. He forgot that he had achieved the very object that was in his mind when he fired the shot: freedom to live a reputable life safe from the menace of the law. His passion for Margaret had become so absorbing that it had obscured all the other purposes of his life; and now that it was gone, it seemed to him that nothing was left.

As he stood thus gloomily reflecting with his eyes fixed on the little picture, he began to be aware of a new impulse. The lighthouse, the black-sailed luggers, the open sea, seemed to take on an unwonted friendliness. They were the setting of something besides tragedy. There, in Cornwall, he had been happy in a way despite the abiding menace of Purcell's domination. There, at Sennen, he had lived under the same roof with her, had sat at her table, had been her guest and her accepted friend. It had not really been a happy period, but memory, like the sundial, numbers only the sunny hours, and Varney looked back on it with wistful eyes. At least his dream had not been shattered then. So, as he looked at the picture, he felt stirring within him a desire to go back and look upon those scenes again. Falmouth and Penzance and Sennen – especially Sennen – seemed to draw him. He wanted to look out across the sea to the Longships, and in the gathering gloom of the horizon to see the diamond and the ruby sparkle as they did that evening when he and the distant lighthouse seemed to hold secret converse.

It was, perhaps, a strange impulse. Whence it came he neither knew nor asked. It may have been the effect of memory and association. It may have been mere unrest. Or it may have been that a dead hand beckoned to him to come. Who shall say? He only knew that he was sensible of the impulse, and that it grew from moment to moment.

To a man in his condition, to feel an impulse is to act on it. No sooner was he conscious of the urge to go back and look upon the well-remembered scenes than he began to make his simple preparations for the journey. Like most experienced travellers he travelled light. Most of his kit, including his little case of sketching materials, was in the studio. The rest could be picked up at his lodgings *en route* for Paddington. Within ten minutes of his having formed the resolve to go, he stood on the threshold, locking the studio door from without with the extra key that he used when he was absent for more than a day. At the outer gate he paused to pocket the key, and stood for a few moments with his portmanteau in his hand, looking back at the studio with a curiously reflective air. Then, at last, he turned and went on his way. But if he could have looked, as the clairvoyant claims to look, through the bricks and mortar of London, he might at this very time have seen Dr John Thorndyke striding up Chancery Lane from Fleet Street; might have followed him to the great gateway of Lincoln's Inn (on the masonry whereof tradition has it that Ben Jonson worked as a bricklayer), and seen him pass through into the little square beyond, and finally plunge into the dark and narrow entry of one of the ancient red brick houses that have looked down upon the square for some three or four centuries – an entry on the jamb of which was painted the name of Mr John Rodney.

But Varney was not a clairvoyant, and neither was Thorndyke. And so it befell that each of them went his way unconscious of the movements of the other.

CHAPTER FIFTEEN

In Which Thorndyke Opens the Attack

As Thorndyke turned the corner at the head of the stairs, he encountered Philip Rodney with a kettle in his hand, which he had apparently been filling at some hidden source of water.

"This is a bit of luck," said Philip, holding out his disengaged hand – "for me, at least; not, perhaps, for you. I have only just arrived, and Jack hasn't come over from the courts yet. I hope this isn't a business call."

"In a sense it is," replied Thorndyke, "as I am seeking information. But I think you can probably tell me all I want to know."

"That's all right," said Philip. "I'll just plant 'Polly' on the gas-stove, and while she is boiling we can smoke a preparatory pipe and you can get on with the examination-in-chief. Go in and take the presidential chair."

Thorndyke entered the pleasant, homely room, half office, half sitting-room, and seating himself in the big armchair began to fill his pipe. In a few moments Philip entered, and sat down on a chair which commanded a view of the tiny kitchen and of "Polly," seated on a gas-ring.

"Now," said he, "fire away. What do you want to know?"

"I want," replied Thorndyke, "to ask you one or two questions about your yacht."

"The deuce you do!" exclaimed Philip. "Are you thinking of going in for a yacht yourself?"

"Not at present," was the reply. "My questions have reference to that last trip that Purcell made in her, and the first one is: When you took over the yacht after that trip, did you find her in every respect as she was before? Was there anything missing that you could not account for, or any change in her condition, or anything about her that was not quite as you expected it to be?"

Philip looked at his visitor with undissembled surprise. "Now I wonder what makes you ask that. Have you any reason to expect that I should have found any change in her condition?"

"If you don't mind," said Thorndyke, "we will leave that question unanswered for the moment. I would rather not say, just now, what my object is in seeking this information. We can go into that later. Meanwhile, do you mind just answering my questions as if you were in the witness-box?"

A shade of annoyance crossed Philip's face. He could not imagine what possible concern Thorndyke could have with his yacht, and he was inclined to resent the rather cryptic attitude of his questioner. Nevertheless, he answered readily:

"Of course I don't mind. But, in fact, there is nothing to tell. I don't remember noticing anything unusual about the yacht, and there was nothing missing, so far as I know."

"No rope or cordage of any kind, for instance?"

"No – at least, nothing to speak of. A new ball of spun-yarn had been broached. I noticed that, and I meant to ask Varney what he used it for. But there wasn't a great deal of it gone, and I know of nothing else. Oh, wait! If I am in the witness-box I must tell the whole truth, be it never so trivial. There was a mark or stain or dirty smear of some kind on the jib. Is that any good to you?"

"Are you sure it wasn't there before that day?"

"Quite. I sailed the yacht myself the day before, and I will swear that the jib was spotlessly clean then. So the mark must have been made by Purcell or Varney, because I noticed it the very next day."

"What was the mark like?"

"It was just a faint wavy line, as if some dirty water had been spilt on the sail and allowed to dry partly before it was washed off."

"Did you form any opinion as to how the mark might have been caused?"

Philip struggled, not quite successfully, to suppress a smile. To him there seemed something extremely ludicrous in this solemn interrogation concerning these meaningless trifles. But he answered as gravely as he could:

"I could only make a vague guess. I assumed that it was caused in some way by the accident that occurred. You may remember that the jib-halyard broke, and the sail went overboard and got caught under the yacht's forefoot. That is when it must have happened. Perhaps the sail may have picked some dirt off the keel. Usually a dirty mark on the jib means mud on the fluke of the anchor, but it wasn't that. The anchor hadn't been down since it was scrubbed. The yacht rode at moorings in Sennen Cove. However, there was the mark; how it came there you are as well able to judge as I am."

"And that is all you know; this mark on the sail and the spun-yarn? There is no other cordage missing?"

"No, not so far as I know."

"And there is nothing else missing? No iron fittings or heavy objects of any kind?"

"Good Lord, no! How should there be? You don't suspect Purcell of having hooked off with one of the anchors in his pocket, do you?"

Thorndyke smiled indulgently, but persisted in his questions.

"Do you mean that you know there was nothing missing, or only that you are not aware of anything being missing?"

The persistence of the questions impressed Philip with a sudden suspicion that Thorndyke had something definite in his mind, that he had some reason for believing that something had been removed from the yacht. He ventured to suggest this to Thorndyke, who answered frankly enough:

"You are so far right, Philip, that I am not asking these questions at random. I would rather not say more than that just now."

"Very well," said Philip; "I won't press you for an explanation. But I may say that we dismantled the yacht in rather a hurry, and hadn't time to check the inventory, so I can't really say whether there was anything missing or not. But you have come at a most opportune time, for it happens that we had arranged to go over to the place where she is laid up, at Battersea, tomorrow afternoon for the very purpose of checking the inventory and generally overhauling the boat and the gear. If you care to come over with us, or meet us there, we can settle your questions quite definitely. How will that suit you?"

"It will suit me perfectly," replied Thorndyke. "If you will give me the address and fix a time, I will meet you there."

"It is a disused wharf with some empty workshops," said Philip. "I will write down the directions, and if you will be at the gate at three o'clock tomorrow, we can go through the gear and fittings together."

Thorndyke made a note of the whereabouts of the wharf, and having thus despatched the business on which he had come, he took an early opportunity to depart, not having any great desire to meet John Rodney and be subjected to the inevitable cross-examination. He could see that Philip was, naturally enough, extremely curious as to the object of his inquiries, and he preferred to leave the two brothers to discuss the matter. On the morrow his actions would be guided by the results, if any, of the survey of the yacht.

Three o'clock on the following afternoon found him waiting at a large wooden gate in a narrow thoroughfare close to the river. On the pavement by his side stood the green canvas-covered "research case," which was his constant companion whenever he went abroad on professional business. It contained a very complete outfit of such reagents and apparatus as he might require in a preliminary investigation; but on the present occasion its usual contents had been reinforced by two large bottles, to obtain which Polton had

193

that morning made a special visit to a wholesale chemist's in the Borough.

A church clock somewhere across the river struck the hour, and almost at the same moment John and Philip Rodney emerged from a tributary alley and advanced towards the gate.

"You are here first, then," said Philip, "but we are not late. I heard a clock strike a moment ago."

He produced a key from his pocket, with which he unlocked a wicket in the gate, and, having pushed it open, invited Thorndyke to enter. The latter passed through, and the two brothers followed, locking the wicket after them, and conducted Thorndyke across a large yard to a desolate-looking wharf, beyond which was a stretch of unreclaimed shore. Here, drawn up well above high-water mark, a small, sharp-sterned yacht stood on chocks under a tarpaulin cover.

"This is the yacht," said Philip, "but there is nothing on board of her. All the stores and gear and loose fittings are in the workshop behind us. Which will you see first?"

"Let us look at the gear," replied Thorndyke; and they accordingly turned towards a large disused workshop at the rear of the wharf.

"Phil was telling me about your visit last night," said Rodney, with an inquisitive eye on the research case, "and we are both fairly flummoxed. He gathered that these inquiries of yours are in some way connected with Purcell."

"Yes, that is so. I want to ascertain whether, when you resumed possession of the yacht after Purcell left her, you found her in the same condition as before, and whether her stores, gear, and fittings were intact."

"Did you suppose that Purcell might have taken some of them away with him?"

"I thought it not impossible," Thorndyke replied.

"Now, I wonder why on earth you should think that," said Rodney, "and what concern it should be of yours if he had."

Thorndyke smiled evasively. "Everything is my concern," he replied. "I am an Autolycus of the Law, a collector of miscellaneous trifles of evidence and unclassifiable scraps of information."

"Well," said Rodney, with a somewhat sour smile, "I have no experience of legal curiosity shops and oddment repositories. But I don't know what you mean by 'evidence.' Evidence of what?"

"Of whatever it may chance to prove," Thorndyke replied blandly.

"What did you suppose Purcell might have taken with him?" Rodney asked, with a trace of irritability in his tone.

"I had thought it possible that there might be some cordage missing and perhaps some iron fittings or other heavy objects. But, of course, that is mere surmise. My object is, as I have said, to ascertain whether the yacht was in all respects in the same condition when Purcell left her as when he came on board."

Rodney gave a grunt of impatience; but at this moment Philip, who had been wrestling with a slightly rusty lock, threw open the door of the workshop, and they all entered. Thorndyke looked curiously about the long, narrow interior with its prosaic contents, so little suggestive of the tragedy which his thoughts associated with them. Overhead the yacht's spars rested on the tie-beams, from which hung bunches of blocks; on the floor reposed a long row of neatly painted half-hundredweights, a pile of chain cable, two anchors, a stove, and other oddments such as water-breakers, buckets, mops, etc.; and on the long benches at the side folded sails, locker cushions, sidelight lanterns, the binnacle, the cabin lamp, and other more delicate fittings. After a long look round, in the course of which his eye travelled along the row of ballast-weights, Thorndyke deposited his case on a bench and asked:

"Have you still got the broken jib-halyard that Philip was telling me about last night?"

"Yes," answered Rodney; "it is here under the bench."

He drew out a coil of rope, and, flinging it on the floor, began to uncoil it, when it separated into two lengths.

"Which are the broken ends?" asked Thorndyke.

"It broke near the middle," replied Rodney, "where it chafed on the cleat when the sail was hoisted. This is the one end, you see, frayed out like a brush in breaking, and the other – " He picked up the second half, and passing it rapidly through his hands held up the end. He did not finish the sentence, but stood, with a frown of surprise, staring at the rope in his hand.

"This is queer," he said, after a pause. "The broken end has been cut off. Did you cut it off, Phil?"

"No," replied Philip; "it is just as I took it from the locker, where, I suppose, you or Varney stowed it."

"I wonder," said Thorndyke, "how much has been cut off. Do you know what the original length of the rope was?"

"Yes," replied Rodney; "forty-two feet. It is down in the inventory, but I remember working it out. Let us see how much there is here."

He laid the two lengths of rope along the floor, and with Thorndyke's spring tape carefully measured them. The combined length was exactly thirty-one feet.

"So," said Thorndyke, "there are eleven feet missing without allowing for the lengthening of the rope by stretching."

The two brothers glanced at one another, and both looked at Thorndyke with very evident surprise.

"Well," said Philip, "you seem to be right about the cordage. But what made you go for the jib-halyard in particular?"

"Because if any cordage had been cut off it would naturally be taken from a broken rope in preference to a whole one."

"Yes, of course. But I can't understand how you came to suspect that any rope was missing at all."

"We will talk about that presently," said Thorndyke. "The next question is as to the iron fittings, chain, and so forth."

"I don't think any of those can be missing," said Rodney. "You can't very well cut a length of chain off with your pocket-knife."

"No," agreed Thorndyke, "but I thought you might have some odd piece of chain among the ballast."

"We have no chain except the cable. Our only ballast is in the form of half-hundredweights. They are handier to stow than odd stuff."

"How many half-hundredweights have you?"

"Twenty-four," replied Rodney.

"There are only twenty-three in that row," said Thorndyke. "I counted them as we came in and noted the odd number."

The two brothers simultaneously checked Thorndyke's statement and confirmed it. Then they glanced about the floor of the workshop, under the benches, and by the walls; but the missing weight was nowhere to be seen, nor was there any place in which an object of this size could have got hidden.

"It is very extraordinary," said Philip. "There is certainly one weight missing. And no one has handled them but Jack and I. We hired a barrow and brought up all the gear ourselves."

"There is just the chance," said Thorndyke, "that one of them may have been overlooked and left in the yacht's hold."

"It is very unlikely," replied Philip, "seeing that we took out the floor-boards, so that you can see the whole of the bilges from end to end. But I will run down and make sure."

He ran out, literally, and crossing the wharf disappeared over the edge. In a couple of minutes he was back, breathing fast, and evidently not a little excited.

"It isn't there," he said. "Of course it couldn't be. But the question is, what has become of it? It is a most mysterious affair."

"It is," agreed Rodney. "And what is still more mysterious is that Thorndyke seemed to suspect that it was missing even before he came here. Now didn't you, Thorndyke?"

"I suspected that some heavy object was missing, as I mentioned," was the reply, "and a ballast-weight was a likely object. By the way, can you fix a date on which you know that all the ballast-weights were in place?"

"Yes, I think I can," replied Philip. "A few days before Purcell went to Penzance we beached the yacht to give her a scrape. Of course we had to take out the ballast, and when we launched her again I helped to put it back. I am certain that all the weights were there then, because I counted them after they were stowed in their places."

"Then," said Thorndyke, "it is virtually certain that they were all on board when Purcell and Varney started from Sennen."

"I should say it is absolutely certain," said Philip.

Thorndyke nodded gravely and appeared to reflect a while. But his reflections were broken in upon by John Rodney.

"Look here, Thorndyke, we have answered your questions and given you facilities for verifying certain opinions that you held, and now it is time that you were a little less reserved with us. You evidently connected the disappearance of this rope and this weight in some way with Purcell. Now, we are all interested in Purcell. You have got something up your sleeve, and we should like to know what that something is. It is perfectly obvious that you don't imagine that Purcell, when he went up the pier ladder at Penzance, had a couple of fathoms of rope and a half-hundredweight concealed about his person."

"As a matter of fact," said Thorndyke, "I don't imagine that Purcell ever went up the ladder at Penzance at all."

"But Varney saw him go up," protested Philip.

"Varney says he saw him go up," Thorndyke corrected. "I do not accept Mr Varney's statement."

"Then what on earth do you suggest?" demanded Philip. "And why should Varney say what isn't true?"

"Let us sit down on this bench," said Thorndyke, "and thrash the matter out. I will put my case to you, and you can give me your criticisms on it. I will begin by stating that some months ago I came to the conclusion that Purcell was dead."

Both the brothers started and gazed at Thorndyke in utter astonishment. Then Rodney said:

"You say 'some months ago.' You must mean within the last three months."

"No," replied Thorndyke. "I decided that he died on the 23rd of last June, before the yacht reached Penzance."

An exclamation burst simultaneously from both of his hearers, and Rodney protested impatiently:

"But this is sheer nonsense, if you will pardon me for saying so. Have you forgotten that two persons have received letters from him less than four months ago?"

"I suggest that we waive those letters and consider the other evidence."

"But we can't waive them!" exclaimed Rodney. "They are material evidence of the most conclusive kind."

"I may say that I have ascertained that both those letters were forgeries. The evidence can be produced, if necessary, as both the letters are in existence, but I don't propose to produce it now. I ask you to accept my statement for the time being and to leave the letters out of the discussion."

"It is leaving out a good deal," said Rodney. "I find it very difficult to believe that they were forgeries or to imagine who on earth could have forged them. However, we won't contest the matter now. When did you come to this extraordinary conclusion?"

"A little over four months ago," replied Thorndyke.

"And you never said anything to any of us on the subject," said Rodney, "and, what is more astonishing, you actually put in an advertisement, addressed to a man whom you believed to be dead."

"And got an answer from him," added Philip, with a derisive smile.

"Exactly," said Thorndyke. "It was an experiment, and it was justified by the result. But let us get back to the matter that we have been investigating. I came to the conclusion, as I have said, that Purcell met his death during that voyage from Sennen to Penzance, and that Varney, for some reason, had thought it necessary to conceal the occurrence; but I decided that the evidence in my possession would not be convincing in a court of law."

"I have no doubt that you were perfectly right in that," Rodney remarked dryly.

"I further considered it very unlikely that any fresh evidence would ever be forthcoming, and that, since the death could not be proved, it was, for many reasons, undesirable that the question should ever be raised. Accordingly, I never communicated my belief to anybody."

"Then," said Rodney, "are we to understand that some new evidence has come to light, after all?"

"Yes. It came to light the other day at the College of Surgeons. I dare say Philip told you about it."

"He told me that, by an extraordinary coincidence, that quaint button of Purcell's had turned up, and that some sort of sea-worm had built a tube on it. But if that is what you mean, I don't see the bearing of it as evidence."

"Neither do I," said Philip.

"You remember that Varney distinctly stated that when Purcell went up the ladder at Penzance he was wearing his oilskin coat, and that the button was then on it?"

"Yes. But I don't see anything in that. Purcell went ashore, it is true, and he went away from Cornwall. But he seems to have gone by sea, and, as I suggested the other day, he probably got a fresh button when he went on board the steamer and chucked this cork one overboard."

"I remember your making that suggestion," said Thorndyke, "and very much astonished I was to hear you make it. I may say that I have ascertained that Purcell was never on board that steamer."

"Well, he might have thrown it into the sea somewhere else. There is no particular mystery about its having got into the sea. But what was there about my suggestion that astonished you so much?"

"It was," replied Thorndyke, "that you completely overlooked a most impressive fact which was staring you in the face and shouting aloud for recognition."

"Indeed!" said Philip. "What fact was it that I overlooked?"

"Just consider," replied Thorndyke, "what it was that Professor D'Arcy showed us. It was a cork button with a Terebella tube on it. Now an ordinary cork, if immersed long enough, will soak up water until it is waterlogged and then sink to the bottom. But this one was impregnated with paraffin wax. It could not get waterlogged and it could not sink. It would float for ever."

"Well?" queried Philip.

"But it *had* sunk. It had been lying at the bottom of the sea for months – long enough for a Terebella to build a tube on it. Then at last it had broken loose, risen to the surface and drifted ashore."

"You are taking the worm-tube as evidence," said John Rodney, "that the button had sunk to bottom. Is it impossible – I am no naturalist – but is it impossible that the worm could have built its tube while the button was floating about in the sea?"

"It is quite impossible," replied Thorndyke, "in the case of this particular worm, since the tube is built up of particles of rock gathered by the worm from the sea bottom. You will bear me out in that, Philip?"

"Oh, certainly," replied Philip. "There is no doubt that the button has been at the bottom for a good many months. The question is how the deuce it can have got there, and what was holding it down."

"You are not overlooking the fact that it is a button," said Thorndyke – "I mean that it was attached to a garment?"

Both men looked at Thorndyke a little uncomfortably. Then Rodney replied:

"Your suggestion obviously is that the button was attached to a garment and that the garment contained a body. I am disposed to concede the garment, since I can think of no other means by which the button could have been held down, but I see no reason for assuming the body. I admit that I do not quite understand how Purcell's oilskin coat could have got to the bottom of the sea, but still less can I imagine how Purcell's body could have got to the bottom of the sea. What do you say, Phil?"

"I agree with you," answered Philip. "Something must have held the button down, and I can think of nothing but the coat to which it was attached. But as to the body, it seems a gratuitous assumption, to say nothing of the various reasons for believing that Purcell is still alive. There is nothing wildly improbable in the supposition that the coat might have blown overboard and been sunk by something heavy in the pocket. As a matter of fact, it would have sunk by itself as soon as it got thoroughly soaked. You must admit, Thorndyke, that that is so."

But Thorndyke shook his head. "We are not dealing with general probabilities," said he. "We are dealing with a specific case. An empty oilskin coat, even if sunk by some object in the pocket, would have been comparatively light, and, like all moderately light bodies, would have drifted about the sea bottom, impelled by currents and tide-streams. But that is not the condition in the present case. There is evidence that this button was moored immovably to some very heavy object."

"What evidence is there of that?" demanded Rodney.

"There is the conclusive fact that it has been all these months lying continuously in one place."

"Indeed!" said Rodney, with hardly concealed scepticism. "That seems a bold thing to say. But if you know that it has been lying all the time in one place, perhaps you can point out the spot where it has been lying."

"As a matter of fact I can," said Thorndyke. "That button, Rodney, has been lying all these months on the sea bottom at the base of the Wolf Rock."

The two brothers started very perceptibly. They stared at Thorndyke, then looked at one another, and then Rodney challenged the statement.

"You make this assertion very confidently," he said. "Can you produce any evidence to support it?"

"I can produce perfectly convincing and conclusive evidence," replied Thorndyke. "A very singular conjunction of circumstances enables us to fix with absolute certainty the place where that button has been lying. Do you happen to be acquainted with the peculiar resonant volcanic rock known as phonolite or clink-stone?"

Rodney shook his head a little impatiently. "No," he answered; "I have never heard of it before."

"It is not a very rare rock," said Thorndyke, "but in the neighbourhood of the British Isles it occurs in only two places. One is inland in the North, and may be disregarded. The other is the Wolf Rock."

Neither of his hearers made any comment on this statement, though it was evident that both were deeply impressed, and he continued:

"This Wolf Rock is a very remarkable structure. It is what is called a 'volcanic neck' – that is, it is a mass of altered lava that once filled the funnel of a volcano. The volcano has disappeared, but this cast of the funnel remains standing up from the bottom of the sea like a great column. It is a single mass of phonolite, and thus entirely different in composition from the sea bed around or anywhere near these islands. But, of course, immediately at its base the sea bottom must be covered with decomposed fragments which have fallen from its sides, and it is with these fragments that our Terebella has built its tube. You remember, Philip, my pointing out to you, as we walked home from the College, that the worm-tube appeared to be built of fragments that were all alike. Now, that was a very striking and significant fact. It furnished *prima facie* evidence that the button had been moored in one place, and that it had therefore been attached to some very heavy object. That night I made an exhaustive examination of the material of the tube, and then the further fact emerged that the material was phonolite. This, as I have said, fixed the locality with exactness and certainty. And I may add that, in view of the importance of the matter in an evidential sense, I submitted the fragments yesterday to one of the greatest living authorities on petrology, who recognized them at once as phonolite."

For some time after Thorndyke had finished speaking the two brothers sat wrapped in silent reflection. Both were deeply impressed, but each in a markedly different way. To John Rodney, the lawyer, accustomed to sworn testimony and documentary evidence, this scientific demonstration appeared amazingly ingenious but somewhat fantastic and unconvincing. In the case of Philip, the doctor, it was quite otherwise. Accustomed to acting on inferences from facts of his own observing, he gave full weight to each item of evidence, and his thoughts were already stretching out to the as yet unstated corollaries.

John Rodney was the first to speak. "What inference," he asked, "do you wish us to draw from this very ingenious theory of yours?"

"It is rather more than a theory," said Thorndyke, "but we will let that pass. The inference I leave to you; but perhaps it would help you if I were to recapitulate the facts."

"Perhaps it would," said Rodney.

"Then," said Thorndyke, "I will take them in their order. This is the case of a man who was seen to start on a voyage for a given destination in company with one other man. His start out to sea was witnessed by a number of persons. From that moment he was never seen again by any person excepting his one companion. He is said to have reached his destination, but his arrival there rests upon the unsupported verbal testimony of one person, the said companion. Thereafter he vanished utterly, and since then has made no sign of being alive; he has drawn no cheques, though he has a considerable balance at his bank; he has communicated with no one, and he has never been seen by anybody who could recognize him."

"Is that quite correct?" interposed Philip. "He is said to have been seen at Falmouth and Ipswich, and then there are those letters."

"His alleged appearance, embarking at Falmouth and disembarking at Ipswich," replied Thorndyke, "rest, like his arrival at Penzance, upon the unsupported testimony of one person, his sole companion on the voyage. That statement I can prove to be untrue. He was never seen either at Falmouth or at Ipswich. As to the letters, I can prove them both to be forgeries, and for the present I ask you to admit them as such pending the production of proof. But if we exclude the alleged appearances and the letters, what I have said is correct: from the time when this man put out to sea from Sennen he has never been seen by anyone but Varney, and there has never been any corroboration of Varney's statement that he landed at Penzance.

"Some eight months later a portion of this man's clothing is found. It bears evidence of having been lying at the bottom of the sea for many months, so that it must have sunk to its resting-place within a very short time of the man's disappearance. The place where it has been lying is one over, or near, which the man must have sailed in the yacht. It has been moored to the bottom by some very heavy object, and a very heavy object has disappeared from the yacht. That heavy object had apparently not disappeared when the yacht started, and it is not known to have been on the yacht afterwards. The evidence goes to show that the disappearance of that object coincided in time with the disappearance of the man, and a quantity of cordage disappeared certainly on that day.

"Those are the facts at present in our possession with regard to the disappearance of Daniel Purcell, to which we may add that the disappearance was totally unexpected, that it has never been explained or accounted for excepting in a letter which is a manifest forgery, and that even in the latter, apart from the fictitious nature of the letter, the explanation is utterly inconsistent with all that is known of the missing man in respect of his character, his habits, his intentions, and his circumstances."

CHAPTER SIXTEEN

In Which John Rodney is Convinced

Once more, as Thorndyke concluded, there was a long, uncomfortable silence, during which the two brothers cogitated profoundly and with a very disturbed expression. At length John Rodney spoke.

"There is no denying, Thorndyke, that the body of circumstantial evidence that you have produced and expounded so skilfully and lucidly is extraordinarily complete. Of course, it is subject to your being able to prove that Varney's reports as to Purcell's appearance at Falmouth and Ipswich were false reports, and that the letters which purported to be written and sent by Purcell were in fact not written or sent by him. If you can prove those assertions, there will undoubtedly be a very formidable case against Varney, because those reports and those letters would then be evidence that someone was endeavouring to prove, falsely, that Purcell is alive. But this would amount to presumptive evidence that he is not alive, and that someone has reasons for concealing the fact of his death. But we must look to you to prove what you have asserted. You could hardly suggest that we should charge a highly respectable gentleman of our acquaintance with having murdered his friend and made away with the body – for that is obviously your meaning – on a mass of circumstantial evidence, which is, you must admit, rather highly theoretical."

"I agree with you completely," replied Thorndyke. "The evidence respecting the reports and the letters is obviously essential. But in the meantime it is of the first importance that we carry this investigation to an absolute finish. It is not merely a question of justice or our duty on grounds of public policy to uncover a crime and secure the punishment of the criminal. There are individual rights and interests to be guarded – those, I mean, of the missing man's wife. If her husband is dead common justice to her demands that his death should be proved and placed on public record."

"Yes, indeed," Rodney agreed heartily. "If Purcell is dead, then she is a widow, and the petition becomes unnecessary. By the way, I understand now why you were always so set against the private detective, but what I don't understand is why you put in that advertisement."

"It is quite simple," was the reply. "I wanted another forged letter, written in terms dictated by myself – and I got it."

"Ha!" exclaimed Rodney. And now, for the first time, he began to understand how Thorndyke had got his great reputation.

"You spoke just now," Rodney continued, "of carrying this investigation to a finish. Haven't you done so? Is there anything more to investigate?"

"We have not yet completed our examination of the yacht," replied Thorndyke. "The facts that we have elicited enable us to make certain inferences concerning the circumstances of Purcell's death – assuming his death to have occurred. We infer, for instance, that he did not fall overboard, nor was he pushed overboard. He met his death on the yacht, and it was his dead body which was cast into the sea with the sinker attached to it. That we may fairly infer. But we have, at present, no evidence as to the way in which he came by his death. Possibly a further examination of the yacht may show some traces from which we may form an opinion. By the way, I have been looking at that revolver that is hanging from the beam. Was that on board at the time?"

"Yes," answered Rodney. "It was hanging on the cabin bulkhead. Be careful," he added, as Thorndyke lifted it from its hook. "I don't think it has been unloaded."

Thorndyke opened the breech of the revolver, and, turning out the cartridges into his hand, peered down the barrel and into each chamber separately. Then he looked at the cartridges in his hand.

"This seems a little odd," he remarked. "The barrel is quite clean and so is one chamber, but the other five chambers are extremely foul. And I notice that the cartridges are not all alike. There are five Eleys and one Curtis and Harvey. That is quite a suggestive coincidence."

Philip looked with a distinctly startled expression at the little heap of cartridges in Thorndyke's hand, and, picking out the odd one, examined it with knitted brows.

"When did you fire the revolver last, Jack?" he asked, looking up at his brother.

"On the day when we potted at those champagne bottles," was the reply.

Philip raised his eyebrows. "Then," said he, "this is a very remarkable affair. I distinctly remember on that occasion, when we had sunk all the bottles, reloading the revolver with Eleys, and that there were then three cartridges left over in the bag. When I had loaded I opened the new box of Curtis and Harvey's, tipped them into the bag, and threw the box overboard."

"Did you clean the revolver?" asked Thorndyke.

"No, I didn't. I meant to clean it later, but forgot to."

"But," said Thorndyke, "it has undoubtedly been cleaned, and very thoroughly as to the barrel and one chamber. Shall we check the cartridges in the bag? There ought to be forty-nine Curtis and Harveys and three Eleys if what you have told us is correct."

Philip searched among the raffle on the bench, and presently unearthed a small linen bag. Untying the string, he shot out on the bench a heap of cartridges, which he counted one by one. There were fifty-two in all, and three of them were Eleys.

"Then," said Thorndyke, "it comes to this: since you used that revolver it has been used by someone else. That someone fired only a single shot after which he carefully cleaned the barrel and the empty chamber and reloaded. Incidentally, he seems to have known where the cartridge-bag was kept, but he did not know about the change in the make of cartridges or that the revolver had not been cleaned. You notice, Rodney," he added, "that the circumstantial evidence accumulates."

"I do, indeed," Rodney replied gloomily. "Is there anything else that you wish to examine?"

"Yes; there is the sail. Philip mentioned a stain on the jib. Shall we see if we can make anything of that?"

"I don't think you will make much of it," said Philip. "It is very faint. However, you shall see it and judge for yourself."

He picked out one of the bundles of white duck, and while he was unfolding it Thorndyke dragged an empty bench into the middle of the floor under the skylight. Over this the sail was spread so that the mysterious mark was in the middle of the bench. It was very inconspicuous – just a faint grey-green, wavy line, like the representation of an island on a map. The three men looked at it curiously for a few moments, then Thorndyke asked:

"Would you mind if I made a further stain on the sail? I should like to apply some reagents."

"Of course you must do what is necessary," said Rodney. "The evidence is more important than the sail."

On this Thorndyke opened his research case and brought forth the two bottles that Polton had procured from the Borough, of which one was labelled "Tinct. Guaiaci Dil." and the other "Aether Ozon." As they emerged from the case, Philip read the labels with evident surprise, remarking:

"I shouldn't have thought that the guaiacum test would be of any use after all these months, especially as the sail seems to have been scrubbed."

"It will act, I think, if the pigment or its derivatives is there," said Thorndyke; and as he spoke he poured a quantity of the tincture on the middle of the stained area. The pool of liquid rapidly spread considerably beyond the limits of the stain, growing paler as it extended. Then Thorndyke cautiously dropped small quantities of the ozonic ether at various points around the stained area, and watched closely as the two liquids mingled in the fabric of the sail. Gradually the ether spread towards the stain, and, first at one point and then at another, approached and finally crossed the wavy grey line; and at each point the same change occurred: first the faint grey line turned into a strong blue line, and then the colour extended to the enclosed space until the entire area of the stain stood out a conspicuous blue patch. Philip and Thorndyke looked at one another significantly, and the latter said: "You understand the meaning of this reaction, Rodney; this is a bloodstain, and a very carefully washed bloodstain."

"So I supposed," Rodney replied; and for a while no one spoke.

There was something very dramatic and solemn, they all felt, in the sudden appearance of this staring blue patch on the sail with the sinister message that it brought. But what followed was more dramatic still. As they stood silently regarding the blue stain, the mingled liquids continued to spread; and suddenly, at the extreme edge of the wet area, they became aware of a new spot of blue. At first a mere speck, it grew slowly, as the liquid spread over the canvas, into a small oval, and then a second spot appeared by its side. At this point Thorndyke poured out a fresh charge of the tincture, and when it had soaked into the cloth cautiously applied a sprinkling of ether. Instantly the blue spots began to elongate; fresh spots and patches appeared, and as they ran together there sprang out of the blank surface the clear impression of a hand – a left hand, complete in all its details excepting the third finger, which was represented by a round spot at some two-thirds of its length.

The dreadful significance of this apparition, and the uncanny and mysterious manner of its emergence from the white surface, produced a most profound impression on all the observers, but especially on Rodney, who stared at it with an expression of the utmost horror, but spoke not a word. His brother was hardly less appalled, and when he at length spoke it was in a hushed voice that was little above a whisper.

"It is horrible," he murmured. "It seems almost supernatural, that accusing hand springing into existence out of the blank surface after all this time. I wonder," he added, after a pause, "why the third finger made no mark, seeing that the others are so distinct."

"I think," said Thorndyke, "that the impression is there. That small round spot looks like the mark of a finger-tip, and its position rather suggests a finger with a stiff joint."

As he made this statement, both brothers simultaneously uttered a smothered exclamation.

"It is Varney's hand!" gasped Philip. "You recognize it, Jack, don't you? That is just where the tip of his stiff finger would come. Have you ever noticed Varney's left hand, Thorndyke?"

"You mean the ankylosed third finger? Yes; and I agree with you that this is undoubtedly the print of Varney's hand."

"Then," said Rodney, "the case is complete. There is no need for any further investigation. On the evidence that is before us, to say nothing of the additional evidence that you can produce, there cannot be the shadow of a doubt that Purcell was murdered by Varney and his body sunk in the sea. You agree with me, I am sure, Thorndyke?"

"Certainly," was the reply. "I consider the evidence so far conclusive that I have not the slightest doubt on the subject."

"Very well," said Rodney. "Then the next question is, what is to be done? Shall I lay a sworn information or will you? Or had we better go to the police together and make a joint statement?"

"Whatever we do," replied Thorndyke, "don't, let us be premature. The evidence, as you say, is perfectly convincing. It leaves us with no doubt as to what happened on that day last June. It would probably be, in an intellectual sense, quite convincing to a judge. It might even be to a jury. But would it be sufficient to secure a conviction? I think it extremely doubtful."

"Do you really?" exclaimed Philip. "I should have thought it impossible that anyone who had heard the evidence could fail to come to the inevitable conclusion."

"You are probably right," said Thorndyke. "But a jury who are trying an accused person on a capital charge have got to arrive at something more than a belief that the accused is guilty. They have got to be convinced that there is, humanly speaking, no possible doubt as to the prisoner's guilt. No jury would give an adverse verdict on a balance of probabilities, nor would any judge encourage them to do so."

"But surely," said Philip, "this is something more than a mere balance of probabilities. The evidence all points in the same direction, and there is nothing to suggest a contrary conclusion."

Thorndyke smiled dryly. "You might think differently after you have heard a capable counsel for the defence. But the position is this: we are dealing with a charge of murder. Now, in order to prove that a particular person is guilty of murder it is necessary first to establish the *corpus delicti*, as the phrase goes – that is, to prove that a murder has been committed by someone. But the proof that a person has been murdered involves the antecedent proof that he is dead. If there is any doubt that the alleged deceased is dead, no murder charge can be sustained. But proof of death usually involves the production of the body or of some identifiable part of it, or at least the evidence of some person who has seen it and can swear to its identity. There are exceptional cases, of course, and this might be accepted as one. But you can take it that the inability of the prosecution to produce the body or any part of it, or any witness who can testify to having seen it, or any direct evidence that the person alleged to have been murdered is actually dead, would make it extremely difficult to secure the conviction of the accused."

"Yes, I see that," said Philip. "But, after all, that is not our concern. If we give the authorities all the information that we possess, we shall have done our duty as citizens. As to the rest, we must leave the court to convict or acquit, according to its judgment."

"Not at all," Thorndyke dissented. "You are losing sight of our position in the case. There are two different issues, which are, however, inseparably connected. One is the fact of Purcell's death, the other is Varney's part in compassing it. Now it is the first issue that concerns us, or at least concerns me. If we could prove that Purcell is dead without bringing Varney into it at all, I should be willing to do so; for I strongly suspect that there were extenuating circumstances."

"So do I," said Rodney. "Purcell was a brute, whereas Varney has always seemed to be a perfectly decent, gentlemanly fellow."

"That is the impression that I have received," said Thorndyke, "and I feel no satisfaction in proceeding against Varney. My purpose all along has been, not to convict Varney but to prove that Purcell is dead. And that is what we have to do now, for Margaret Purcell's sake. But we cannot leave Varney out of the case. For if Purcell is dead, he is dead because Varney killed him; and our only means of proving his death is to charge Varney with having murdered him. But if we charge Varney we must secure a conviction. We cannot afford to fail. If the court is convinced that Purcell is dead, it will convict Varney, for the evidence of his death is evidence of his murder; but if the court acquits Varney, it can do so only on the ground that there is no conclusive evidence that Purcell is dead. Varney's acquittal would therefore leave Margaret Purcell still bound by law to a hypothetical husband, with the insecure chance of obtaining her release at some future time either by divorce or presumption of death. That would not be fair to her. She is a widow, and she is entitled to have her status acknowledged."

Rodney nodded gloomily. A consciousness of what he stood to gain by Varney's conviction lent an uncomfortable significance to Thorndyke's words.

"Yes," he agreed, half reluctantly, "there is no denying the truth of what you say, but I wish it might have been the other way about.

If Purcell had murdered Varney I could have raised the hue and cry with a good deal more enthusiasm. I knew both the men well, and I liked Varney but detested Purcell. Still, one has to accept the facts."

"Exactly," said Thorndyke, who had realized and sympathized with Rodney's qualms. "The position is not of our creating, and whatever our private sentiments may be, the fact remains that a man who elects to take the life of another must accept the consequences. That is Varney's position so far as we can see, and if he is innocent it is for him to clear himself."

"Yes, of course," Rodney agreed; "but I wish the accusation had come through different channels."

"So do I," said Philip. "It is horrible to have to denounce a man with whom one has been on terms of intimate friendship. But apparently Thorndyke considers that we should not denounce him at present. That is what I don't quite understand. You seemed to imply, Thorndyke, that the case was not complete enough to warrant our taking action, and that some further evidence ought to be obtained in order to make sure of a conviction. But what further evidence is it possible to obtain?"

"My feeling," replied Thorndyke, "is that the case is at present, as your brother expressed it just now, somewhat theoretical, or, rather, hypothetical. The evidence is circumstantial from beginning to end. There is not a single item of direct evidence to furnish a starting-point. It would be insisted by the defence that Purcell's death is a matter of mere inference, and that you cannot convict a man of the murder of another who may conceivably be still alive. We ought, if possible, to put Purcell's death on the basis of demonstrable fact."

"But how is that possible?" demanded Philip.

"The conclusive method of proving the death of a person is, as I have said, to produce that person's body or some recognizable part of it."

"But Purcell's body is at the bottom of the sea."

"True. But we know its whereabouts. It is a small area, with the lighthouse as a landmark. If that area were systematically worked over with a trawl or dredge, or, better still, with a set of creepers attached to a good-sized spar, there should be a very fair chance of recovering the body, or at least the clothing and the weight."

Philip reflected for a few moments. "I think you are right," he said at length. "The body appears, from what you say, to be quite close to the Wolf Rock, and almost certainly on the east side. With a good compass and the lighthouse as a sailing mark, it would be possible to ply up and down and search every inch of the bottom in the neighbourhood of the Rock."

"There is only one difficulty," said Rodney. "Your worm-tube was composed entirely of fragments of the Rock. But how large an area of the sea bottom is covered with those fragments? We should have to ascertain that if we are to work over the whole of it."

"It would not be difficult to ascertain," replied Thorndyke. "If we take soundings with a hand-lead as we approach the Rock, the samples that come up on the arming of the lead will tell us when we are over a bottom covered with phonolite débris."

"Yes," Rodney agreed, "that will answer if the depth is within the range of a hand-lead. If it isn't we shall have to rig the tackle for a deep-sea lead. It will be rather a gruesome quest. Do I gather that you are prepared to come down with us and lend a hand? I hope you are."

"So do I!" exclaimed Philip. "We shall be quite at home with the navigation, but if – er – if anything comes up on the creepers, it will be a good deal more in your line than ours."

"I should certainly wish to come," said Thorndyke, "and, in fact, I think it rather desirable that I should, as Philip suggests. But I can't get away from town just at present, nor, I imagine, can you. We had better postpone the expedition for a week or so until the commencement of the spring vacation. That will give us time to make the necessary arrangements, to charter a suitable boat, and so forth. And, in any case, we shall have to pick our weather, having regard to the sort of sea that one may encounter in the neighbourhood of the Wolf."

"Yes," agreed Philip, "it will have to be a reasonably calm day when we make the attempt, so I suggest that we put it off until you and Jack are free; and meanwhile I will get on with the preliminary arrangements, the hiring of the boat and getting together the necessary gear."

While they had been talking the evening had closed in, and the workshop was now almost in darkness. It being too late for the brothers to carry out the business that had brought them to the wharf, even if they had been in a state of mind suitable to the checking of inventories, they postponed the survey to a later date, locked up the workshop, and in company with Thorndyke made their way homeward.

CHAPTER SEVENTEEN

In Which There is a Meeting and a Farewell

It was quite early on a bright morning at the beginning of April when Thorndyke and the two Rodneys took their way from their hotel towards the harbour of Penzance. Philip had been in the town for a day or two, completing the arrangements for the voyage of exploration; the other two had come down from London only on the preceding evening.

"I hope the skipper will be punctual," said Philip. "I told him to meet us on the pier at eight o'clock sharp. We want to get off as early as possible, for it is a longish run out to the Rock, and we may have to make a long day of it."

"We probably shall," said Rodney. "The Wolf Rock is a good departure for purposes of navigation, but when it comes to finding a spot of sea bottom only a foot or two in extent, our landmark isn't very exact. It will take us a good many hours to search the whole area."

"I wonder," said Thorndyke, "what took them out there. According to Varney's description and the evidence of the button, they must have had the Rock close aboard. But it was a good deal out of their way from Sennen to Penzance."

"It was," agreed Philip. "But you can't make a bee-line in a sailing craft. That's why I chartered a motor-boat for this job. Under canvas you can only keep as near to your course as the wind will let you. But Purcell was a deuce of a fellow for sea room. He always liked to keep a good offing. I remember that on that occasion he headed straight out to sea and got well outside the Longships before he turned south. I watched the yacht from the shore, and wondered how much longer he was going to hold on. It looked as if he were heading for America. Then, you remember, the fog came down, and they may have lost their bearings a bit; and the tides are pretty strong about here."

"Yes," said Thorndyke, "and as we may take it that the trouble, whatever it was, came to a head while they were enveloped in fog, it is likely that the yacht was left to take care of herself for a time, and may have drifted a good deal off her course. At any rate, it is clear that at one time she had the Rock right under her lee, and must have drifted past within a few feet."

"It would have been a quaint position," said Philip, "if she had bumped on to it and gone to the bottom. Then they would have kept one another company in Davy Jones' locker."

"It would have saved a lot of trouble if they had gone down together," his brother remarked. "But from what you have just said, Thorndyke, it seems that you have a more definite idea as to the position of the body than I thought. Where do you suppose it to be?"

"Judging from all the facts taken together," replied Thorndyke, "I should say that it is lying close to the base of the Rock on the east side. We have it from Varney that the yacht drifted down towards the Rock during the fog, and I gathered that she drifted past close to the east side. And we also learned from him that the jib had then come down, which was, in fact, the cause of her being adrift. But the bloodstains on the sail prove that the tragedy occurred either before the halyard broke or while the sail was down – almost certainly the latter. And we may take it that it occurred during the fog; that the fog created the opportunity; for we must remember that they were close to the lighthouse, and therefore, apart from the fog, easily within sight of it. For the same reason we may assume that the body was put overboard before the fog lifted. All these circumstances point to the body being close to the Rock, and the worm-tube emphatically confirms that inference."

"Then," said Philip, "in that case there is no great point in taking soundings."

"Not in the first instance," Thorndyke agreed. "But if we get no result close to the Rock, we may have to sample the bottom to see how far from the base the conditions indicated by the worm-tube extend."

They walked on in silence for some time. Presently Rodney remarked:

"This reminds me of the last time I came down to a rendezvous on Penzance pier, when I expected to find Varney waiting for me and he wasn't there. I wonder where he was, by the way."

"He had probably gone to post a letter to Mr Penfield at some remote pillar-box, where collections were not too frequent," said Thorndyke.

Rodney looked at him quickly, once more astonished at his intimate knowledge of the details of the case. He was about to remark on it when Thorndyke asked:

"Have you seen much of Varney lately?"

"I haven't seen him at all," replied Rodney. "Have you, Phil?"

"No," replied Philip; "not for quite a long time. Which is rather odd, for he used to look in at Maggie's flat pretty often to have tea and show her his latest work. But he hasn't been there for weeks, I know, because I was speaking to her about him only a day or two ago. She seemed to have an idea that he might have gone away on a sketching tour, though I don't think she had anything to go on."

"He can't have smelt a rat and cleared out," mused Rodney. "I don't see how he could, though I shouldn't be altogether sorry if he had. It will be a horrid business when we have to charge him and give evidence against him. But it isn't possible that he can have seen or heard anything."

This was also Thorndyke's opinion, but he was deeply interested in the report of Varney's disappearance. Nor was he entirely without a clue to it. His observations of Margaret and Varney suggested a possible explanation, which he did not think it necessary to refer to. And, in fact, the conversation was here interrupted by their arrival at the pier, where an elderly fisherman, who had been watching their approach, came forward and saluted them.

"Here you are then, skipper," said Philip; "Punctual to the minute. We've got a fine day for our trip, haven't we?"

"Ay, sir," replied the skipper; " 'tis a wonderful calm day for the time of year. And glad I am to see it, if we are to work close into the Wolf, for it's a lumpy bit of water at the best of times around the Rock."

"Is everything ready?" asked Philip.

"Ay, sir. We are all ready to cast off this moment," and in confirmation he preceded the party to the head of the ladder, and indicated the craft lying alongside the pier beneath it – a small converted Penzance lugger with a large open cockpit, in the fore part of which was the engine.

The four men descended the ladder, and while the skipper and the second fisherman, who constituted the crew, were preparing to cast off the shore ropes, Philip took a last look round to see that all was in order. Then the crew, who was named Joe Tregenna, pushed off and started the engine, the skipper took the tiller, and the boat got under way.

"You see," said Philip, as the boat headed out to sea, "we have got good strong tackle for the creeping operations."

He pointed over the boat's side to a long stout spar which was slung outside the bulwarks. It was secured by a chain bridle to a trawl-rope, and to it were attached a number of creepers – lengths of chain fitted with rows of hooks – which hung down into the water and trailed alongside. The equipment also included a spirit-compass, fitted with sight-vanes; a sextant; a hand-lead, which lay on the cockpit floor, with its line neatly coiled round it; and a deep-sea lead, stowed away forward with its long line and the block for lowering and hoisting it.

The occupants of the cockpit were strangely silent. It was a beautiful spring day, bright and sunny, with a warm blue sky overhead and a tranquil sea, heaving quietly to the long swell from the Atlantic, showing a sunlit sparkle on the surface and clear sapphire in the depths. "Nature painted all things gay," excepting the three men who sat on the side benches of the cockpit, whose countenances were expressive of the deepest gravity and even, in the case of the two Rodneys, of profound gloom.

"I shall be glad when this business is over," said Philip. "I feel as nervous as a cat."

"So do I," his brother agreed. "It is a gruesome affair. I find myself almost hoping that nothing will come of it. And yet that would only leave us worse off than ever."

"We mustn't be prepared to accept failure," said Thorndyke. "The thing is there, and we have got to find it; if not today, then tomorrow or some other day."

The two brothers looked at Thorndyke, a little daunted by his resolute attitude. "Yes, of course you are right," the elder admitted, "and it is only cowardice that makes me shrink from what we have to do. But when I think of what may come up, hanging from those creepers, I – bah! It is too horrible to think of! But I suppose it doesn't make that sort of impression on you? You don't find anything repulsive in the quest that we are engaged in?"

"No," Thorndyke admitted. "My attention is occupied by the scientific and legal interest of the search. But I can fully sympathize with your feelings on the matter. To you Purcell is a real person, whom you have known and talked with; to me he is a mere abstraction connected with a very curious and interesting case. The really unpleasant part of that case – to me – will come when we have completed our evidence, if we are so fortunate – I mean when we have to set the criminal law in motion."

"Yes," said Philip, "that will be perfectly beastly."

Once more silence fell upon the boat, broken only by the throb of the engine and the murmur of the water as it was cloven by the boat's stem. And meanwhile the distant coast slipped past until they were abreast of the Land's End, and far away to the south-west the solitary lighthouse rose on the verge of the horizon. Soon afterwards they began to overtake the scattered members of a fleet of luggers, some with lowered mainsails and hand-lines down, others with their black sails set, heading for some distant fishing-ground. Through the midst of them the boat was threading her way, when her occupants suddenly became aware that one of the smaller luggers was steering so as to close in. Observing this, the skipper was putting over the helm to avoid her, when a seafaring voice from the little craft was heard to hail.

"Motor-boat ahoy! Gentleman aboard wants to speak to you!"

The two Rodneys looked at one another in surprise and then at the approaching lugger.

"Who the deuce can it be?" exclaimed Rodney. "But perhaps it is a stranger who wants a passage. If it is we shall have to refuse. We can't take anyone on board."

The boat slowed down, for at a word from the skipper Joe Tregenna had reversed the propeller. The lugger closed in rapidly, watched anxiously by the two Rodneys and Thorndyke. Suddenly a man appeared standing on the bulwark rail and holding on by the mast stay, while with his free hand he held a binocular to his eyes. Nearer and nearer the lugger approached, and still the two Rodneys gazed with growing anxiety at the figure on the bulwark. At length the man removed the glasses from his eyes and waved them above his head, and as his face became visible both brothers uttered a cry of amazement.

"God!" exclaimed Philip. "It's Varney! Sheer off, skipper! Don't let him come alongside."

But it was too late. The boat had lost way and failed to answer her helm. The lugger sheered in, sweeping abreast within a foot, and as she crept past Varney sprang lightly from her gunwale and dropped on the side bench beside Jack Rodney.

"Well!" he exclaimed, "this is a queer meeting. I couldn't believe my eyes when I first spotted you through the glasses.

Motor-boat, too! Rather a come down, isn't it, for seasoned yachtsmen?"

He looked curiously at his hosts, evidently a little perplexed by their silence and their unresponsive bearing. The Rodneys were, in fact, stricken dumb with dismay, and even Thorndyke was for the moment disconcerted. The lugger which had brought Varney had already gone about and was standing out to sea, leaving to them the alternative of accepting this most unwelcome passenger or of pursuing the lugger and insisting on his returning on board of her. But the Rodneys were too paralyzed to do anything but gaze at Varney in silent consternation, and Thorndyke did not feel that his position on the boat entitled him to take any action. Indeed, no action seemed to be practicable.

"This is an odd show," said Varney, looking inquisitively about the boat. "What is the lay? You can't be going out to fish in this craft. And you seem to be setting a course for the Scillies. What is it? Dredging? I see you've got a trawl-rope."

As the Rodneys were still almost stupefied by the horror of the situation, Thorndyke took upon himself to reply.

"The occasion of this little voyage was a rather remarkable marine worm that was sent to Professor D'Arcy, and which came from the locality to which we are bound. We are going to explore the bottom there."

Varney nodded. "You seem mighty keen on marine worms. I remember when I met you down here before you were in search of them, and so was Phil, though I don't fancy he got many. He had the bottles labelled ready for them, and that was about as far as he went. Do you remember that button you made, Phil, from the cork of one?"

"Yes," Philip replied huskily, "I remember."

During this conversation Thorndyke had been observing Varney with close attention, and he noted a very appreciable change in his appearance. He looked aged and worn, and there was in his expression a weariness and dejection that seemed to confirm certain opinions that Thorndyke had formed as to the reasons for his sudden disappearance from surroundings which had certainly not been without their attractions to him. And, not for the first time, a feeling of compunction and of some distaste for this quest contended with the professional interest and the sense of duty that had been the impelling force behind the long, patient investigation.

Philip's curt reply was followed by a rather long, uncomfortable silence. Varney, quick and sensitive by nature, perceived that there was something amiss, that in some way his presence was a source of embarrassment. He sat on the side bench by Jack Rodney, gazing with a far-away look over the sea towards the Longships, wishing that he had stayed on board the lugger or that there were some means of escaping from this glum and silent company. And as he meditated he brought forth from his pocket his tobacco-pouch and cigarette-book, and half unconsciously, with a dexterity born of long practice, rolled a cigarette, all unaware that three pairs of eyes were riveted on his strangely efficient maimed finger, that three minds were conjuring up the vivid picture of a blue handprint on a white sail.

When he had lit the cigarette, Varney once more looked about the boat, and again his eye lighted on the big coil of trawl-rope, with its end passed out through a fair-lead. He rose, and, crossing the cockpit, looked over the side.

"Why," he exclaimed, "you've got a set of creepers! I thought you were going dredging. You won't pick up much with creepers, will you?"

"They will pick up anything with weeds attached to it," said Thorndyke.

Varney went back to his seat with a thoughtful, somewhat puzzled expression. He smoked in silence for a minute or two, and then suddenly asked:

"Where is the place that you are going to explore for these worms?"

"Professor D'Arcy's specimen," replied Thorndyke, "came from the neighbourhood of the Wolf Rock. That is where we are going to work."

Varney made no comment on this answer. He looked long and steadily at Thorndyke; then he turned away his head, and once more gazed out to sea. Evidently he was thinking hard, and his companions, who watched him furtively, could have little doubt as to the trend of his thoughts. Gradually, as the nature of the exploration dawned on him, his manner changed more and more. A horrible pallor overspread his face, and a terrible restlessness took possession of him. He smoked furiously cigarette after cigarette. He brought various articles out of his pockets, fidgeted with them awhile, and put them back. He picked up the hand-lead, looking at its arming, ran the line through his fingers, and made fancy knots on the bight. And ever and anon his glance strayed to the tall lighthouse, standing out of the sea with its red and white ringed tower, and drawing inexorably nearer and nearer.

So the voyage went on until the boat was within half a mile of the Rock, when Philip, having caught a glance and a nod from Thorndyke, gave the order to stop the engine and lower the creepers. The spar was cast loose and dropped into the water with a heavy splash, the trawl-rope ran out through the fair-lead, and meanwhile Jack Rodney took a pair of cross-bearings on the lighthouse and a point of the distant land. Then the engine was re-started, the boat moved forward at half-speed, and the search began.

It was an intensely disagreeable experience for all excepting the puzzled but discreet skipper and the unconscious Joe. Varney, pale, haggard, and wild in aspect, fidgeted about the boat, now silent and moody, now making miserable efforts to appear interested or unconcerned, picking up and handling loose objects or portions of the gear, but constantly returning to the hand-lead, counting up the "marks" on the line, or making and pulling out various knots with his restless but curiously skilful fingers. And as his mood changed, Thorndyke watched him furtively, as if to judge by his manner how near they were to the object of the search.

It was a long and wearisome quest. Slowly the boat plied up and down on the eastern side of the Rock, gradually approaching it nearer and nearer at each return. From time to time the creepers caught on the rocky bottom, and had to be eased off; from time to time the dripping trawl-rope was hauled in and the creepers brought to the surface, offering to the anxious eyes that peered over the side nothing on the hooks but, perchance, a wisp of Zostera or a clinging spider-crab.

Calm as the day was and quiet as was the ocean, stirred only by the slumberous echoes of the great Atlantic swell, the sea was breaking heavily over the Rock; and as the boat closed in nearer and nearer, the water around boiled and eddied in an unpleasant and even dangerous manner. The lighthouse keepers, who had for some time past been watching from the gallery the movements of the boat, now began to make warning signs, and one of them bellowed through a megaphone to the searchers to keep farther away.

"What do you say?" Rodney asked in a low voice. "We can't go any nearer? We shall be swamped or stove in? Shall we try another side?"

"Better try one more cast this side," said Thorndyke; and he spoke so definitely that all the others, including Varney, looked at him curiously. But no one answered, and as the skipper made no demur the creepers were dropped for a fresh cast still nearer the Rock. The boat was then to the north of the lighthouse, and the course set was to the south, so as to pass the Rock again on the east side. As they approached, the man with the megaphone bawled out fresh warnings and continued to roar at them and flourish his arm until they were abreast of the Rock in a wild tumble of confused waves. At this moment, Philip, who had his hand on the trawl-rope between the bollard and the fair-lead, reported that he had felt a pull, but that it seemed as if the creepers had broken away. As soon, therefore, as the boat was clear of the backwash and in comparatively smooth water, the order was passed to haul in the trawl-rope and examine the creepers.

The two Rodneys looked over the side eagerly but fearfully, for both had noticed something new – a definite expectancy – in Thorndyke's manner. Varney, too, who had hitherto taken but little notice of the creepers, now knelt on the sidebench, gazing earnestly into the clear water whence the trawl-rope was rising. And still he toyed with the hand-lead, and absently made clove-hitches on the line and slipped them over his arm.

At length the spar came into view, and below it, on one of the creepers, a yellowish object, dimly visible through the wavering water.

"There's somethin' on this time," said the skipper, craning over the side and steadying himself by the tiller, which he still held. All eyes were riveted on the half-seen yellowish shape, moving up and down to the rise and fall of the boat. Apart from the others, Varney knelt on the bench, not fidgeting now, but still, rigid, pale as wax, staring with dreadful fascination at the slowly rising object. Suddenly the skipper uttered an exclamation.

"Why, 'tis a sou'wester! And all laced about wi' spun-y'n! Surely 'tis – Steady, sir; you'll be overboard! My God!"

The others looked round quickly, and even as they looked Varney fell, with a heavy splash, into the water alongside. There was a tumultuous rush to the place whence he had fallen, and arms were thrust into the water in vain efforts to grasp the sinking figure. Rodney darted forward for the boat-hook, but by the time he was back with it the doomed man was far out of reach; yet for a long time, as it seemed, the horror-stricken onlookers could see him through the clear, blue-green water, sinking, sinking, growing paler, more shadowy more shapeless, but always steadily following the lead sinker, until at last he faded from their sight into the darkness of the ocean.

Not until some time after he had vanished did they haul on board the creeper with its dreadful burden. Indeed, that burden, in its entirety, was never hauled on board. As it reached the surface,

Tregenna stopped hauling and held the rope steady; and for a sensible time all eyes were fixed upon a skull, with a great jagged hole above the brows, that looked up at them beneath the peak of the sou'wester, through the web of spun-yarn, like the face of some phantom warrior looking out through the bars of his helmet. Then as Philip, reaching out an unsteady hand, unhooked the sou'wester from the creeper, the encircling coils of spun-yarn slipped, and the skull dropped into the water. Still the fascinated eyes watched it as it sank, turning slowly over and over, and seeming to cast back glances of horrid valediction; watched it grow green and pallid and small, until it vanished into the darkness, even as Varney had vanished.

When it was quite invisible, Philip turned, and, flinging the hat down on the floor of the cockpit, sank on the bench with a groan. Thorndyke picked up the hat and unwound the spun-yarn.

"Do you identify it?" he asked; and then, as he turned it over, he added: "But I see it identifies itself."

He held it towards Rodney, who was able to read in embroidered lettering on the silk lining "Dan Purcell."

Rodney nodded. "Yes," he said, "but, of course, there was no doubt. Is it necessary for us to do anything more?" He indicated the creepers with a gesture of weariness and disgust.

"No," replied Thorndyke. "We have seen the body and can swear to its identity, and I can certify as to the cause of death. We can produce this hat, with a bullet-hole, as I perceive, in the back, corresponding to the injury that we observed in the skull. I can also certify as to the death of Varney, and can furnish a sworn declaration of the facts that are within my knowledge. That may possibly be accepted by the authorities, having regard to the circumstances, as rendering any further inquiry unnecessary. But that is no concern of ours. We have established the fact that Daniel Purcell is dead, and our task is accomplished."

"Yes," said Rodney, "our quest has been successful beyond my expectations. But it has been an awful experience. I can't get the thought of poor Varney out of my mind."

"Nor I," said Philip. "And yet it was the best that could have happened. And there is a certain congruity in it, too. They are down there together. They had been companions, in a way, friends, the best part of their lives, and in death they are not divided."

R Austin Freeman

The D'Arblay Mystery
A Dr Thorndyke Mystery

When a man is found floating beneath the skin of a green-skimmed pond one morning, Dr Thorndyke becomes embroiled in an astonishing case. This wickedly entertaining detective fiction reveals that the victim was murdered through a lethal injection and someone out there is trying a cover-up.

Dr Thorndyke Intervenes
A Dr Thorndyke Mystery

What would you do if you opened a package to find a man's head? What would you do if the headless corpse had been swapped for a case of bullion? What would you do if you knew a brutal murderer was out there, somewhere, and waiting for you? Some people would run. Dr Thorndyke intervenes.

R Austin Freeman

Felo De Se
A Dr Thorndyke Mystery

John Gillam was a gambler. John Gillam faced financial ruin and was the victim of a sinister blackmail attempt. John Gillam is now dead. In this exceptional mystery, Dr Thorndyke is brought in to untangle the secrecy surrounding the death of John Gillam, a man not known for insanity and thoughts of suicide.

Flighty Phyllis

Chronicling the adventures and misadventures of Phyllis Dudley, Richard Austin Freeman brings to life a charming character always getting into scrapes. From impersonating a man to discovering mysterious trapdoors, *Flighty Phyllis* is an entertaining glimpse at the times and trials of a wayward woman.

R Austin Freeman

Helen Vardon's Confession
A Dr Thorndyke Mystery

Through the open door of a library, Helen Vardon hears an argument that changes her life forever. Helen's father and a man called Otway argue over missing funds in a trust one night. Otway proposes a marriage between him and Helen in exchange for his co-operation and silence. What transpires is a captivating tale of blackmail, fraud and death. Dr Thorndyke is left to piece together the clues in this enticing mystery.

Mr Pottermack's Oversight

Mr Pottermack is a law-abiding, settled homebody who has nothing to hide until the appearance of the shadowy Lewison, a gambler and blackmailer with an incredible story. It appears that Pottermack is in fact a runaway prisoner, convicted of fraud, and Lewison is about to spill the beans unless he receives a large bribe in return for his silence. But Pottermack protests his innocence, and resolves to shut Lewison up once and for all. Will he do it? And if he does, will he get away with it?